SAVING PARIS

ALSO BY RONN MUNSTERMAN

FICTION

Brutal Enemy – A Sgt. Dunn Novel
Behind German Lines – A Sgt. Dunn Novel
Operation Devil's Fire – A Sgt. Dunn Novel

NONFICTION

Chess Handbook for Parents and Coaches

Available on Amazon.com

SAVING PARIS

A SGT. DUNN NOVEL

RONN MUNSTERMAN

SAVING PARIS – A SGT. DUNN NOVEL

Copyright © 2015 by Ronn Munsterman
www.ronnmunsterman.com

Cover Design by David M. Jones and Nathalie Beloeil-Jones
www.beloeil-jones.com

Cover Photo of the Eiffel Tower by Jessica Welter (2015)

Printed in the United States of America
1 3 5 7 9 10 8 6 4 2

ISBN-13: 978-1522859864
ISBN-10: 1522859861

BISAC: Fiction / War & Military

Acknowledgments

The men who served during World War II will tell you they were only doing what had to be done. Perhaps so, but nevertheless, the world was in flames and they stopped not one, but two brutal and evil regimes who fully intended to rule the world at the cost of lives of people who were viewed as worthless. The Sergeant Dunn books are first, stories, but second are my attempts to reveal the strength of character these men displayed and their mental, physical, and emotional power.

The liberation of France, and Paris in particular, shows the unyielding courage displayed by the French. Some of the grateful behaviors of some French characters in this book are based on historic films I've seen and books I've read. In today's world, and with the separation of seventy-one years we might not be able to fully understand the depth of gratitude showered upon American, British, and French soldiers. However, it's not difficult at all to imagine the horror of having your country occupied for years by the Nazis. Thank you to the people of France, especially the members of the Resistance, without whom the war might have taken much longer and cost many more lives.

From my readers' emails, I've learned one thing in particular that sticks with me through all of the writing of these books: they're not just stories. This is because you, the reader, have made connections, based on your own experiences and family history, with the stories and the characters that I couldn't have foreseen. Thank you for sharing those connections with me. It's a very humbling experience and I am grateful to you for it.

I have an Author's Notes section at the end of the book. Please save it until last because it has spoilers.

Thank you to my FIRST READERS who take a messy first draft and help turn it into the book you have in front of you. It just wouldn't be possible without their insight and help. Steven E. Barltrop, Dave J. Cross, David M. Jones, Nathan Munsterman, Robert (Bob) A. Schneider II, John Skelton, Steven D. White, and Derek Williams. It's not by chance that some of characters in the Sgt. Dunn books have the names they do. A special thanks to my wife for her brutal editing.

A heartfelt thank you to my family for their love and support.

David M. Jones (Jonesy) created the cover using a color photo of the Eiffel Tower taken by Jessica Welter, my friend Christian's wife. Thank you Christian and Jessica Welter. I'm glad you took a convenient (for me) vacation to Paris. This is Dave's third cover for Sgt. Dunn.

For the people of France who suffered under Nazi tyranny
1940 – 1944

And the people of Paris who suffered under terrorism
13 November 2015

I do not see why man should not be just as cruel as nature.

Adolf Hitler

Maybe because we have a brain!

Wars may be fought with weapons, but they are won by men. It is the spirit of men who follow and of the man who leads that gains the victory.

General George S. Patton

It had to be done.

Sergeant First Class Thomas Dunn

SAVING PARIS

Prologue

Pingfan, Manchuria
Unit 731 compound
4 March 1943, 1135 Hours

There were no screams of agony, no grunts of despair, just . . .
death.

Dr. Gebhard Teichmann watched the dying with no visible
reaction, except perhaps a slight furrowing of the eyebrows from
his intense concentration. Beyond the glass lay a dozen men and
women in the last stages of dying.

One of the Chinese victims managed to turn his head and
look through the rubber-sealed window at the three men
observing his tortuous death. Teichmann thought the man might
be looking directly at him, so the doctor . . . waved. Then the man
died. Over the next hour, Teichmann watched as, one by one, the
victims succumbed.

When it was all over, Teichmann finally spoke to the short,
squat Japanese general standing to his left.

"How long from exposure to death?"

Teichmann's assistant, SS Major Dolf Egert, translated into Japanese.

Lieutenant General Masaji Kitano, commander of Unit 731 replied, "Eight days."

Unit 731 was the Japanese Army's biological and chemical weapons group. It specialized in lethal human testing that by anyone else would be called what it was: torture of the cruelest kind.

Teichmann nodded. "That's quite good. What do you call it?"

"Floating death."

Teichmann nodded his approval.

All three men's speech was muffled slightly by the white surgical masks over their faces. Earlier, the men had walked amongst the dying so the German guests could view the subjects close up and wore safety gear. Although they were outside of the death room, they kept their gear on until they could decontaminate themselves.

White headgear with flaps protected their heads and draped over the collar. Only their eyes were visible, but were guarded by goggles similar to those on a gas mask. White tunics with long sleeves reached to the knees. The trousers were white. Protecting their lower legs and feet were black rubber boots. On their hands were white rubber gloves.

The Japanese host had to special order the protective gear for the much larger German officers. He was grateful that the clothing had fit properly. It would have been an embarrassment if otherwise. And someone would have been shot for it. It would not be him.

General Kitano had taken over command of the unit two years prior from his predecessor, General Shiro Ishii, who had himself just been promoted to Chief of the Medical Section of the Japanese First Army. The transition of command had been smooth, and Kitano had ensured the experimental programs instituted by Ishii continued with no interruption.

Like Egert, Teichmann was a member of the Nazi SS, but he rarely wore his uniform while working, although he'd purposely worn it on this trip to Manchuria with his rank of colonel. He knew if he did the Japanese military men would hold him in higher esteem.

General Kitano glanced over his shoulder back into the death room. Several men wearing the same protective gear were carefully wrapping the infected bodies in white sheets. They would be taken to another sealed room in preparation for autopsy, which would take place immediately. It was the only way to document and prove the internal damage caused by the biological agent.

Turning his attention back to his guests, the general lifted an arm in invitation toward the exit. "May I interest you gentlemen in lunch?"

Neither Nazi was offended by an offer of a meal while standing outside a room where innocent people had been murdered in an effort to further science, and more specifically, weaponized science.

"Lead the way, General," replied Teichmann with a smile that was hidden by his mask.

After following decontamination procedures to the letter and then changing back into their uniforms, the men had walked across the compound to the building housing the mess hall. After loading their wooden bowls with sticky rice and, to Teichmann's eyes, barely cooked fish, they seated themselves at a round table near the window looking out to the south, and the noontime sunshine.

For a few moments, no one said anything, and just ate a few bites, and drank some hot tea.

Still holding his chopsticks in midair, Teichmann started to speak, but remembered at the last second that it was rude to wave the chopsticks around like batons. He carefully laid them across his bowl, side by side, never cross them, he'd been taught.

"What is your mortality rate?" Egert translated.

Kitano also put his chopsticks down in the same manner. "Ninety percent."

"Treatment?"

"None."

"What's your dispersal method?"

"Biologic."

Teichmann raised an eyebrow.

"Infected fleas. We'll be spraying them from airplanes by the hundreds of thousands."

Teichmann's expression was incredulous. Speaking in a low voice to his interpreter, he said, "That's just crazy, Egert. We can't rely on that method."

General Kitano didn't understand the words, but certainly did the tone.

He gave a chilling smile to Dr. Teichmann and said, "Fleas were effective enough to depopulate Europe by two-thirds, were they not?"

Teichmann turned away, thinking. The Black Death was indeed thought to be responsible for wiping Europe almost completely clean of human life due to the bacteria carried by the Oriental rat fleas. They had been carried in turn by the black rats aboard ships and probably over land caravans from Asia. It had first arrived in Sicily in October 1347, aboard twelve Genoese galleys and then spread across the island. Next it went to Genoa and Venice in January 1348. After a ship was expelled from Italy, it went to Marseilles. From there, Europe began to die by the tens of thousands. Paris went from one hundred thousand to fifty thousand.

Teichmann looked at the Japanese doctor. The man was willing to release an uncontrollable plague on the Chinese citizens. He understood that, admired it. Exterminating a group of people was not exactly foreign to Teichmann. However, what would keep the plague from spreading to Europe as it had done six hundred years earlier? And back to Japan?

"Containment?"

"All outbound transportation from the target area will cease."

"How can you guarantee that?"

Kitano smiled. "Rest assured, Doctor, we can and shall do exactly that."

"Your purpose for depopulation?"

"I would have thought it obvious: food. Food and supplies originally intended for the target area can be redirected elsewhere, even to Japan itself."

Teichmann nodded. It was really no different from Hitler's *lebensraum*, living space, in the east and the mass killings of Russians to make room for Germans. Unfortunately, it hadn't come to fruition according to the *Führer's* plans. This had been due to the generals in the east failing to adhere to Hitler's orders to the letter, especially the disgraced Field Marshal Friedrich Paulus, who had blatantly disregarded Hitler's order to fight to the last man. In January 1943 Paulus had refused to commit suicide and handed Stalingrad back to the Russians.

Teichmann stopped asking questions and began eating again, and the other men followed suit. After finishing the meal, the men rose and Teichmann begged off a tour of the labs saying he was fatigued from his travels. His hosts bowed and he nodded in return.

As Teichmann and Egert walked across the compound again, Teichmann spoke softly, "Fleas! Can you believe it? And I thought we were clever investigating the use of mosquitoes."

Glancing up at the bright, clear midday sky, he said, "I would love to have been able to spray London."

Egert chuckled. "Yes, sir. I imagine it would have made invasion much easier. After a suitable amount of time for the English to all die, that is."

Teichmann laughed, then said, "Yes." He turned more serious. "I think we need to examine an aerosol delivery method. Yes, I need to focus on that. Then we can more easily control distribution."

"Yes, sir," replied Egert, who looked at his boss for a moment. The doctor's expression was intent on something inside his brilliant mind, even as he walked. Egert recognized it and understood the man was already mentally back in his own lab, on Insel Riems Island.

Chapter 1

Hitler's Office, The Chancellery
Berlin, Germany
9 August 1944, 1556 Hours

Lieutenant General Dietrich von Choltitz closed the door to the *Führer's* office. He immediately looked to his left where the leader of the German nation was seated behind his massive desk. Hitler's head was down, reading, thought Choltitz.

The entire Reich Chancellery was designed to intimidate foreign visitors and Hitler's office followed that theme. Choltitz estimated it to be thirteen by thirty meters with a ceiling ten meters high. The doors he'd just stepped through were over five meters tall. Straight ahead was a dark gray marble table set in front of the middle of five tall, narrow windows through which the afternoon sun shone.

To his right was a sitting area in front of a fireplace. Facing the fireplace were a blue fabric, wood-trimmed sofa for six, and two matching chairs. Across from, and facing toward the sofa were four wing chairs evenly spaced apart. Four lamps were stationed around the area.

The general made his way to Hitler's study area where a three-meter-wide desk held books, a blotter, and a black phone, and a report Hitler was reading. Once there, Choltitz stood at attention until the German leader graced him with a glance.

"*Mein Führer!*" von Choltitz saluted with a raised arm.

Hitler returned the salute with a flip of his hand, his version of the royal wave.

"Be seated," said Hitler, as he resumed reading.

Von Choltitz sat in one of the three chairs facing the desk. He placed his peaked, officer's hat in his lap and waited. The general was a well-fed man, with a round face and body. His dark, almost black, hair was parted on the left, and just above the ears was trimmed close to the skull. He wore the Knight's Cross of the Iron Cross, the highest order of medal in Germany after the Grand Cross, which had been awarded only once: to Hermann Göring.

The general studied his master, thinking about the last time he'd seen the man in person. It had been shortly after the assassination attempt of twentieth July. The *Führer* had been ranting and raving like a true lunatic about revenge on all who had participated. He was shouting so fast that spittle flew from his twisted lips. At that moment Choltitz knew the *Führer* had devolved into sheer madness. He worried about the survivability of Germany if Hitler continued as the *Führer*. While he would not condone the attempt to kill Hitler, he understood perfectly the why of it. One cannot reason with a man who has none left.

Hitler finished reading and looked at his general. "You were blamed by Field Marshal von Kluge." As always, to the point.

The general tensed up, but said, "Yes, *mein Führer*, I was."

"Do you think it was deserved?"

"No, *mein Führer*, I do not."

"I examined the maps of the day in question and the orders from Kluge." Hitler's tone was accusatory.

Choltitz had been the commander of the 84th Corps in the Cotentin Peninsula when Kluge, the commander of the 7th Army, had ordered von Choltitz to move his unit south-southeast. Choltitz had immediately seen the problem with the order and protested that the Americans would then be able to advance straight into Brittany. Kluge had pressed the order and after

Choltitz complied, the Americans had done exactly as he'd predicted. The field marshal had quickly tried to blame Choltitz, but Choltitz had been able to exonerate himself, and presumably, this was why he was sitting in a soft chair in front of the *Führer*.

"I agree that you were correct."

"Thank you."

Hitler rewarded Choltitz with a smile that reminded the general of the many times he'd seen Hitler speaking to masses of people. Each person had fallen under the spell of the charm he could invoke, seemingly at will. With some sadness, Choltitz mentally compared that man with the one sitting in front of him. The days of German greatness appeared to be over and the nation's very existence was threatened. Choltitz was a soldier and he would defend the Fatherland as long as possible. Where his next stop would be was definitely not clear to him, even in this moment when Hitler had praised him. Before stepping into the office, from the moment of the summons, he'd harbored dark thoughts of the eastern front.

"You are wondering why you are here."

"Yes, *mein Führer*. I await your illumination."

Hitler appeared to enjoy Choltitz's response and rewarded the general with another smile.

"Paris. You are the new governor of Paris, effective this moment, General."

"Paris?"

"Yes. I need someone there I can trust and you were the first man I thought of."

"I don't know what to say."

"Prepare yourself to leave tonight."

"Yes, *mein Führer*."

Hitler's face changed suddenly and Choltitz braced for whatever was coming. Madness seemed to have crept back into the man's eyes again.

"You are to be prepared to leave no Parisian religious buildings or historical monuments standing, should matters prove to worsen against the enemy."

Choltitz blinked rapidly, trying to think of a reply to such an order. Nothing came to mind, so he repeated the *Führer's* words,

"The order is for me to leave no Parisian religious buildings or historical monuments standing?"

"Correct." Hitler stared at the general for a long moment, then asked, "Any questions?"

"None whatsoever, *mein Führer*."

"You are dismissed."

Choltitz stood up, holding his hat in his left hand, and gave the salute. "*Heil* Hitler!"

Hitler gave a hand flap return salute.

Choltitz turned and left the office. Out in the long, beautiful marble gallery, he glanced around at the opulence of the seat of Nazi power. How much food would this have provided for Germans? Shaking his head at the misery that had befallen his country, he marched away, his heels clicking on the marble floor.

Chapter 2

Colonel Kenton's Office, Camp Barton Stacey
Andover, England
10 August, 1750 Hours, London time

Sergeant First Class Thomas Dunn stood outside the headquarters building sitting on the spacious grounds of Camp Barton Stacey. The camp was less than a year old, and his boss, Colonel Mark Kenton, had his office inside this main building.

A twenty-four-year-old Iowan, Dunn was six-two and weighed about one hundred eighty pounds. He was a handsome soldier with short brown hair and dark brown eyes that sometimes turned black. Being on the receiving end of the black eyes was unenviable, just ask any solider not doing his job properly.

Dunn was waiting for his British friend, Sergeant Malcolm Saunders, to arrive so they could enter the office together for a cooperative meeting with their respective bosses. Kenton's counterpart was British Colonel Rupert Jenkins.

One of Dunn's favorite cigarettes, a Lucky Strike, dangled from his lips as he smoked anxiously. He leaned against one of

RONN MUNSTERMAN

the rail posts on the building's steps, his right jump boot crossed comfortably over the left. There was little traffic on the main camp thoroughfare: one two-and-a-half-ton truck and a couple of jeeps had wandered by headed to or from some location within the confines of the camp.

Dunn was feeling uneasy, an uncommon feeling for him. Not due to the upcoming assignment, whatever that was going to be, but rather for his wife of twelve days, Pamela, who was soon leaving for the continent, France in particular, to work as a battlefield nurse with the Queen Alexandra's Imperial Military Nursing Service. She'd told him just a few days ago and when he'd tried to get her to change her mind she more or less laid into him, making him quickly see the error of his ways.

They'd worked through it, meaning he'd come around to her point of view, and had gone back to Hayling Island, just thirty-five miles south on the coast of England, to resume their interrupted honeymoon. Tonight, after this meeting, Dunn would drive out to her parents' farm about five miles south of Andover, and spend the night with Pamela in the extra, but small, house there. He figured when he came back to camp, he'd be staying in the barracks, and she was due to fly out sometime soon.

"Excuse me, Sergeant, have you by chance seen an ugly, stupid fellow around? Goes by the name of Dunn?" Saunders gruff voice came from behind Dunn.

Without bothering to turn around, Dunn replied, "I heard he was with some red-headed British idiot."

Saunders moved smoothly around in front of the steps and looked up at his friend. "Ah, there you are." He grinned, and the tips of his red handlebar moustache twitched in delight. Saunders was a heavily muscled, wide-shouldered man who moved with an unexpected gliding grace. A Londoner from the east end, he was a true Cockney. He'd joined the army in September 1939 and like Dunn, had first seen action in North Africa.

The two men, the American Ranger and the British Commando shook hands, both pleased to see each other. It hadn't always been this way. They'd been at the British Commando School, Achnacarry House, at the same time, along with their squads. Saunders and his men had made it their life's ambition to make Dunn and his men's lives as miserable as possible. They had greatly succeeded. The pranks weren't just one way after the first one or two. Dunn and his second in command, Dave Cross, had managed to replace Saunders' assigned map coordinates for a field exercise with new ones. Saunders and his men had ended up two miles off target and received a thrashing from Colonel Jenkins, who was the school commander at the time.

"How's Sadie doing?"

Saunders smiled. His fiancé had been in London, shopping for a new dress to surprise Saunders on his return from a mission, when a buzz bomb exploded nearby. She'd been unconscious for almost a week, and also suffered breaks in her right femur and tibia bones. She was in a cast from her ankle to her hip. It had been while waiting for her to wake up, afraid she might not ever, that Saunders came to realize he'd been a fool to put off what he knew he wanted: to marry her.

"Doctor says she's healing nicely. Might get the cast off in two or three weeks."

"Set a date yet?"

Saunders shrugged his broad shoulders. " 'ave to wait and see. She wants to be able to walk down the aisle with 'er dad." Saunders' accent was as strong as ever, but Dunn was used to it now.

"I hope the cast comes off sooner rather than later and you get that date set." Dunn tossed his cigarette butt on the ground and stomped it out with his boot. "I expect an invitation, of course."

"I suppose, if we have to."

"You do. Although I don't know whether Pamela will be able to come."

Saunders raised an eyebrow. "Really? Why not?"

"She signed on with Queen Anne's Nursing Service. I can't quite recall the whole name of it, but you get the idea."

"Yeah, sure, I know of it. Although, it's Alexandra's not Anne's." Saunders chuckled at Dunn's mistake.

"Ah, yeah. Anyway, she's leaving very soon."

Saunders lifted his hands, palm up, and gave Dunn an expectant look.

"She's going to the continent. She thinks maybe France. It scares me and I tried to talk her out of it. I suggested she stay here where it was safe."

"You told Pamela to stay here . . . where it's safe? Bloody hell, you really are fooking stupid!"

Dunn looked at his feet.

Saunders picked up on Dunn's reaction and asked, "What the hell else did you say?"

"Oh, ah. I asked what her parents thought since she'd moved back home to be near them after her brother Percy died at Dunkirk."

Saunders roared with laughter, bending over at the waist and grabbing his knees. Eventually, he stood up wiping his eyes with the back of a massive hand. He put a hand on Dunn's shoulder and squeezed. "You dolt. You're never going to make it to your first anniversary, you keep this shite up."

"She forgave me," Dunn countered defensively.

"I'm glad I know you, mate. I can learn from your daft mistakes. That makes me a wise man."

"Wiseass, perhaps." Dunn grinned and Saunders punched him lightly in the arm.

Dunn checked his watch. "Time to go see what awaits us."

Minutes later, after the niceties were over, Dunn and Saunders stood on one side of the six-foot-square map table in Colonel Kenton's office, Dunn on the left and close to the corner of the table. Four officers stood along two other sides, two American and two British. Evening light shone through the window behind Kenton's desk, but the ceiling light was on, too. The map spread out on the pine table was of France.

Colonel Mark Kenton, Dunn's commanding officer, on Dunn's left, was also nearest the table corner. Next to him was his aide, Lieutenant Samuel Adams. On the side opposite the sergeants were the Brits, Colonel Rupert Jenkins, Kenton's counterpart for special operations, and his aide, Lieutenant Carleton Mallory. Jenkins had started bringing his aide along for meetings with Kenton to make sure he wasn't outnumbered. To say Jenkins didn't see eye to eye with Kenton would be a disservice to the phrase. They never made it through a meeting without arguing about something.

Kenton stood just south of five-nine, but had an extraordinarily deep voice that surprised everyone the first time they heard him speak. Just forty years old, Kenton already had gray hair along the temples. He liked to call them his sergeant stripes, as in his sergeants caused them. A West Point graduate, Kenton's eighteen-year-old son was following his dad and was about to start his time at the academy.

Where Kenton was short, Jenkins was tall, just over six feet and slender. His dark hair was combed straight back. His narrow face tended toward a permanent scowl and he typically looked down his long nose at everyone. Just a couple of years older than Kenton, Jenkins had graduated from Sandhurst in 1920. He'd been sorely disappointed at being too young for the Great War.

Samuel Adams, who'd had more than his fair share of troubles having the name of a famous American Revolution figure, had worked for Kenton since the inception of the unit in February 1944. With an open and friendly face, Adams often played the part of mediator between the two strong personalities of the colonels.

Carleton Mallory had been Jenkins' aide for just over a month, after his predecessor had committed one too many small mistakes for the unforgiving colonel. Mallory adopted his boss's attitude and rarely smiled, even when Adams had told a quick joke in an attempt to break the ice. Dunn and Saunders had cracked up, though, and Kenton grinned. Adams had simply shrugged and ignored the glares from the British officers.

"Let's get started, shall we," said a frowning Jenkins.

"By all means, Colonel, please go ahead," replied an unruffled Kenton.

Jenkins cleared his throat, but it came across as an honest to goodness, "Harrumph." He had a wooden, rubber-tipped pointer in his hand. He raised it, then leaned over and tapped a spot on the map. It was about sixty miles southwest of Paris.

"General Patton and his Third Army are getting close to breaking out and rushing toward Paris. Of course, General de Gaulle will undoubtedly insist that a French unit be the first to march into the capital." If it was possible, Jenkins disliked the French even more than the Americans.

"Patton has requested the use of a few Commandos and Rangers to secure a bridge at Chartres and hold it until his armored units can arrive. The bridge in question crosses the L'Eure River in Chartres. It's the only one big enough for the armored units. You'll be flown to a landing strip near Nogent-le-Rotrou, where you'll meet with Patton's chief of operations and planning, Colonel Edwards. He'll give you the particulars and coordinate with you for the supplies you'll need and the attack itself."

Jenkins looked directly at Saunders and said, "I'm sorry you'll be reporting to Patton and not Monty, but that's the way it is, I'm afraid."

"Of course, sir, I understand perfectly." Almost all British soldiers wanted to be a part of General Montgomery's Army. Saunders, though, preferred not to be. If anyone was more arrogant than Jenkins, it was Montgomery.

Dunn glanced at Kenton, but the American colonel's face was expressionless at Jenkins' latest insult to Americans. Dunn wondered briefly what kind of personal life the British colonel had, and what he was like with people he might actually . . . not dislike. Dunn was about to grimace and shake his head, but caught himself just in time. Wouldn't do to let Jenkins know he'd gotten under his skin.

"Any questions?" asked Jenkins.

Dunn glanced at Saunders, who shook his head. "Not at this time, Colonel."

"Very well. That's all."

Jenkins said a quick, perfunctory goodbye and then he and Mallory departed.

Typically, after receiving an assignment, Dunn and Saunders would retire to their barracks and work up a plan, but it would have to wait until they arrived in France.

Dunn's last mission, to rescue a missing colonel in Italy who knew too much about the invasion of southern France had been successful. He'd been forced to devise an outrageous plan to attack a German prison camp to rescue the British and American men there, but it had gone perfectly. Then, he'd learned that the Gestapo and a platoon of elite SS soldiers were going to destroy an Italian village. It had not gone well for the Nazis. In the end, Dunn had killed the murderous Gestapo agent in charge during brutal hand-to-hand combat.

"Is there anything either of you need from me?" asked Colonel Kenton.

Dunn shook his head. "No, sir." He paused, then said, "Thanks for signing the orders transferring the men I selected from Bagley's squad so quickly. I got them into the barracks today to officially meet the men, although they all know each other slightly."

Dunn had lost three men in the attack on the SS unit, plus Squeaky Hanson who had gotten his right leg blown off below the knee by a German potato masher grenade while diving into a young Italian partisan fighting alongside the Rangers. It had saved the seventeen-year-old boy's life, but Hanson would never return to duty.

Sergeant Bagley, who had another squad of Rangers, had been injured in a training exercise, and Kenton offered Dunn his pick of Bagley's men to bring his own squad back up to strength.

"You're welcome." Kenton turned to Saunders. "I'm sorry to hear about Owens."

"Thank you, sir."

Owens had been killed in Italy on a successful mission to blow up an important train bridge north of the Gothic Line.

"Have you found a replacement?"

"I have, sir."

Kenton nodded. "Okay, good. I'm glad you guys are going to be full strength. I do believe you'll need every hand you can get."

"Yes, sir. I agree," Dunn said.

The non-coms said their farewells to the two officers, saluted, then made their way back onto the steps in front of the building.

"We're having breakfast tomorrow at the Star and Garter. Do you think Sadie would be up to joining us?" Dunn asked.

"We have a wheelchair with a support brace built onto it for her damned cast. I can ask her if she wants to. What time?"

Dunn glanced at his wrist watch. "How about 0700 hours?"

Saunders nodded. "We could make that if I give her a call first, so she can get ready. You know she and her mum are staying with friends in Andover?"

"No. When did that happen?"

"While we were in Italy. Sadie insisted because she wanted to be closer than Cheshunt."

Cheshunt was fifteen miles northwest of London and a good hour and a half from Andover.

"I hope she can make it. You're welcome, even if she can't, you know."

"Aye. But I doubt I would. Rather be with her than you."

"Hard to imagine why."

"Right," replied Saunders with a grin.

They shook hands and went off in their separate directions.

Chapter 3

Apartment building rooftop
Northeast Paris
10 August, 1922 Hours, Paris time

The sniper stared unblinking over the stolen Mauser's steel sights at the brick roadway, waiting. She didn't have a scope on the weapon, but at a range of fifty meters, she wouldn't need one. Even the light breeze was not going to be a problem as it was coming from her right, the south, which at street level was blocked by all of the buildings. There were no alleyways between the buildings.

She had been holding a kneeling position for nearly fifteen minutes, but was able to lean her right side against the parapet for support, as well as prop her right elbow there to support the weapon. The flat roof was atop a three-story apartment building, and the sniper knew she was nearly invisible from the ground because she was in a shadow created by the slightly taller building to her west. Others in her group were stationed at street level, and were armed with a variety of weapons, some British, some American, and others German like hers. She was patient, and didn't bother checking her watch. The Germans were famously punctual and the target would be coming within a couple of minutes.

The street ran east-west and was bordered on both sides by apartment buildings, although directly across from the shooter was a smaller two-story building housing a café on the first floor, with the owners living in the apartment above.

The evening sun shone directly onto the street below, and it wouldn't set for another two hours, providing ample light for the ambush. Additionally, the Germans would be coming from the east driving into the low sun. Their ability to see what was happening was going to be severely restricted.

She heard and then sighted the target and the escorting sidecar motorcycle a few blocks away. They appeared to be moving at about forty kilometers an hour, not very fast at all for a sniper.

The second the truck hit the predetermined spot, she fired one shot through the windshield. A sustained burst of weapons fire erupted on the street. The cyclist and his sidecar companion died and the motorcycle veered off course, crashing into a parked car and tipping over, throwing the driver onto the street. The truck slowed down when the dead driver's foot slipped off the gas pedal. It rolled forward and finally came to a stop in the center of the street, where the engine died because the truck was still in gear.

From buildings on both sides of the street, four French Resistance men ran out into the street. Two darted to the back of the truck and then on a count of three, one pulled back the canvas revealing a cargo area half full of crates of all sizes. The men clambered aboard and the other pair climbed in the cab. The man on the driver's side shoved the dead German out of the way. He restarted the truck and drove it away.

At the same time, two more men dragged the motorcyclists off between two buildings, then got the motorcycle back on its wheels. It was only slightly damaged, and one of them was able to get it started after a few leg kicks. After his partner jumped into the dented sidecar, the driver revved up the engine and the motorcycle tore off down the street.

Above the street, the sniper, who had been keeping vigilant watch for additional Germans since her single shot, rose to a standing position and stretched her muscles. She reached up and pulled off a beret. This released her long auburn hair, which glistened in the evening light. Her emerald green eyes burned with the intensity of her hatred for the Nazis, which was shared by virtually all French Resistance fighters.

Madeline Laurent was twenty-five years old, and had been fighting the Germans since late 1940. Most of her fighting had been around the Pas Calais area, where she'd grown up. Her father had died of cancer when she was only eleven. Her uncle, Remi Laurent, who lived in Saverne, had kept a promise to his dying brother by watching over Madeline and her mother and helping out financially.

Madeline had arrived in Paris two weeks ago. The trip from Calais had been danger filled and she'd nearly been caught near Amiens, about one hundred twenty kilometers north of Paris. She'd received word of a planned large and systematic uprising which would soon begin in Paris. It would coincide with a general strike by the Paris Metro, the Gendarmerie, and the postal service. Madeline had known immediately she would have to go to Paris and be a part of the liberation of the capital.

Slinging the Mauser over her shoulder, the French Resistance fighter turned away and ran across the roof to the door that led to the hallway on the building's top floor. Shortly after, she was at the downstairs front door. She opened it and leaned out, looking in both directions before stepping out onto the sidewalk. Seeing no traffic, she crossed the street and entered the café. The place was empty and the proprietor watched the red-headed woman warily as she got closer to the counter.

"All clear, *monsieur*," Madeline said in a friendly tone.

The short, thin man nodded and turned away, walking to an opening behind the counter that led to the back of the café.

"It's safe."

A group of older men and women stepped through the opening and returned to their interrupted dinners, eyeing Madeline and her rifle as they went by. At the sound of gunfire, the small crowd had bolted to the back of the store with no need to be prompted.

The owner said to Madeline, "It would have been nice to know ahead of time."

Madeline shrugged. "Not possible. You know we can't risk a collaborator hearing about it."

The man sighed. "I hope it was worth it."

"It's always worth it to kill a German."

Madeline turned away and left the café, ignoring the irritated glances from the patrons.

Turning left at the door, then left again at the corner, Madeline was nearly run over by a boy on a bicycle. She darted to the right to get out of the way and the boy slammed on his coaster brake, skidding a few meters before coming to a stop. He was about ten with a great shock of black hair hanging into his face. He tilted the bike so his left foot could rest on the ground while his right foot stayed on the right pedal, as if to be prepared for a quick escape if the woman got angry.

Madeline just smiled at him.

Disarmed by her reaction, he braved a question, "Are you all right, *mademoiselle*?"

"*Oui*. Where are you headed in such a hurry?"

The boy noticed the rifle for the first time and his eyes lit up. "Did you shoot a German? I heard gunshots. I wanted to see!"

Madeline stepped close to the boy and ruffled his hair. "It's all over now. Go home. Be careful."

"But did you?" the boy persisted.

"*Oui*."

"I want to be like you, but I'm too young."

Madeline stared at the boy for a moment, crafting a careful response.

"I don't want you to be like me. I want you to be a good little boy. Can you do that for me?"

The boy wasn't sure what to make of the woman's comment, but he saw something in her eyes that alarmed him. Fear, sadness, maybe? No pride or satisfaction in killing the Germans. This was not what he expected at all.

Madeline was suddenly fearful and grabbed the boy by the shoulders.

"I want you to be very careful over the next few weeks. Stay away from gunfire. You are too young to be killed this late in the war. Bullets don't care if you're a little boy or a grown man. Promise me!"

Suddenly frightened, not by the woman's act of grabbing him, but by the intensity of her expression, the boy nodded and said, "I promise."

Madeline let go and stepped back.

"Please go home now. Be with your family."

"*Oui, mademoiselle.*"

As the boy turned his bike around and pedaled away, Madeline began to cry for her own lost childhood, her father's early death, her involvement with the Resistance, and that she had no family of her own at the age of twenty-five. Suddenly overwhelmed, she took two quick steps and leaned against the building. She stayed there a long time. Alone in all possible ways.

Chapter 4

Mess hall
Camp Barton Stacey
14 August, 1845 Hours, London time

Dunn's men were seated at a long table in the camp's mess hall. Evening light shone through the windows on the west side of the building. Another dozen or so soldiers were seated elsewhere around the large, plain mess hall. All of the windows were open, as was the main door. A slight breeze made its way into the hall making the room fairly comfortable.

Dunn had already briefed the men on the upcoming mission, giving what few details he had. The men had quickly packed their gear and then beat it over to the mess to eat and relax together. The flight out from Hampstead would be at 1000 hours the next day. Dunn and Cross had stayed behind in the barracks to discuss the squad's new organization.

Most of the men had a small glass bottle of Coca Cola next to their tray, although Stanley Wickham, whose peculiar British-Texas accent drove the English girls crazy, was sipping a cup of unsweetened tea. Wickham sat in the middle of one side of the table. He held the unenviable position of being the last original member of the squad, other than Dunn and Cross, having trained with both men.

Seated around the table were the rest of the squad members: the sniper, Dave Jones, Jonesy, who was the best shooter in a squad of outstanding shooters, Bob Schneider, who was six-four and had grown up an army brat, living in many places across the U.S. and who was the squad's German and French translator, and Eugene Lindstrom. Clustered at one end of the table were the four men who'd recently joined the squad. Alphonso Martelli, who went along on the mission to Italy because he could speak the language, Leonard Bailey, Rob Goerdt, and Clarence Waters.

Wickham swallowed a mouthful of dinner, then said, "You guys," he pointed lazily at the new men with a fork, "this is the last time you sit together. From now on, you are members of this squad and you'll sit amongst everyone else."

They had all been reassigned as Dunn's picks from Sergeant Bagley's squad. Dunn had immediately selected Martelli, who had done a terrific job in Italy. Dunn knew everyone in the other squad, and had picked the additional three based on previous interactions with them, and Bagley's comments during a recent conversation.

Martelli grinned at Wickham and rose, taking his tray with him. He moved over behind Lindstrom and said, "Scoot over, Eugene from Eugene."

Lindstrom grinned back and moved over to make room. Martelli was seated directly across from Wickham. The other three new men got up and the squad rearranged themselves so that it was new-old around the table.

After the men got seated and started digging back into their chow, Wickham said, "Much better."

Leonard Bailey, next to Lindstrom, asked, "What's the story behind Eugene from Eugene?"

"I'm from Eugene, Oregon. My parents were rather unimaginative."

Bailey chuckled, then said, "Why not use your middle name, then, if you don't like it?"

"I didn't say I didn't like it. Besides, the ladies seem to find it cute."

"Well, that settles it. I wonder if there's a Leonard somewhere . . . ?"

Bailey turned back to his meal.

Clarence Waters asked Wickham, "Is it true about Sergeant Dunn getting the Medal of Honor?"

"Where'd you hear that?"

"Around."

"Don't spread rumors."

"Don't get wound up. I'm just asking, is all."

Wickham stared at Waters, noting a disagreeable smirk. "If Sarge is getting the medal, he'll tell us when he sees fit."

"What, you don't hear what's going around?" Waters' smirk broadened.

Wickham took a deep breath, and laid his fork down on his plate. "Listen, you little shit, you don't come into this squad thinking you're in charge. You keep your bullshit to yourself, or we're going to have a big problem."

"What, you're going to take me out back and teach me a lesson?"

Waters started to get up, but Martelli grabbed him by the upper arm yanked him down.

"Shut the fuck up, Waters. You're not going to keep on doing the bullshit that Sergeant Bagley ignored. You've got a big mouth. Just because you're a great shot doesn't mean you can shoot off your mouth."

Waters started to say something, but Martelli squeezed Waters' arm. "Shut it. The only thing we want to know is if when it comes down to it, we can count on you to do your job."

Waters tried to shake off the grip, but couldn't. "Fine. Yes, you can count on me. Let go so I can eat."

Martelli gave a final squeeze, then let go. He glanced at Wickham, who nodded once. Martelli nodded in return and resumed eating, as if nothing had happened. The rest of the men had watched the exchange silently, and then continued their chatter.

"So you're from Iowa, too, like Dunn?" asked Schneider.

Rob Goerdt nodded. "Yep. Northeast Iowa. Small town, Dyersville. Not too far from the Mississippi."

"Family?"

"Big one, nine brothers and sisters."

Schneider lowered his voice, *"Sprechen Sie Duetsch?"*

"Ja." Goerdt tipped his head in the direction of Waters, who was looking the other way, and said, *"Ist ein esel."* Is an ass.

Schneider, *"Ja, er ein esel ist!"*

Goerdt laughed. The two continued their conversation in whispered German, learning about each other.

"Jones, I hear you're the sniper," Bailey said.

"Yeah, I am."

"What are you shooting?"

"A 1903 Springfield A4."

Bailey nodded. "Nice." He raised a fork in salute. "I'd love to see you shoot sometime."

"Sure. I'll let you know next time I'm heading out to the range."

"You do that. Do you take it on all your missions?"

"Yeah, a standing order from the Sarge."

"Maybe I can be your spotter sometime."

Jonesy shrugged. "Up to the Sarge. Eugene does it."

"Sure, I understand."

The rest of the meal was spent with the men all chatting to get to know each other, the veterans trying to get a feel for the new men's reliability, the new men trying to impress the veterans. Exaggeration was thrown in, but was recognized for what it was, and discounted.

Everyone who was honest with themselves came away with the feeling that only time and a mission would truly answer the question.

Combat was the ultimate truth-finder.

Chapter 5

Hut 3
Bletchley Park, England
14 August, 1905 Hours

Located just over forty miles northwest of downtown London, Bletchley Park was home to the biggest, single most important Allied intelligence facility in the world. Bletchley Park was tasked with intercepting, decrypting, translating, and analyzing secret messages the Nazis sent all across Europe using the Enigma cipher machines. The resulting intelligence was referred to by the code name Ultra.

The two-story brick and stone mansion was the centerpiece of the property, measuring a hundred feet by one hundred fifty. The monstrosity's architecture was some kind of bizarre combination of Victorian Gothic, Tudor, and Dutch Baroque styles. Using his own money in early 1938, Admiral Hugh Sinclair, who was the MI6 British Secret Intelligence Service chief, purchased the mansion and fifty-eight acres. The location was ideal for many reasons, one of which was its proximity to the railway line connecting Oxford and Cambridge, the universities from which the codebreakers were expected to be drawn. Only a select few knew the truth of the goings on at Bletchley Park.

North of the mansion were numerous smaller wooden buildings, all known simply as Hut and a number. It was inside these huts that the real work took place.

Mathematicians, crossword puzzle experts, and chess masters ruled the day here, and they had worked tirelessly to unlock the secrets of the German Enigma encrypting machine. Hundreds of messages were handled on a daily basis by the analysts, among whom was Reginald Shepston. He was in Hut 3 where translation and analysis of intercepted message took place, while the decrypting occurred in Hut 6.

Sitting stone still at his desk, Shepston read the last message he had in his stack for the day. Shepston wasn't a mathematician, but could have been, but instead he was an analyst for MI6. At thirty-three, he fit right in amongst the other analysts age-wise. He shared many of the same qualities that an outstanding analyst should have: attention to minute detail, able to draw accurate conclusions from incomplete information, and reliable.

Shepston wore a dark blue suit with his favorite brown shoes, although to be honest they were his only pair. His blue tie was knotted but not snugged into its proper place. By this time of the day, it had been loosened and was askew with the bottom of the knot pointing toward his right hip instead of his belly button.

As was often the case, Shepston was the last one to leave for the day. He never left anything for the next day, not that the others did either, but he typically got the messages deemed most important.

He was leaning over and staring straight down at the message lying on his desk. Next to it was a notepad on which a worn-down pencil rested, its eraser completely intact. He would have preferred using a pen, like he did when doing *The Times* crossword, but pencils were required. His first reaction was this message was about something entirely new, and his brain was searching its didactic memory for previous messages containing the same or similar words. Shortly, after finding no earlier reference, he confirmed his first thoughts.

Sliding the message and notepad to the side, he leaned down and lifted a massive world atlas off the floor next to his chair. He quickly flipped to the city index in the back of the book and found Germany. He scanned the list until he found the location mentioned in the message, and its page number and coordinates.

Flipping to the page, he found the location quickly on the map and discovered it was an island off the German coast in the Baltic Sea about one hundred twenty miles north of Berlin. The island was curved going roughly west to east, resembling a dolphin leaping from the sea, and measured about a mile in length. A narrow causeway on the western end was the only access to the mainland.

The map's detail was insufficient to determine what might be there. He'd have to submit a request for a search of aerial reconnaissance photos from that area, if any existed.

Frustrated, he closed the atlas and placed it back on the floor gently. He pulled the notepad closer and wrote down his thoughts on the message, as well as the page number and map coordinates for Insel Riems. He didn't do this for himself, he'd remember tomorrow or in a month, but for anyone who might have to follow behind him if he got hit by the infamous pie truck and never returned.

When he was done, he grabbed another piece of paper, a request form, and filled it out. The form would go to the research team, a number of women at Bletchley Park. He wanted them to locate all messages where either Insel Reims or small cylindrical airtight containers were mentioned. He knew the request would take time, but this was the only way to find out what the Germans might be up to on the island. He added a note to find out everything known about the island, what had been done there in the past, if anything. He filled out another form requesting recon photos of the island. He reached across the desk and selected a rubber stamp from a little turnstile holder. He pressed it onto a red inkpad, then stamped all of his requests: URGENT. As if nothing else was, he thought dryly.

He slipped the forms into a manila envelope and sealed it. Instead of throwing it into his out basket, he set it aside. He cleaned off his desk, putting everything carefully in a desk drawer. After pulling a key ring from his pocket with two keys on it, he locked the desk with one. Standing up, he picked up the envelope.

As he exited the hut's lone door, he switched off the overhead lights, stepped through the door and locked it with the other key, then he returned the key ring to his trousers pocket. He strode off quickly toward another hut where he would hand deliver the envelope. After that, he'd bike into town and have a well-earned pint and some dinner. If the other fellows were there, great, if not, that'd be great, too.

Chapter 6

German Biological Weapon Facility, Building 6
Insel Riems Island, Germany
14 August, 2042 Hours, Berlin time

Situated in a central complex on Insel Riems Island, Building 6 was an older brick building, constructed just before the Great War by the German government. It was about thirty by fifteen meters in size and two stories tall, although there was no second floor, just a high ceiling under a flat roof with narrow eaves all around. There were no windows anywhere, which gave the building a sinister, brooding appearance. It was at this facility and in this very building where mustard gas was first tested on unsuspecting throwaway people, inmates from Germany's worst offender prison, murderers and rapists.

Dr. Gebhard Teichmann was too young to remember any news about that, as if the government would have made it public knowledge, but after joining the ranks of renowned and elite biologic scientists, he'd soon learned of the details. Depending on one's point of view, those details were either a sordid example of the horrors unleashed by the military or a worthy accomplishment by brilliant men. Teichmann fell clearly into the second camp. In his mind, his end goal would be a far greater accomplishment, one that would permanently etch his name in history.

Born is 1906, Teichmann was almost thirty-eight. His early childhood was spent in Munich, and he did remember Hitler's and the Nazis' rise in that city. An early believer, as were his parents, Teichmann attended some of Hitler's rousing, patriotic speeches and he had been impressed by the power Hitler held over his audiences. The failure of the Beer Hall Putsch had disappointed Teichmann deeply, and he came to fear for his nation.

It was shortly after this, in December 1923, that Teichmann's parents decided he should experience higher education in the United States, and they departed the next summer. The young Teichmann's initial reaction was anger, believing his parents to have turned their backs on Germany. But not long after arriving in America, and enrolling at Princeton University, he came to appreciate what they'd done. He had graduated in three years, carrying a tremendous workload each semester. Although he'd made friends along the way, he never forgot that he was living in a nation that had killed his own countrymen.

When they returned home to Munich in the summer of 1927, he was thrilled to be back home. He had learned many things at Princeton, chief among them was an unexpected love for biology, and specifically virology. He continued his education in Munich earning his doctorate in 1931. He'd applied for and was immediately hired to work at the Insel Riems facility, a place he'd grown to love. That love, and his fascination for, and expertise in, viruses, had all led to this moment.

The interior of Building 6 was divided into four rooms. On the west side, a long narrow hallway ran the entire length of the building and was the only room with access to the outside world. At the south end were two identically sized rooms, three by five meters, running the width of the building. Between the two rooms was a double-door airlock and between the west room and the long hallway was another airlock. The main area covered the rest of the building's space. All the rooms were open to the ceiling, but the walls between the rooms reached all the way to the top, ensuring that they were all truly and safely segregated from each other.

Teichmann and two other men were in the southwest room, out of sight of the test subjects. The men wore white protective gear from head to toe, and gasmasks, possibly leftover from the Great War. They surrounded a small metal table.

In addition to Dr. Teichmann's assistant, Major Dolf Egert, another virologist, Dr. Rikard Baer, was present for the test. All the other members of the team, fifteen in all, were still working in the lab, which was in a nearby building.

Following Teichmann's visit to Unit 731 almost a year and a half ago, he and his team had worked incredibly hard and long to find a better delivery method than using *ficken flöhes,* fucking fleas, as the doctor liked to say. The end result of their work was on the metal table.

The object of the scientists' attention was a cylinder measuring fifty centimeters tall with a diameter of ten centimeters. It was nearly the same size as an 88mm shell casing, but instead of brass, it was constructed of brushed aluminum, which reflected the ceiling lights. For stability, the cylinder had an extra two centimeters around the base on which it could stand. On top of the tube, a lid was screwed on as tight as it would go, and then two clip latches were flipped into a locked position. In the center of the lid was a red button. Next to it was a small opening, the nozzle.

"What's the timer set for?" Teichmann asked.

"Five minutes," Major Egert replied.

"Once the device is triggered, it can't be stopped?"

"No, sir. There's no safety switch at all."

"Well, we'd better be damned certain we're ready and then get to the safe room."

"I'd be happy to trigger the device."

"I know you would be, but I need to do it. You understand, don't you?"

"Certainly, I do, Doctor."

Turning to the third man in the safety gear, Teichmann asked, "Baer, is the fan unit ready to go?"

"Yes, it is. I have it set to mimic a typical summer breeze of fifteen kilometers per hour."

Teichmann nodded his satisfaction.

Above the men, a large, enclosed, two-meter-diameter fan was set high in an otherwise blank wall separating the men from the test subjects. It drew air from the outside through a maze of filtered tubes designed to ensure that air was always flowing into the building, never out. The door leading to the viewing room was actually a pair of doors designed like a submarine passageway door with a wheel to complete the closure and framed with rubber so as to be sealed airtight. The airlock could never have both doors open at the same time. Each door had a port hole that was convex shaped toward the inside of the airlock.

Teichmann lifted a gloved hand and pointed toward the north end of the building. "Are the subjects prepared?"

"They are," Egert said.

"Time for you two to leave then," Teichmann said.

"Yes, sir," replied both men.

Teichmann waited, feeling both impatient and excited at the same time. When the two men entered the airlock and closed the door, Teichmann stepped back to the table and looked at the device. So much was riding on this. His career and perhaps life were at stake depending on the outcome of the next few days.

The virus was far more virulent, or aggressive, than its forebears. Just watching it grow under the microscope had been thrilling and shocking at the same time. It spread three times faster than any previous generation. When introduced into the test mice, the effects could be measured in hours not days, which indicated that on the larger human mammals it would be fast spreading also, much faster than the Japanese virus.

A horn sounded one minute later signifying that Egert and Baer had arrived in the safe room.

A group of six men and six women was gathered at the north end of the large main area. Several lunch tables were set about and about half of the people sat on some metal chairs at a table, while the others stood around. Each had a clipboard in hand and a pencil. Over their heads, bright lights made the room seem almost . . . pleasant. Sleeping areas for each gender were positioned on opposite sides of the common area.

The test subjects all turned their attention to the written tests on their clipboards. They'd been told it was a civil service exam and how well they did would determine whether they would be able to leave the work camp and go to work in Berlin for the government. That some of them would have to take the test while standing was explained that some of the jobs might entail working at a counter all day. The fact that all twelve people had been sent to the work camps because they were communists was no longer a problem according to the nice young man in charge. All was forgiven.

Dangling from the high ceiling above the test subjects were several microphones that fed sound into a speaker in the safe room.

Teichmann focused on the cylinder. It was necessary to pay close attention to what he was doing. No need to hurry and be careless. With a steady hand, Teichmann put the tip of his gloved right forefinger on the red button, and without hesitation, pushed it. He was rewarded with a soft click.

Five minutes, he thought as he turned away, being careful not to knock over the device, and walked toward the exit. He made it through the airlock with plenty of time to spare. Egert and Baer stood next to a window that was two meters square between the fatally dangerous test area and the safe room. The window had been treated to be a two-way mirror.

"Should be about ten seconds now, sir," said Egert, who had started a stop watch when, through the airlock portholes, he'd observed his boss press the red button.

Teichmann nodded as he glanced through the large window into the test area. He was satisfied to see the subjects doing exactly what they had been told. Looking through the port hole, he concentrated intently on the top of the device.

"Now," Egert said.

Teichmann noted that Egert had timed it exactly right because almost immediately a clear mist began to flow from the top of the cylinder. The aerosol was working perfectly. The mist rose steadily straight up and into the breeze created by the fan where it seemed to just disappear, but the doctor knew it was just dispersing in the moving air.

Teichmann leaned close to the window and craned his neck to look up. He imagined what was happening and tracked his gaze along a path from the fan to the subjects as if he could actually see the virus flying across the open space. He knew that the miniscule weight of the virus cells would bring them down from the ceiling over the distance.

Dr. Teichmann, Major Egert, and Dr. Baer stood at the window, much like children admiring toys in a Christmas display in downtown Berlin. Egert picked up a large pair of binoculars from a table nearby and handed them to Teichmann. The doctor focused in on the group of twelve subjects. After a few minutes, he lowered them.

"Now we wait, gentlemen. The hardest part."

Both men replied, "Yes, sir."

Egert said, "Why don't you go get a bite to eat, sir? We can keep watch and call you as soon as something happens."

Teichmann shook his head. "No. I want to be here when the first symptoms appear."

"Of course, sir. Would you care to sit?" Egert waved his gloved hand in the direction of a nearby chair.

"I believe I *will* sit. Thank you."

Three hours later, near midnight, at the far end of the test area, which had some minimal lighting on, the subjects all appeared to be asleep, perhaps dreaming of a government job back home. Teichmann lifted binoculars to his eyes. Ten minutes later he was rewarded with the sound of the first cough. Teichmann unconsciously held his breath as he waited for confirmation. A few seconds later, a series of coughs came. As he watched, a woman rose from her cot and made her way unsteadily toward the lunch tables.

"Turn up the lights."

Egert flipped a couple of switches and the test area brightened.

The woman sat down heavily and then poured herself a glass of water, which she drank until the glass was empty. She put the glass down and rubbed her throat, fingers on one side and thumb on the other.

Teichmann zoomed in on the woman's face. She was perhaps in her mid-twenties. Sitting sideways to Teichmann's view, she put her right hand in front of her mouth and coughed again. Her skin was shiny. Teichmann knew this was sweat from a rising fever.

"It's starting, gentlemen," the doctor said. "It worked. It worked!"

"Congratulations, Doctor."

"Now to begin the monitoring. I can't wait to learn how much faster death arrives with this strain."

"Yes, sir."

"Have the staff prepare the subjects."

An excited and pleased Egert said, "*Jawohl*, Doctor Teichmann. *Heil* Hitler." The major gave a stiff-armed salute.

Both scientists retuned the salute and the enthusiasm.

Baer seemed unable to contain his own excitement and said with a gleam in his eyes, "Doctor Teichmann, where would you like to see the weapon used first?"

That Teichmann perceived this question as normal, would have made a non-German bystander sick.

"Wherever the *Führer* sees fit would be fine with me."

"Yes, of course, but surely there's some city you'd like to see hit first."

Teichmann glanced at the SS major. The glance was merely to gauge the SS man's reaction to the question. He had full faith in Egert's loyalty to the program, and unlike most SS members, Teichmann knew he could trust Egert not to go telling tales to the Nazi party.

Egert gave a small smile, evidently wondering the same thing himself.

"I do confess, I've been dreaming of killing Winston Churchill, so I must say London would be first choice!" Teichmann admitted.

"Me, too," blurted Baer.

"And then after that, maybe Washington. Get that Jew-lover, Roosevelt."

"Excellent."

The three men smiled at each other, then began the process of entering another large airlock between them and the outside of the building, and in which they would be able to discard their safety gear.

"Anybody hungry? I'm starving," said Dr. Teichmann, as he thought back to the meal at Unit 731 after watching Chinese men and women die from the Japanese virus. His virus was much better, he knew it for certain. He doubted he would ever share the knowledge with the Japanese.

Chapter 7

5 miles northeast of Paris
15 August, 0225 Hours, Paris time

The black matte painted British Lysander soared across the French countryside at only a thousand feet in altitude. The pilot, who was on his twelfth insertion and recovery mission, focused on the task at hand. Up ahead, four burning torches marked his very short landing and takeoff field.

"About two minutes, sir," the pilot said to his lone passenger.

"Righto. I'm ready." The man pulled his back pack closer to his body.

Right on the pilot's predicted two minute mark, the tires hit the grassy field, bounced once and settled into a smooth roll. The four torches blinked out. Not needed for takeoff.

The passenger slid back the canopy over his seat and unhooked his harness as cool French morning air rushed into the cockpit.

The rollout was short and the pilot deftly turned the plane around to head back out the way it came.

The passenger climbed up and out of the plane saying, "Thanks for the ride."

"Any time."

With the plane still rolling, the passenger went down the permanently attached ladder and jumped to the ground. From his left, a dark figure ran right by him and jumped onto the ladder as the pilot revved the engine. Neither agent had spoken. It wasn't done.

One minute after dropping off one agent and picking up another, the Lysander soared back into the black French sky.

The British spy slipped his pack on his back, and ran off in the moonlight toward the trees, not those closest to him, but the ones that were farthest away. This was because they were in the direction he was supposed to go to meet the French Resistance, the same people who'd brought the other agent to be picked up.

The night air was cool and a slight southerly breeze blew against his blackened face. He wore all black including a black watch cap. On his hip he wore a Smith & Wesson Model 10, something he'd rarely done, and never had in his four years in Berlin. He preferred the lighter .38 caliber to the massive Webley .455 caliber.

MI5 agent Neil Marston was slender, but had a surprising strength. He'd needed every ounce of it in the last weeks of his time in Berlin when a lone sentry had caught him on the street in the middle of the night. Marston had just left a German Minister's office where he'd taken photos of a top secret document. The soldier seemed about to let Marston go, apparently believing the spy's story of working late, but suddenly he ordered Marston to empty his pockets while bringing his Mauser to bear. Marston couldn't allow that, so he used his sleeve knife to kill the sentry after an exhausting struggle for the knife during which Marston had been stabbed in the upper left arm. Afterwards, Marston had vomited on the way back to his apartment, where he patched up the wound. He had some trouble with what he'd done, even though he understood it had been a him-or-me situation. Over time, he had come to grips with it and it rarely occurred to him anymore.

In 1939 Marston had been a happy linguist and professor of English at Oxford when an MI5 recruiter had told him he'd make a terrific spy. Marston had laughed at the idea, but when Nazi Germany invaded Poland, he'd called the recruiter and said, 'yes.' Another reason MI5 had been interested in the thirty-two-year-old professor was hidden under his cap: blond hair over brilliant blue eyes. Fluent in German, Marston spoke as if he'd grown up in Berlin instead of London's West End. Marston also spoke French and Italian, and a smattering of other European languages; he collected languages like some people collected coins.

It was Marston who had led Sergeant Dunn and his men to the Nazis' atomic bomb facility, and he had even provided transportation in the form of a "requisitioned" German truck. He'd been stabbed in the upper chest by the German physicist, Dr. Herbert, because Marston was wearing a stolen SS colonel's uniform. Herbert, who was trying to escape because he'd sabotaged the Nazi atomic bomb program, saw an enemy and plunged a letter opener into the British spy. In the nearly two months since returning from that mission, after a few days in the hospital to make sure his wound was healing properly, he'd been assigned to train new spies. While he loved teaching, he had come to love what he'd done as a spy on a mission. Two weeks ago, he'd gone to his commander and requested reassignment to active status so he could go on another mission.

And so, here he was back in France, just miles from the great European capital city, Paris.

He slipped through the grove of trees and saw a small dark car parked on the side of the road. A lone person stood outside the car. Marston veered toward it and slowed down as he got closer. When he was about ten feet away, he called out in French, "It's my birthday today."

He received the coded response he expected and stepped closer. The man was short and heavyset. The men exchanged handshakes and then the Frenchman waved a hand at the car.

"Get in."

After both men settled into the front seat, the Frenchman started the car and drove off to the southwest, towards Paris.

Chapter 8

Star & Garter Restaurant
Andover, England
15 August, 0703 Hours, London time

Dunn and Pamela loved the Star & Garter. It was here they'd had their first date, albeit one that ended badly. Pamela had made a comment that Dunn had taken the wrong way and he cut the date off, and drove her home without a word.

While on a mission to Calais, France, which had been a failure due to the treachery of a French Resistance traitor, Dunn had come to realize he'd been wrong. As soon as he'd returned, he apologized and asked Pamela if they could try again. Only after giving him a rough time over the phone, then giving away her real intentions by laughing away the seriousness in her voice, she'd forgiven him and things had gone remarkably well thereafter.

Seated at their favorite table by a window that had a view out onto High Street, both had coffee to drink while they waited for Saunders and Sadie. Dunn took a sip of the steaming, black liquid, then set his cup down. He eyed his wife of seventeen days.

Pamela's long blond hair was tied up, or rolled up, he wasn't sure which to call it, into a thing called a bun. Her blue eyes, which never failed to mesmerize him, focused on him. She smiled, and Dunn thought his heart would explode. This was the most beautiful woman he'd ever seen and why she'd picked him still flummoxed him daily. This was because when he looked into the mirror, all he saw was, well . . . himself. Nothing special, he'd always thought. But he'd seen the way *her* eyes always seemed to catch fire and light up at the sight of him, and he believed her when she said she loved him.

Their honeymoon had been interrupted by a phone call from Colonel Kenton. The assignment resulting from that phone call, a rescue mission to northwest Italy that had become much more, had concluded less than a week ago. They were able to resume their honeymoon for a few days before it was time for Pamela to depart for France.

"Where are Malcolm and Sadie?" Pamela asked.

Dunn checked his watch. "He did say he wasn't sure they'd be able to come. Getting Sadie from place to place is a logistical problem."

Pamela nodded, she understood what life was like for someone in a cast from ankle to hip. She'd helped with plenty of those.

Pamela's gaze shifted from Dunn's face to a point over his left shoulder; she was facing the entry to the restaurant, which came from the hotel's lobby. "Oh, there they are!"

Dunn stood and turned to face the door.

The huge bulk of his Commando friend dwarfed the young woman in the wooden wheelchair he was pushing with the greatest care. Sadie's right leg was sticking straight out resting on a wooden support. Dunn glanced at the table and said, "Here, Pamela, let's have you move to my side."

Pamela understood what Dunn wanted, and said, "Sure." She got up and pulled out the chair farthest from the window, and pushed it against an empty table nearby.

Saunders rolled Sadie to a spot just past the table, then he carefully turned her around and slid the chair forward until she was seated at the table.

"Pamela, 'ello. May I introduce my fiancé, Sadie? Sadie, this is Pamela and her 'usband, Tom."

Sadie lifted a hand and Pamela, then Dunn shook it gently.

"I'm so pleased to finally meet you both!" said Sadie, her voice smooth, like soft music. Sadie wore a white blouse and a black skirt, so much easier to get on and off what with the gigantic cast. Sadie's hair had recovered from the bandages that had covered it for most of a week. A red line streaked from her lip toward her right ear for a length of two inches. The stitches had been expertly done and when the doctor had removed them, he'd said over time the scar would be nearly unnoticeable. However, even though she was smiling, she turned her head slightly to the right, away from Pamela and Dunn.

Dunn shook Saunders' hand and clapped him on the shoulder.

As Saunders and Pamela seated themselves, Dunn found the waitress and waved at her, then he sat down across from Saunders.

The waitress arrived, and after placing their orders, the conversation got started with the ease of old friends.

Breakfast arrived, and everyone dug in. Dunn grabbed the catsup he'd asked for and dumped about half the bottle on his breakfast selection. Oblivious to the three pairs of eyes staring at him, he used his fork to cut off a corner and then he stuffed it in his mouth. Glancing at the others, he was greeted with open mouths and wide eyes.

"What?"

"Is that the infamous Spam and Egg sandwich?" asked Saunders.

Dunn looked down at the item in question. "Yeah. Why?"

"And you smother it with catsup?"

Dunn grinned. "It's an American thing."

Pamela shook her head. "Oh no, you don't. That is most definitely a Tom thing."

Everyone laughed.

Pamela turned her attention to Sadie and asked, "So when does the cast come off?"

Before speaking, Sadie unconsciously placed her right hand against her right cheek when everyone turned their attention on her.

Pamela noticed.

"Two more weeks. Ugh. It itches something awful."

"I know. That's quite common. I'm afraid I don't know of any remedies that really work. Just hang in there."

Sadie shrugged as if to say what else can I do? "When are you leaving for France? Mac told me."

"Tomorrow morning."

"Do you know where you're going? Or can you say?"

"I'm not sure exactly, but it's somewhere near Caen."

"Oh dear. I read there's been terrible fighting around that part of France."

"I'm afraid so. That's why they need me."

Saunders and Dunn ate while the women talked, glancing at each other once in a while, but both were really alone with their pre-combat thoughts. Saunders had once given Dunn advice on how to deal with leaving a girl behind when heading off to combat, to compartmentalize things. But the advice didn't cover what to do when your girl herself was heading to a combat zone.

Pamela and Sadie stopped talking suddenly and the men looked at them.

Sadie grinned. "Would you like me to repeat the question, Tom?"

Tom grinned back at her. "If you would, please."

"How long have you been in the army?"

"Oh, ah, I signed up the day after Pearl Harbor."

"Oh, dear. So many killed."

"Yes, but we're making the Japs pay for what they did. Did you know we sank four of their carriers involved in the attack on Pearl within six months? At Midway, it was."

"No, I didn't realize that. I mean I know about Midway, but not about the specific carriers. Do you think we'll win this war?"

Dunn put his fork down, glanced at Malcolm, then said, "Yes. I have no doubts that we'll win. It will be difficult, but in the end, we'll win." What he didn't say were his thoughts about how tough the fighting would be once the Germans retreated to the borders of the Fatherland. It was one thing to defend foreign territory gained in battle, and quite another when it's your own countryside.

"Do you think it'll be over by Christmas?" Sadie had a hopeful expression on her face. "It would be so nice to have Mac home for Christmas. It'd be the first time for us."

Dunn wanted to say yes, but he didn't believe the scuttlebutt going around since D-Day. "It's a long shot, but we can certainly hope for that, can't we, Malcolm?"

"Aye. We can always hope for that. You know, recently I had occasion to talk with a captured German SS soldier. He told me that as far as he was concerned, the war was already over, on sixth June. What I don't understand is that if some of their best soldiers think that, why do they continue to fight?"

No one at the table had an answer for that.

Pamela changed the subject. "Have you two set a date for the wedding?"

Sadie leaned into Mac, and he wrapped an arm around her.

"As soon as I can walk down the aisle. The doctors say I'll have to do some rehabilitation to gain back strength and confidence in walking. I'm not sure how long that'll take, though, but I am going to work very hard."

Pamela grasped Sadie's hand across the table. "Just remember that every moment of pain you experience is a sign that you are getting better."

"I haven't thought about it quite like that, thank you. Have you two decided on how many children you want to have?"

Dunn blushed at the question and Saunders chuckled at his friend's discomfort.

"Oh, shouldn't I have asked that?" Sadie frowned.

Pamela patted Sadie's hand. "It's all right. Yes, we've discussed it. Right now we're thinking four children would be right for us." Pamela smiled and took Dunn's left hand in hers. "Two boys and two girls, right, Tom?"

"Yep."

Dunn got a wicked grin on his face and asked, "How about you, Malcolm? Having a bunch of little Saunders running around?"

Impossible to embarrass, Saunders just roared in laughter. "You are correct, mate, all over the house."

"Red-headed boys and brown-haired girls. That's what I want," Sadie said.

The conversation drifted toward the future and each couple expressed their plans: Dunn and Pamela to Iowa and Saunders and Sadie to Cheshunt.

Dunn glanced at his watch and said, "I'm sorry, but Malcolm and I need to get going." He rose to go take care of the bill.

Pamela got up and went over to Sadie. She opened her purse and removed a small round object. She bent over to whisper in Sadie's ear while she handed it to her. "I think this might be your color. I won't need it where I'm going. It's old, from before the war, but it's still good."

Sadie's eyes brimmed and she said, "Thank you so much."

"My pleasure. Now you get better soon, so you can marry this guy." Pamela patted Saunders on the shoulder. She then kissed the big redhead on the cheek, and turned to join the returning Dunn.

Together, they walked out of the Star & Garter, not knowing when or if they'd ever be back.

Chapter 9

15 miles northwest of Le Mans, France
15 August, 1522 Hours, Paris time

Surprise on the battlefield is not unlike the feeling you get when you reach to open a door and someone on the other side yanks it open except it's not very likely that the person opening the door is about to try and kill you and your four friends.

The American Sherman tank's commander and gunner both were surprised when the German Mark V Panther burst into view from a stand of trees. They'd thought the trees were too thick for armor to make it through.

Even as the commander was giving him directions to the Panther, Corporal Rick Gordon rotated the turret quickly to bring the 76mm cannon to bear on the much larger, more powerful, more deadly Panther. He lined up the shot. The German tank was moving from Gordon's right to left at an oblique angle generally toward the Sherman. The Panther's gun pointed to its own right about forty-five degrees, meaning its gunner was looking the wrong way.

RONN MUNSTERMAN

"Confirming Mark V Panther, Sergeant, one thousand yards. AP round."

Gordon felt the nudge of a boot in the shoulder from his loader, who stood slightly above him, to let him know the armor piercing round was locked in the breech.

"Confirmed," replied the commander.

Gordon flipped the fire switch, and then mashed a foot pedal. "On the way!"

The thirty-three ton Sherman tank fired, its 76 mm round streaking from the long barrel.

The tank gunner watched through his view scope, maintaining a track on the target tank. The breech kicked back and ejected the round. Gordon heard the loader slam the breech closed, and without waiting for the kick in the shoulder, fired again.

The first round reached the target and Gordon shouted, not in celebration but shock, "What the fuck?"

The round had hit the tank dead on at the lower edge of the hull and . . . bounced off. The second round hit the rear left of the hull and also skipped away.

The Panther's turret began to rotate and its own gun, a 75mm, arced toward the Sherman.

Gordon lowered his aim and fired again. Just as the German gun was coming into line with him, Gordon saw the front left drive sprocket explode in a shower of flame and sparks. The Panther came to a halt as the track unraveled.

Gordon's commander shouted, "Back us out of here, Ted. Take a right angle as you go."

Ted Ritter, the driver, didn't need to be told twice. Even though he would be moving blind, he trusted the commander to know the way was clear. He yanked the steering handles backwards, the left one a little farther to facilitate a small turn, and the tank changed directions.

Gordon watched the Panther's gun continue its rotation, but it was moving more slowly now: the gunner was acquiring them. The Panther's gun barrel rose slightly.

Then the Panther exploded in a massive fireball.

Near the right edge of the view screen, Gordon spotted the distinct shape of an American Tank Destroyer.

"I think we owe someone dinner, Sarge."

"Damn straight." There was a pause, and Gordon knew the tank commander, Mike Lynch, was searching for a new target. "Ass end of a Mark III, bearing three-forty, twelve hundred yards, AP."

Gordon quickly rotated the turret and acquired the new target. The loader slammed a round into the breech and nudged his gunner. Gordon fired. The round shrieked out of the muzzle at over twenty-six hundred feet per second. About one and a half seconds later, the Mark III exploded and then sat burning. Gordon didn't see anyone get out.

Gordon didn't see any other tanks, so he asked, "Anything else out there?"

The tank commander grunted, then said, "I can't see a fucking thing with all the smoke. I'm going to pop up for a quick look."

Something fairly close to the Sherman caught Gordon's eye in his viewfinder and he rotated the turret a little bit. "Hang on, Sarge!" He reached up and grabbed hold of his commander's pant leg. "Load HE!"

Traversing the barrel and then depressing it almost as far as he could, he waited for the kick, then he fired. At the same time, a clang sounded throughout the tank as the fourteen pound panzerfaust round bounced off the upper part of the turret.

The Sherman's high explosive round hit the ground where the German soldier who'd fired the rocket was kneeling. He disappeared in fount of flame and dirt.

Gordon let go of his commander's leg.

"Thanks, Rick. I owe you."

"A beer would be nice, Sarge."

"Yeah, I'll see what I can do here in the middle of fucking nowhere."

The commander swung his periscope around in a full circle using the little crank handle. He spotted a dozen other Shermans, but no German tanks.

"It looks clear out there, the wind is helping with the smoke. Let me see what I can find out." He got on the radio and asked a few questions.

"Okay, I have the word. We're going to advance northeast another five hundred yards with the platoon, and stop short of the ridge for the night." Speaking for the benefit of the driver, he continued, "Ted, do you see the ridge?"

"Sure do."

Gordon heard the commander unlock the hatch above him, and then the clang of the hatch being tossed open. Fresh air, or at least less stale air considering the smell of gunpowder and smoke, poured into the Sherman as a welcome relief.

Gordon continued watching through his scope, just in case they'd missed something. As they'd just seen, a split second could make the difference between living and dying. If the tank destroyer hadn't shot the Mark V exactly when it did, Gordon and the rest of the crew would be dead. Gordon had learned not to dwell on these thoughts too long; they could drive you over the edge. Instead you celebrated making it through one more day of battle.

Ted Ritter goosed the four hundred plus horsepower engine and the Sherman sped off at ten miles per hour, keeping pace with the surviving tanks on either flank. Just downslope of the ridge, Ritter stopped the tank, but left the engine running. He was waiting for Lynch to give the word.

Sergeant Lynch had binoculars to his eyes, and he scanned the ridge from as far left to the right as possible. Over the low rumbling of the engine below and behind where he stood in the commander's cupola, he heard a jeep coming his way. He lowered the glasses and watched as a two-man scout team ran the jeep right past the Sherman and then another fifty yards uphill. They stopped and the passenger jumped out with a Thompson .45 submachinegun in his hands. He took a couple of steps then belly crawled to the top of the ridge.

The scout scanned the view in front of him for several minutes, then he put binoculars to his eyes. He seemed to be focusing on one spot for a long time.

Trouble, thought Lynch. He spoke quietly into his radio set, "Chuck, load an AP."

"Roger," replied Chuck Billington.

The scout crawled back toward the jeep, then rose and jumped in. He said something to the driver, who backed up the jeep and turned a hard left. They were coming straight back to Lynch's Sherman.

When the jeep pulled up next to the Sherman, Lynch looked down at the men expectantly.

The passenger, a corporal, spoke. "Sarge, there's a Tiger sitting inside a barn way down the other side. We're probably five hundred feet above him, and he's about fifteen hundred yards. Do you think you can get a plunging shot onto him if I guide your shots?"

Lynch knew the Tiger tank's frontal armor was almost four inches thick, but the top was only one inch, the only vulnerable spot, other than the rear end.

"Sure, but do you really want to do that?"

The corporal, a freckle-faced red head, smiled wanly. "Gots to be done."

Lynch nodded. "Okay, do what you can to give my gunner directions."

"Will do."

The jeep driver spun the jeep's wheels and shot back toward the ridge. He stopped in a spot that wouldn't interfere with the corporal's line of sight to the Sherman.

While the jeep was driving off, Lynch gave instructions to Gordon.

The corporal crawled up to the ridge, then glanced over his shoulder to make sure he was lined up between the Sherman and Tiger. He seemed to brace himself, and stood up.

Gordon visualized where he was in relation to the target and set his rangefinder at a little less than fifteen hundred yards to account for the drop, and lined up his sight right over the head of the corporal. He fired. The corporal didn't even flinch as the supersonic round roared over his head, perhaps by only six feet.

A couple of seconds passed. The corporal held up two fingers, and indicated that the shot was left. He then held up four fingers and indicated it was short.

Gordon adjusted and fired again.

The corporal began hopping up and down and waving his arms. In his excitement, he ran back to the jeep, forgetting to crawl.

When the jeep got back to the tank, the corporal was grinning wide. "Direct hit, Sarge! Went up in a huge explosion. The barn's gone, too. That was some shooting."

"That took guts to stand up there, son. What's your name?"

"Waterson. John."

Lynch nodded. "Well, thank you, John Waterson. Hell of a job."

"You're welcome. Well, we have to go. Need to report back." Waterson waved as the jeep roared away.

Lynch waved back.

"Okay, Ted, shut her down. Everyone come on out for the night."

"Roger, Sarge," replied the driver. The engine wound down.

Lynch unhooked his radio headset and microphone and slipped them over a hook near his right knee.

A few minutes later, the five men were sitting behind the tank digging into some C-rations.

The Sherman tank, "home" to the crew, had been named *Ghost Devil* by the men. They'd argued for some time about whether to name it with a *"II"* because this was an upgraded M4A2 version that replaced their first tank. The one that had kept them alive across North Africa and Sicily.

The men had first met in January 1942 at tank school located in Pine Camp, New York. That they had remained together for two and a half years was remarkable. Plenty of crews had been killed off piecemeal in various battles.

They gathered behind the tank, and shared dinner and coffee, followed by cigarettes. Within minutes of the last cigarette and long before the French sunset arrived, all five men were sound asleep.

Chapter 10

Hut 3
Bletchley Park, England
15 August, 1430 Hours

A timid tap on his desk caused Reginald Shepston to glance up to find a pretty, young brunette standing next his desk with a sheaf of papers in her hand. In her other hand was a large brown case like a barrister might carry.

"Mr. Shepston, you marked your inquiries 'urgent.' I wanted to hand deliver what I found to you as soon as I'd finished the report."

Shepston held out his hand and took the papers from the girl without a word. His attention was immediately on the contents of the report. He read it completely, flipping through the six pages quickly.

He was oblivious the whole time to the young woman, who had remained standing, her only movement an occasional shifting of her weight from one foot to another. She seemed unperturbed by the fact that the handsome young man had clearly forgotten she was there.

When he finished reading, Shepston placed the papers on his desk. He suddenly felt the young woman's presence and looked at her as if wondering where she'd suddenly come from. "Oh, sorry about that." He waved a hand at a chair to the side of this desk. "Won't you please be seated?"

"Why, thank you, Mr. Shepston," she replied with a smile. She sat down, placing the brown case on the floor next to her. She sat with her feet flat on the floor and her slim hands in her lap. Her hair was fixed up and away from her oval-shaped face.

Shepston flipped the papers to the last page, where the summary was located.

He read aloud the salient facts the young woman had coalesced. " 'Insel Riems was used to create mustard gas for the First World War. It's currently receiving radio traffic on a daily basis. The man in charge is Doctor Gebhard Teichmann, who reports to Himmler.' How did you track all this down in such a short time?"

The young woman spoke smoothly, "Well, I backtracked messages sent to Insel Riems that had a repeating name in it. It was Teichmann's, so then I followed where *his* outbound messages went if they contained 'Insel Riems.' There were only three: one was Berlin's central supply office, which handles all orders for materiel, and one the office for logistics, transports and such, and the last was Himmler's office, as one might expect.

"Next, I followed messages *sent* from those three offices that contained 'Insel Riems,' but did *not* go back to Insel Riems. Those are listed there at the bottom of the summary, sir. A number of highly specialized medical manufacturing facilities, plus the outlier, the one that makes the cylinder you asked about."

She held her hands up, palm facing each other about two feet apart. "The thing is about this long and about," she formed a rough circle with her hands about four inches apart, "this big in diameter."

She leaned forward, excited by the next part, but she managed to keep her voice low, "I guessed they were trying to create a new weapon, sir, so I checked further on the cylinders. They are not shell casings, so the weapon will not be fired from a cannon." She paused, evidently waiting for some reaction from Shepston.

Through all of this, Shepston simply listened rather stone-faced, but inside he was growing excited, too, but also intensely worried that this girl was about to confirm his worst fear. He merely nodded for the young woman to continue.

"Right. Well, then I wondered how else they might trigger a weapon and I wonder if it might not be some sort of aerosol sprayer, you know, like a smoke bomb."

Shepston nodded.

"I found some messages that were to a supplier who makes aerosol devices. The devices are all small enough to fit on top of those cylinders. Sir." She stopped, suddenly worried she may have blathered on too long.

Shepston was silent for a moment, nearly afraid to ask the question. Finally, after what seemed like an age to the girl, he said, "And have any of these devices been sent to Insel Riems?"

Although he'd spoken softly with no obvious change in expression, the girl did notice something in his eyes. Was it fear? Apprehension?

Certainly smart enough to have tracked down all of the information now laid out in the report, she was also smart enough to connect the dots, and understand her next sentence was about to change something big.

"Yes, sir. A dozen were received there only last week."

Shepston picked up a pencil and used it like a drumstick against the sheaf of papers. "Any of the messages to Himmler's office explain what's going on there at Insel Riems?"

Before the woman could answer, Shepston held up his hand, palm out. "Wait. I've seen you around, but what's your name?"

Surprised by the interruption, the young woman, who was only twenty years old, stared at Shepston as if he'd asked a terribly difficult question. She caught up mentally to the change of direction and said, "Eileen."

"Eileen. Eileen what?"

"Oh, Lansford. Eileen Lansford."

Shepston held his hand out. "Nice to meet you, Eileen Lansford."

Eileen shook his hand. "You too, sir."

"Oh, please, just Reggie."

"Reggie." Eileen looked at Shepston, suddenly aware of the handsome analyst's eyes taking in her face and her hair, evidently seeing her clearly for the first time. She successfully fought off the urge to plump her hair with a hand. It was then she noticed she was still holding the man's hand, having forgotten to let go. They both looked down at the same time, and then pulled back their hands, then looked away.

A spot of red appeared on both of Shepston's cheeks.

After a moment, Shepston cleared his throat, then said, "So, uh, Miss Lansford."

"Eileen, Reggie."

"Yes, of course, Eileen. About those messages . . . uh." Shepston started tapping the pencil harder than ever, possibly a jazz tempo.

A smile grew on Eileen's lips when she realized he'd forgotten what he'd asked her just two minutes ago.

"None of the messages stated anything clearly about what's going on at Insel Riems. For that matter, they don't really imply much of anything either," she offered.

She pronounced the last word as 'eye-ther,' which caused Shepston to smile. Memories of an old school chum had come to him, his best friend, who was now working at 10 Downing Street. They'd argued endlessly on which way was proper, then when they tired of that debate, they moved on to mathematics where at least the answer was more likely to be finite unless, of course, you were talking about linear partial differential equations, which don't always have solutions. In that instance, they would argue their point with the same fervor as if the problem did have a solution.

"Is everything all right, sir?"

"Reggie," Shepston replied automatically. He hadn't realized he'd slipped farther away into those memories than he thought. He focused on Eileen's face. He suddenly thought her eyes were a lovely hazel. Or maybe that was green? Maybe it depended on the light? Or on what she was wearing?

"Yes, yes. So nothing useful?"

"No, I'm afraid not." She looked up at the ceiling, thinking. "Well, wait. There was something odd."

She picked up the brown case and started to lay it on Shepston's desk. "May I."

"By all means."

She opened the case and pulled out a thick stack of papers, the messages she'd analyzed. She quickly flipped through the papers, which were obviously superbly organized, and found the one she wanted. She read it quickly, to make sure she had remembered it correctly.

"Yes. This is it. Doctor Teichmann asked the logistics office to work up an estimate of transit time from Insel Riems to various locations by rail, air, and roadway, trucks that is. Here you go, sir." She handed over the sheet of paper.

Shepston read the locations, "The Russian front, Bologna, Italy, Brussels, Caen. All front lines."

"Yes, sir."

Shepston rubbed his face with his hands and then ran a hand through his hair. "Bugger all."

"My thoughts, exactly, sir," said Eileen with a wry smile.

Shepston's cheeks turned red again. "Oh, I am sorry."

"Not to worry. I've heard worse, believe me. Three brothers."

Shepston gave her a weak 'thank you' smile.

"You've done great work here, Eileen. You can leave this all with me. I'll sign for it."

"Certainly, sir." Eileen pulled a log sheet out of the brown case and slid it across the table.

Shepston signed it quickly and handed it back.

Eileen put the paper away, but didn't get up.

Shepston looked at her. "Something else?"

"One other oddity. There's an early message from Teichmann to Himmler. You'll find it at the bottom of the stack. It's from March of forty-three. It says something about the 'Japanese methodology is too inefficient.' "

Shepston mulled this over briefly. "Thank you. I'll take a look at it."

Eileen surmised that the meeting was over and stood up to leave. She picked up the brown case and said, "Anything else, sir?"

Shepston started to speak, stopped himself, then said something else, or so it seemed to Eileen.

"No, thank you for a job well done, Miss Lansford."

Because he hadn't said what he first meant to, and he had reverted to formality, Eileen was pretty sure he had been about to ask her to go out with him, perhaps for dinner. "You're quite welcome, Mr. Shepston." She nodded, then turned and left the hut. She was smiling.

Shepston stared after her for a few moments, shook his head, then started reading through the stack of messages the lovely Miss Lansford had gathered for him.

It took him nearly an hour to glean the important facts, which he detailed on a notepad. He picked up all of the papers and neatened them, then laid them back down on his desk.

Leaning back in his chair, he stretched, then rubbed a hand through his hair.

He didn't have to think about what he'd read. The conclusion was inescapable.

He picked up the black phone and dialed a number from memory. All numbers were automatically memorized, he didn't have to think about it.

"Mr. Finch's office, may I help you?"

"Shepston for Mr. Finch, please."

"One moment."

A click and a few seconds later, Shepston heard his old friend come on the line, "Finch, here, Shepston. How are you, old boy?"

"I'm just fine, Finch. Yourself?"

"Busier and busier. "

"I should think so. Me, too. I have something urgent. Can we meet? Right away?"

"How urgent?"

"Your standing order."

There was a long silence on the line, followed by a deep sigh. "How soon can you be here?"

"Four o'clock."

"Get going."

Chapter 11

General George Patton's field headquarters
2 miles west of Nogent-le-Rotrou, France
15 August, 1556 Hours

By definition, a field headquarters is mobile, which meant tents were the only architectural structures in view. Large and small tents were spaced roughly evenly across a large grassy field, in places awnings, supported by evenly-spaced metal posts, provided some shade to the men and tables and chairs underneath. It was under one of the larger tents that Dunn and Saunders found themselves.

The day was hot for France in August, almost ninety, and the sky was clear of clouds making the late afternoon sun seem like a heat lamp. The sides of the tent were all rolled up to allow the summer breeze to flow through.

A craggy-faced colonel with gray hair stepped forward, and accepted and returned the sergeants' salutes.

"Edwards."

"Hello, Colonel, it's good to meet you," replied Dunn.

"Colonel." Saunders said with a nod.

"This way."

The colonel, who was Patton's chief operations and planning officer, led the men toward a small table in the center of the tent, offset slightly due to the main support pole. A radio operator sat nearby at a folding desk just big enough to hold the set and provide a writing surface. He was listening intently through a headset, and writing on a large notepad. A captain and a major were conversing animatedly at the edge of the tent, under it just enough to stay in the shade. The major seemed to be doing most of the talking and hand gesturing. Dunn thought he was angry.

From somewhere in the distance, to the east, came sounds of small arms fire and the *whump* of artillery and tank cannon fire. Jeeps seemed to be racing everywhere inside the headquarters area.

Edwards pointed at a nearby table on which a map of France was laid out. Small rocks acting as paperweights were on the map's corners.

Dunn and Saunders leaned over the map and oriented themselves mentally. The map had been set up with north in the correct direction, as you would expect from any military operation. Blue and red pencil marks indicated American and German unit locations. Some of the red marks included the names of the German officers who were known or thought to be in command.

The colonel picked up a number two pencil and pointed at a small blue oval on the map. "This is where we are. You can see Le Mans is to our southwest. To our east-northeast is Chartres." He tapped the location with the eraser end of the pencil. "General Patton intends to charge straight through that city, liberate it, then move on to the east to be able come up west of Paris. He wants to be in Paris within ten days."

The two officers finished their conversation and joined everyone at the table. The colonel introduced them as Captain Alford and Major Willis. Alford was young, perhaps Dunn's age of twenty-four, with an open friendly face oftentimes associated with a Kansas farm boy. The major was closer to thirty, and had blue eyes that probably stood him well with the girls. Both men were slender and fit, although their uniforms looked a bit worse for the wear. Being on the battlefield did that.

After the men exchanged salutes, Major Willis abruptly said, "So you're the hot shots who will save our ass in Chartres?"

Dunn eyed the major briefly without responding. It was clear the major was still pissed off about something. Dunn finally spoke in a soft tone, "We're just here to provide whatever help we can. Sir."

"Trying to horn in on the Third Army's success, I'd say. We've made it this far without your 'help.' " The major's face looked like he'd just bit into a lemon.

With a calm expression Dunn replied, "Whatever you need, sir, we're here to help."

"So what do you think two squads are going to do for us?"

"We don't know what the assignment is yet, sir."

"It's to win the fucking war, you idiot."

Dunn remained silent, although inside he was steaming. He'd run across plenty of assholes in his life, and especially in the army, but this guy was rapidly climbing to the top of the 'A' list. He made Colonel Jenkins seem downright chummy.

Colonel Edwards had heard enough. "Time to move ahead, gentlemen." The colonel was more than a little irritated with the major, who had managed to embarrass not only himself, but the other officers in front of the sergeants. As far as Edwards was concerned this was talking out of school. He would have a conversation with Willis afterwards. In private.

The major harrumphed once, but was quiet, and looked away briefly as if perhaps he realized he'd crossed the line in front of the colonel.

Edwards picked up a stack of eight-by-ten reconnaissance photos and spread them out on top of the map. He rotated the first one so Dunn and Saunders could see it better.

"These are from this morning. There's only one bridge in Chartres that's big enough for our tanks. You see it here?" He tapped a spot on the picture.

The photo was excellent and the resolution sharp. It looked like it was taken from about a thousand feet, but Dunn knew the recon flights flew much higher than that. A river ran through the city, north and south, cutting the city into one-quarter and three-quarter segments. The bridge in question was clearly visible. It crossed the river east to west. Using the buildings nearby as a measuring tool, Dunn guessed, "Is the river about a hundred feet wide, sir?"

The colonel's eyebrows went up. "Correct."

The river flowed through the city in two branches until just south of the target bridge where it merged into one. About a third of a mile to the south-southwest, a long shadow cast across the ground. "What's this?"

Saunders leaned closer and spoke first, "Has to be a cathedral. See the cross shape, here?"

"Okay, yes," Dunn replied.

"That's the Cathedral Basilica of Our Lady of Chartres. Dates back to around twelve hundred A.D.," Edwards explained.

Saunders was awestruck and said, "I bet it's gorgeous." Saunders loved architecture.

"Couldn't tell you, sergeant," replied Edwards.

"You want us to take the bridge and hold it for you? And I expect we'll need to prevent the krauts from blowing it up?" Dunn asked.

"That's right. We need you there by the night of the seventeenth. We plan to be rolling through on the next day. You have to secure the bridge a few hours prior to our tanks moving in. We'll also need to coordinate the timing, not too soon, but not too late either, if you see what I mean"

"I do see," was all Dunn said, as he thought about the problem.

"We can't drop you in there."

"I figured that, sir. Antiaircraft?"

"Yes, quite a bit more than we can risk."

Dunn and Saunders both quietly examined the map. After a minute, Dunn placed his finger on the notation indicating the headquarters where they were standing. He eyed the terrain between his finger and Chartres, then he plopped his other forefinger on a different spot and traced a path toward the beleaguered city.

Saunders saw the same thing Dunn did. "Interesting idea."

The colonel and the other officers leaned over to see what Saunders was talking about, but Dunn had lifted his finger off the map and stood back.

"How far do you expect to be the night of the seventeenth, sir? South of the city?" Dunn asked.

Edwards touched a spot on the map. "At or near Morancez."

Using his right thumb and forefinger as a measuring stick, Dunn widened them until they were a scale mile apart, then gauged the distance from Morancez to the bridge. "About four miles. Okay that's not too bad." He looked up from the map and asked Edwards, "Who do we see about special weapons and logistics, sir?"

"Uh, that's me," replied Captain Alford. "What is it you're going to need?"

Dunn told him, listing most everything he could think of, plus some extras that he didn't expect to get, the fluff of the request that could be thrown out without harming the mission.

Alford raised his eyebrows at some of the items. He glanced at Colonel Edwards, who merely shrugged and said, "We have to have that bridge, Captain."

"Yes, sir."

Dunn handed the captain a scrap of paper. "I wrote it all down, sir."

"Hm, yes. Okay," Alford replied, taking the paper and checking it over quickly. It was neatly written and organized. If only supply sergeants were so precise, he thought.

The colonel had heard a lot about Dunn and Saunders from above, and had talked with both of the sergeants' commanders, Kenton and Jenkins. What he had learned during those conversations was the quick thinking and high success rate both men had. Each had their own style, but the successful results spoke for themselves. Kenton in particular had mentioned that while he couldn't get into the top secret particulars, both men and their squads had contributed significantly to the war effort on numerous occasions, from France to Germany to Italy.

One thing Edwards had learned from Patton was that sometimes you had to just trust your men and get out of their way to get the job done. Once Patton gave responsibility to someone, that person also had the authority necessary to accomplish the task at hand. Right now, that person was Edwards. If Edwards was going to emulate his boss, the responsibility had just shifted to a Ranger and a Commando. And that was that.

Edwards looked at Captain Alford. "Give them everything they ask for. Keep me informed." To Dunn, he said, "The job is yours now. Provide Captain Alford with the details of your attack and the plan for holding the bridge. Do you have any questions?"

"Do you have any recon photos of the entire city?"

"We do. They're right here." Edwards picked up a stack and handed it to Dunn.

Dunn and Saunders examined the half-dozen sharp photos for a few minutes. To Saunders he said, "Look, they're ten on this side and only five on the other one."

"Aye,"

"We can keep these?" Dunn waved the photos in the air as he asked the colonel.

"Yes, you can. I have others. Any other questions?"

"Not right now, sir."

"If any come up later, you can find me here. In the meantime, work with Captain Alford." He started to turn away, then stopped to glance back and asked, "Both of your squads are full strength?"

Dunn and Saunders both answered, "Yes, sir."

Edwards nodded. "Major Willis, you're with me." Edwards didn't wait for a reply and moved away from everyone to stand at the edge of the tent.

Major Willis studiously ignored the sergeants and followed the colonel.

Dunn wondered whether the major was about to be dressed down for being an ass.

Captain Alford asked, "I expect you'll be needing ground transport?"

"Not exactly, sir."

"What? Why not? How do you plan to get there? What are the details of your attack?"

Dunn and Saunders told him.

As he listened, Alford noted that they seemed to have a close enough relationship where one would start a sentence or an idea, and the other would finish it. He couldn't tell whether they were adlibbing the plan or if they had worked up some possibilities prior to their arrival. When they got to the transportation part of the plan, his mouth plopped open at the mention of the required equipment.

"What the hell?" he said. At first, Alford thought the two soldiers were kidding him, but when they calmly stared at him, he realized they weren't. He shook his head at the audacity of the plan, but understood immediately that it could work. Like most officers, Alford was not easily impressed, but he was this time.

"I'll get to work on that right away. I have to ask: what made you think of it?"

Dunn shook his head and shrugged. "I don't really know, sir. Stuff just pops into my head."

"And the bull shite pops out of your mouth," muttered Saunders, who elbowed Dunn in the ribs, even in front of the captain, who grinned.

"Your men all squared away?"

"Yes, sir. A few tents not far from here. I told them to either sack out or grab some chow," Dunn replied.

"Okay, good to hear. You can join them. I'll send for you in a couple of hours after I get these things," he waved the equipment list, "for you."

"Thank you, sir."

The sergeants stepped back and saluted. Alford returned it and then he turned away.

The two sergeants walked toward the tents where the two squads were billeted.

"So do you think the captain will come through?" Saunders asked.

"Yeah, I do. He didn't bat an eye at the thirty calibers."

Saunders nodded. "Aye. Although I thought his eyes were going to bug out of his head with the rest of the stuff."

"That *was* priceless."

"I can't wait to see the expression on our men's faces when we tell them."

Dunn laughed. "Oh, me too, Malcolm. Me, too."

Chapter 12

Open field 10 miles west of the remnants of Caen, France
16 August, 1604 Hours

Pamela Dunn stared out the C-47's window as the aircraft began its swooping descent into a rough airstrip in France. On her first airplane ride ever, she had looked out through the small window in wonder for the whole trip across the gray English Channel. She couldn't help thinking about her husband and his frequent flights. He routinely flew in these contraptions, and then to top it off, jumped out of them with nothing but cords and silk between him and certain death. While she didn't seem to have problems with airsickness or have a fear of heights, the thought of falling through the clear blue sky under a parachute was overwhelming.

The transport carried Pamela, two other nurses, and a dozen American soldiers who were sound asleep, their gear stowed at their feet and in the aisle.

Turning away from the window, Pamela glanced at her traveling companions, two young women, also nurses in the Queen Alexandra's Military Nursing Service. Both were just twenty years old, and recently completed their training. This was their first assignment. Pamela would be their mentor, even though it was also her first assignment, because of her experience. At the young age of twenty-two, Pamela already had nearly four years behind her. The QA, as the nursing service was known, had awarded her a commission and the rank of Lieutenant.

When she'd learned of this and told Dunn that she outranked him now, he'd simply and wisely replied, "You've always outranked me, dear."

She had rewarded him with a not-so-girlish snort, and a kiss.

One of the younger women noticed Pamela's glance and returned it with a grim smile.

"Are you feeling any better, Irene? We're almost there."

Holding her head perfectly still, Irene said, "As long as I don't move my head and don't look out the windows." Underneath Irene's place on the bench seat was a partially filled bag with the late lunch that had come up shortly after takeoff. "And maybe if I stop breathing."

The other nurse, Edith, wrapped her arm around Irene and gave her friend a squeeze.

A clunking sound came from below their feet, and the plane suddenly lurched. Irene's eyes grew wide.

Pamela looked forward into the cockpit. The pilot and copilot seemed to be calm, so Pamela deduced that the landing gear must have locked into place.

"It's okay. That's just the wheels going down so we can land."

"Maybe I should close my eyes."

Pamela said, "Oh, no, don't do that. I've heard it can make things worse." Pamela got up and took one step across the plane to sit down on the other side of Irene. She grasped one of Irene's hands and held it between her own. She looked out the window on the other side of the aircraft and noted that they seemed to be at tree level.

"Tell you what, Irene. As soon as the wheels touch the ground, shall we shout and cheer? Does that sound like fun?"

"Yes, okay." Irene looked dubious.

Edith leaned forward slightly and glanced at Pamela, giving her a nod and mouthing 'thank you.'

Pamela smiled in return.

The wheels smoothly hit the ground.

The three nurses shouted and cheered, and a relieved Irene broke into a wide grin. With a dead pan expression she quickly said, "See, I told you it was going to be okay."

The three nurses laughed. Two friends became three.

None of the soldiers even woke up until the plane came to a stop and the engines shut down.

The soldiers, replacements who were along for the ride, exited the plane first, not to be rude or ungentlemanly, but because the nurses would have had to climb over their gear to get out the rear door. Once the men hit the ground, they formed up and took off at double-time.

Pamela went last, and climbed carefully down the ladder backwards. When her feet touched French soil, she took a quick step to the side and looked around. The airfield was merely an open field in a larger expanse of farmland between French villages. It looked just like England, but then again, not. Off in the distance to the south were some hills. When Pamela examined them, she noted something seemed . . . off. Then it hit her. Instead of green grass, shrubs and trees, the hilltops were brown, almost an ugly gray. What trees there were appeared to be free of foliage and many were missing limbs and others were broken clean off part way up.

"Oh, dear God," she whispered.

Edith, who was closest to Pamela asked, "What?"

Pamela lifted her hand and pointed at the hills.

Edith and Irene followed Pamela's point and their eyes widened. After a moment the three nurses exchanged uneasy glances.

Irene spoke first. "Makes me think of London in nineteen forty."

"Me too," Edith said.

Pamela took a deep breath, as if preparing herself for an unpleasant task, then said, "We're here. Let's focus on our job." She led them toward the lone tent across the field. At the same moment, a black four-door sedan veered off the road that ran parallel to the field, and raced across the grass toward them.

The nurses stopped walking, waiting for the car to reach them.

The car skidded to a stop a few feet from the women. The female driver shouted at them through the already rolled down window, "Hop in! We've got to go! Casualties coming in. Throw your bags in the boot, it's unlocked."

Each woman had a duffle bag containing all of her belongings. The nurses ran to the back of the car where Edith twisted the handle and lifted the lid. After the bags were in, she slammed the boot closed. Pamela went around the left side of the car and got in the front passenger seat, while the other two jumped in the back seat.

The moment the car doors closed the driver, a woman in her early thirties, stomped on the gas pedal and let out the clutch. Grass and dirt spewed out from underneath the torqued tires. A few seconds later, with the new arrivals holding on for dear life, the car careened onto the blacktop road and sped away to the east.

Without looking at the women, the driver said, "I'm Agnes. Which of you is Pamela?"

"That's me."

"Good to meet ya."

"You, too. Edith is behind me and Irene is behind you."

"Hi girls." Agnes took her left hand off the steering wheel and gave a little wave. "I'm your supervisor. We'll be at the hospital in a few minutes. We're located a few miles from Caen, although not much of anything is left of that city. When we get there, I want each of you to change and scrub up. You'll have exactly five minutes to accomplish that." She went on to explain what each nurse would be doing.

The more she talked, the more somber grew the faces of the new arrivals.

Pamela spotted the hospital after the car zipped around a curve in the road. She could scarcely believe her eyes.

Tucked into a huge clearing, and surrounded by trees on three sides, were somewhere around fifty tents. All of them were adorned with the international hospital symbol: large white circles with red crosses on both sides of the sloping roofs. Pamela thought the largest of the tents were big enough to hold thirty cots, her reference point being an ambulance parked near one of them; three of the vehicles could fit inside, parked nose to tail. Smaller, but not small, wall tents were interspersed throughout the camp. She assumed some of these would be for recuperation, and others would be quarters for the doctors, nurses, and other staff required to make a hospital run properly.

People were moving around the hospital grounds, not running, but not dilly-dallying either.

Agnes turned off the road into the hospital field following a path created by many vehicles passing over the grass. She pulled the car into a space near one of the large tents and shut off the engine.

"All right, ladies. Grab your bags and let's go."

As the women climbed out of the car, two ambulance trucks roared into camp and stopped only a few yards from them. Moments later, men on litters were placed gently on the ground in rows. Four nurses from another tent had run out at the sound of the vehicles arriving, and were kneeling beside the new patients, performing triage while calming the wounded men.

A moment later, Pamela and her group of nurses were all inside the tent, which was the size of a nice flat in London. Only one end of the tent had its door flaps pulled back, which were tied off with canvas strips.

One area to the right was curtained off and Agnes pointed toward it. "You can change into your uniforms over there. I laid everything out for you. But don't get used to that!" She smiled to take out the sting, but the new arrivals knew she was serious.

Chapter 13

Alan Finch's Office
10 Downing Street, London
17 August, 1555 Hours

Shepston found Finch's office on the third floor and down a narrow hallway filled with doors, number thirty-six. The door was open and he walked right in. He appraised the office and the man sitting behind the dark wood desk.

"You've moved up in the world."

Alan Finch stood up with a smile. He walked around the desk and shook hands with his old friend.

At thirty-three, Finch was the same age as Shepston, older by a few months. He wore a neatly pressed black suit, white shirt and for color added a narrow blue tie. A slender five-eleven, Finch's thin face sported a new, dark Clark Gable moustache.

Finch arrived in 10 Downing Street by way of MI5, where he'd been an analyst for almost six years. Just a little over two months ago, Finch had hand-delivered a message to the Prime Minister. It was based on information he'd pulled together, and indicated that the German rocket plans were more advanced than first thought. He'd ended up working on Operation Devil's Fire with Harold Lawson of the American Office of Strategic Services, then with Dunn and Saunders.

He had come up with a brazen plan to fly the two elite units into Germany, and land at abandoned airfields instead of parachuting. Dunn's squad destroyed the atomic bomb facility. Saunders' job was to blow up the Nazis' jet bomber meant to carry the bomb to the United States, but an American pilot on fighter escort for the flight had other ideas. He'd convinced Saunders to help him steal the German bomber and had flown it back to England.

The twin successes of that mission had deeply impressed Winston Churchill. He immediately hired Finch away from MI5. Now Finch provided analysis of various situations and missions to the Prime Minister.

Finch spread his arms out wide. "Look, I can't touch both walls at the same time."

"That was a shithole tiny office you had over at five."

"Indeed." Finch went back around his desk and sat down, waving a hand for Shepston to be seated. "And look, I have a window." Behind Finch was a small window looking out onto Downing Street. "I can tell when the sun is shining."

Shepston chuckled. "Yeah, as if you'd ever actually go outside. You practically live here, I'll wager."

Finch shrugged. His friend was right; sixteen hour days were the norm.

Shepston examined Finch's face closely. He knew why Finch had thrown himself into his work. It had been four years.

"How have you been?"

Finch knew what his friend meant. He glanced away briefly, then back at Shepston. Finch's wife and unborn child had been killed by German bombers in 1940.

"Day by day, Reggie."

Shepston nodded. "Let me take you to dinner tonight."

"Steak?"

"Dream on."

Finch gave a little lopsided grin that Shepston recognized. It was the one Finch always wore as a boy. It had died with Finch's wife. Shepston was happy to see it.

"Anyone special in your life?" Finch asked.

For a split second, the image of Eileen Lansford popped into Shepston's mind. He started to smile, but stopped himself. Instead, he shook his head. "No. Too busy for that, don't you know?"

Finch grinned at his friend; he'd seen the twitch of the almost smile. "Whatever you say."

Shepston knew he was caught out. "Fine. I just met someone at work. Seems a nice girl. But that's all there is to it. I really am too busy."

"You have to eat don't you? Maybe take her to dinner instead of me." Finch grinned.

"You won't give up will you?"

Finch had tried to get Shepston to settle down before the war, touting the wonderfulness of marriage. "Just trying to help, old son."

Shepston shrugged. "We'll see."

Finch shrugged in return. The personal time ended and he asked, "Tell me, what did you find that is related to my standing order about information on new German weapons?"

Shepston leaned forward. "The bastards. I'm certain the Nazis are working on a chemical weapon."

"Explain."

Shepston laid out what he'd found, and what Eileen Lansford had discovered in the messages outbound from Insel Riems to Himmler, the logistics and transportation offices in Berlin. Finch listened without comment, letting Shepston go through all of the information first.

Only when Shepston stopped and leaned back in his chair did Finch say anything. "How far back do these messages go?"

"The first one to Himmler was a reference that the 'Japanese methodology was too inefficient' and was sent in late March last year."

"No indication of what that methodology was?"

"None. We're inferring the delivery system for the poison."

"You mean gas, don't you? Like or similar to mustard gas."

"I do."

Finch picked up a brand new Argentine *Biro* ballpoint pen, a gift from the Prime Minister after he'd joined the staff at 10

Downing Street. Finch rarely used it without thinking of the RAF bomber crews who used the new pens because they wouldn't leak at high altitude like other brands.

He jotted down a couple of notes, and drew a cylinder underneath the text. He doodled a cloud above the cylinder. Looking up at his friend, he said, "As I recall, the Germans used cylinders only early on in the First World War because of difficulties they encountered. They had to bury sometimes over ten thousand devices, and then were forced to rely on favorable winds before releasing the gas, which could take weeks. Only when they finally switched to using artillery gas shells did they become much more effective."

"So you don't think they're trying to resurrect the gas?"

Finch shook his head. "Not in the way we're thinking about it."

"But they had that list of locations for which Teichmann asked questions about transit time. Surely they plan to send the cylinders to them?"

"Yes, I agree, but two things trouble me: first, the message about the Japanese method being too inefficient, and the fact they only ordered a small number of the cylinders."

"Why?"

"Well, how many different ways can there be to deliver poison gas?"

Shepston tilted his head in a half-nod, acquiescing the point. "Just the two that we know about."

"Right."

"So that makes me think the Japanese method has nothing to do with gas, but something else."

"Something else? What?"

"What else could you deliver in a cylinder?"

"Other than poison?"

"Think about death in European history."

Shepston knew Finch already had something in mind, but he was expecting Shepston to arrive at the same conclusion through the Socratic Method, which they both enjoyed.

Shepston only had to think for a few seconds. "That's easy: the Black Death. Bubonic plague. Some kind of pathogen, a biological weapon."

Finch nodded grimly.

"Why would they unleash something they can't control? Once it's out, it could spread back to Germany."

Finch shrugged again and the men sat in silence for a few minutes, each trying to figure what out the Germans were up to.

Shepston had a sudden thought and sweat began to bead up on his forehead. "They aren't worried about it spreading to Germany. They have the vaccine."

Chapter 14

1/4 mile south of Thivars, France
18 August, 0112 Hours, Paris time

Three deuce-and-a-half trucks followed the narrow road into the southern edge of the village Thivars. They were driving slowly and without lights in the near dark of a quarter moon. All had their canvas tops rolled up so the men could see.

The lead truck carried Dunn's squad, with the Ranger sitting in the cab so he could see better to the front. The middle truck carried the equipment Dunn had requested from Captain Alford, every single item. Alford had pulled some strings and favors and got the special items, including the two big ones.

The last truck held Saunders and his men. The British Commandos sat half on each side of the truck, Saunders and his second in command Steve Barltrop sat across from each other, with Saunders behind the American driver.

Barltrop was Saunders' best friend and second-in-command. Barltrop's father was a mechanic at a garage in Cheshunt, the same town where Saunders' fiancé Sadie lived. While Barltrop was a year younger than Saunders' twenty-six, he was three years older than Sadie. He often said he wished he could take credit for introducing them, but he only knew of her in school. Barltrop's dream was to work on race cars, preferably Grand Prix, if only England would develop a car worthy of the race.

Along the same bench seat as Barltrop were four others. Geoffrey Kopp and James Pickering were replacements who had gone on the recent missions to Italy with the squad and held up their end of the job well. Kopp was skinny man and a Cockney like Saunders. Pickering was quick to smile and people were glad to be around him. William Endicott was a quiet fellow, prone to long periods of silence. Then out of the blue, he would quip something that would make the squad burst out laughing. George Mills from Manchester sat next to the rear gate.

Sitting on Saunders' side of the truck were the remaining members of the squad. Edward Redington, Tim Chadwick, Christopher Dickinson and a new replacement, Arthur Garner, who arrived just a few days ago after the loss of veteran squad member Neville Owens. Owens had been killed in Italy while the squad was on a mission to blow up a rail bridge. Saunders and the squad had brought Owens' body all the way back to Corsica, where he rested in a British military cemetery.

Garner, a corporal, had been selected for his expertise in explosives, which had been Owens' job. While all the men were more than capable of handling explosives of all manner, having someone who'd spent more time with dangerous things was still valuable.

Dunn looked out at the darkened streets of the French village of Thivars as the truck passed through. In a short time, the convoy drove out of the town. The driver downshifted, then braked, which was followed by a left turn. The truck rolled off the road and down a small hill, then stopped. Saunders' truck stopped next to Dunn's, but the middle one rolled on past, around the vehicles, before stopping.

Leaving their gear, Dunn's men were out of the truck the moment it came to a halt. They ran to the equipment truck and began unloading the first of the two assault boats, which were stacked piggyback. Just as they finished getting the cumbersome flat-bottomed boat off the truck, Saunders' men arrived and got their boat unloaded. Within minutes, the two boats were in the waters of the L'Eure River and tied off to keep them from floating free.

Dunn and Saunders stood together on the bank of the slow-moving river while the men set about gathering all the gear, which included the Sten submachineguns with suppressors, as well as two .30 caliber Browning machineguns. The more difficult items to store in the wide boats were two long cylindrical devices and the crates that went with them.

"Think of anything else we should have brought with us?" Dunn asked.

"It feels like we brought too much, but when we get there it won't seem like that at all."

Dunn snorted. "So true. Pity we can't bring a Sherman along to help."

"Aye."

"I'm still estimating two hours to cover the four miles to the southern edge of Chartres."

"Yes. It looks like that water is barely moving north."

"Yeah, this makes the Mississippi look like a speedster and the Missouri a downright jet."

The Mississippi River moved along at a stately three miles per hour, while the Missouri roared past Kansas City at seven miles per hour, making it the fastest flowing clear channel river in the United States.

The L'Eure River appeared black in the night, simply a darker space than its surroundings. It was about forty feet wide at this point. Dunn knew it wound its way northwards, through their target city of Chartres, and across the French countryside until it met its much larger and faster sister, the Seine.

"I'll take your word for it, mate."

"We'll take the lead. You staying back about thirty yards?"

"That's right."

The two sergeants spent the next few minutes going over the plan in detail, asking questions like what if certain things happened how would we handle them? Meanwhile, the rest of the men completed their tasks of loading the equipment into the boats.

"See you when we get there, Malcolm."

"Aye. Be careful."

"Always am."

The men separated and Dunn went to the first truck. "We're all set. Thanks for the ride."

The soldier nodded. "Welcome, sergeant."

As the trucks roared away into the night, Dunn made his way down to the boats. The men had already boarded and were waiting for their sergeants.

The U.S. Army assault boat M2 was five feet, nine inches wide by thirteen feet, four inches long. Constructed of plywood, it weighed just over four hundred pounds and was very maneuverable in the water. The bow and stern were both square, although the bow tapered slightly inboard. Eight of the men would row with canoe-style paddles while another man used a paddle as a rudder.

Dunn stepped into the boat with the help of Wickham. The rest of the men were kneeling and had their paddles at the ready. After settling into a kneeling position himself on the starboard bow, Dunn said in a whisper, "Jonesy, push us off."

Jonesy was right behind Dunn. He placed the paddle against the river bank and pushed the craft's nose away. As soon as a gap of a few feet opened up, Dunn said quietly, "Start paddling, men."

Nine paddles dipped into the water and eight men began smooth silent strokes through the black water. Dave Cross, who knew his way around boats, manned the rudder. He was the son of a Maine fisherman, and had spent many days on the Atlantic Ocean. He helped guide the boat into the weak current about ten feet from the east bank. This would be where they'd stay, rather than the center of the channel.

The quarter moon visibility worked both ways, and a boat on a shiny surface looked big and black and, most importantly, obvious. Saunders' boat followed in the small wake of Dunn's boat, staying the thirty yards behind.

The night sky was star filled and Dunn made out the Milky Way, something that always left him feeling awestruck, primarily by the enormity of it. Trees lined the river, living directly upon the fresh water flowing by. Their branches and leaves formed a partial tunnel on each side of the river. If the river were to become narrower and the branches touched, the tunnel effect would be complete. There were just a few sounds of nature, some insects, and perhaps some bullfrogs. An occasional splash in the center of the channel might have been a fish snagging a flying insect for a late night snack.

The boats moved quietly, their flat bottoms making only a slight rasping sound as they slid across the river's surface. Even fully loaded, the draft was merely fifteen inches, making the boat capable of cruising the shallowest of rivers.

The river was full of turns, and because of the trees lining the banks, seeing ahead was a problem. At each blind corner, Dunn would order the men to stop paddling. While the boat drifted forward with the current, Cross would keep it straight. Dunn would peer ahead as soon as he had a clear view of the next section of the river. He thought of Mark Twain and Mississippi river boat pilots who might only know a one-mile stretch of the twenty-three hundred mile long river. But they knew it better than anyone in the world and safely guided the boats and their precious cargo, both people and goods.

Dunn was on the alert for German patrol boats, although he didn't really believe one would be cruising the small river. The Seine was more likely to be under guard. However, Dunn was a cautious man when being careful was prudent. He'd take risks when necessary to complete the mission, but everything was a calculated risk. His ambush attack on a platoon of elite Nazi SS troops to save the village of Ville di Murlo, Italy just a couple of weeks ago had been planned and calculated down to the minute. He had optimized Saunders' and his squads, and deployed Jonesy the sniper with specific targets.

The first sign of trouble occurred two hours into the journey. Dunn judged they were within a quarter mile of the southern edge of the city of Chartres. They were on a long straight stretch of the river and he could see a bridge ahead, the first of several. These were the things he'd pointed out to Saunders on the map back in the headquarters tent: ten on one side and five on the other.

A road ran parallel to the river on the east side, only about twenty yards from the water. A sound grew louder slowly, but soon Dunn realized it was a motorcycle coming from the south, behind them. Dunn gave the order to stop paddling. Saunders, who was watching Dunn's men closely, saw them ship their paddles so he gave the same order.

The boats drifted in silence. The motorcycle engine sounds grew louder and louder. Suddenly, through a break in the trees Dunn spotted it, a standard German cycle-sidecar affair. It was also easy to see that the sidecar, which was on the side opposite him, was also occupied. The riders gave no indication they'd seen anything, and they'd certainly never be able to hear the small sounds of the boats over that of the motorcycle's engine. The problem as Dunn quickly saw, was the road crossed the first bridge the boats would go under when they entered Chartres.

Dunn gave the order to paddle toward the east river bank to get farther under the tree canopy and out of sight He planned to sit there until the Germans crossed the bridge and rode on to their destination. Saunders' boat followed. When they reached the bank, a couple of men on the starboard side of each boat grabbed onto low hanging tree limbs to keep them moored in place. The boats were only about fifty yards from the bridge.

At this point the river was about thirty feet wide. The simple stone bridge ahead of the men had low walls, just enough to keep cars from rolling off into the drink. Two arches supported the structure, forming black, half-moon shapes above the water.

Dunn expected the motorcycle to roar across the bridge and on into the city, but that didn't happen. When the vehicle reached the middle of the bridge, the driver slowed, then stopped, turning the cycle toward the south side of the bridge. He shut off the engine and got off, and the passenger climbed out of the sidecar. Both men stretched, then walked over to the bridge's south wall. In unison, they put their left boot on the low stones. Then one of the men lit a cigarette and offered one to the other. Two red dots flared.

"Oh for fuck's sake," muttered Dunn.

Chapter 15

French Resistance meeting place
Paris, France
18 August, 0332 Hours

The building where Marston was set up was the fourth one in as many days. Staying in the same place too long just invited the Germans to track you down. He sat at a large metal desk in the basement of a three story apartment building. At sunset the evening before, Marston had climbed to the roof and looked westward. There, a half mile distant, stood the fifty-meter-tall *Arc de Triomphe de l'Étoile*, the one-hundred-eight-year-old monument to veterans of the French Revolutionary and Napoleonic Wars. Marston longed to touch it, but he knew it was unlikely until the Allies freed Paris.

The two basement windows behind the agent, which would normally provide a view up onto the passing sidewalk, were covered with blackout drapes. The room itself was for extra storage for the tenants, at least during peacetime. It was empty except for a few wooden chairs and a table for the French Resistance members to sit around to plan, eat and drink, and play cards. Stairs leading to the ground floor were just outside the room to the left and a backdoor was to the right at the end of the long hallway.

Three young men were sitting at the table talking, but Marston ignored them. He was examining a stack of papers provided by many Resistance members. The information varied from troop strength and location to how well the trains, taxis, and streetcars were running this particular day. Other reports covered what other Resistance factions were doing. Between the communists and the socialists, among others, it was difficult to keep track of their activities, not to mention attempting to coordinate action.

Also on the desk, on Marston's right was a Morse code key and transmitter. He finished encoding his notes and turned on the transmitter, and turned the knob to the frequency specified for the day.

While he keyed his messages, the three men broke out a deck of cards and began arguing about what to play. One of the men, the eldest about thirty-five, interrupted the discussion by standing up abruptly and declaring he had to take a piss. The other two men sat back in exasperation. The one holding the unopened deck of cards tossed them back onto the table.

By the time the man returned from the bathroom on the first floor, Marston had completed sending the messages. While clicking the key, part of his brain was tracking the conversation. He got up, stretched his back, and then walked over to join the men at the table.

"Need a fourth for Belote?" he asked.

"Oui."

Marston joined the men and the one who had thrown the pack picked it up with a smile. He shuffled the cards and then put the deck in the center of table. Marston, who was sitting opposite the dealer, and therefore his partner, cut the deck and pushed both halves back. After the first hand, the player to the dealer's right would cut the deck.

The game soon proved to be serious and loud, with players trying to win the bid, evidently by out-shouting the others. Cigarette smoke hung in the air.

Marston's partner wore a dingy white shirt and brown slacks with suspenders. His cigarette never left his mouth except to flick the ash onto the floor. The other men wore similar clothing. Each had a black Modèle 1935A automatic, which held eight 7.65mm rounds, tucked in shoulder holsters. Marston carried his Smith & Wesson .38 in a belt holster.

Marston's partner laid down a winning hand down and said, "We win!"

Marston grinned and said, "We did. Another, gentlemen?"

The two opponents grumbled, but agreed and the one on Marston's right dealt.

"So where are you from?" asked the dealer, looking at Marston.

"Across the channel."

"Yes, I figured. Just curious. I guess you're not supposed to say."

"Correct."

Marston's partner said, "You look more German than English."

"I do, yes."

"I bet that's been a big help for you."

"Well, I can't say."

"Oh come on, where else have you been?"

"Here and there."

"I bet you've actually been in Germany. Do you speak the language? I bet you do."

Marston shrugged.

"As you wish."

The group fell silent for a few minutes, then resumed their shouting and arguing about the game, the cards, and the bids.

Almost an hour of playing elapsed and Marston's partner put his cards down after the hand was over and said, "My turn to go to the bathroom." He rose and left the room.

Once in the apartment on the first floor where the nearest bathroom was located, the man pulled his pistol out and double-checked the clip. He gently pulled back the slide to make sure there was a round in the chamber. He found the black telephone next to the bed. He picked it up and dialed a number, which was answered on the first ring.

"Ja?"

"He's here."

A click on the other end was his only reply and he lowered the handset to the cradle quietly. He went into the bathroom, relieved himself of whatever was ready to go, then flushed the toilet. A minute later he sat down across from the spy and smiled.

"Shall we try to win this game?"

Marston returned the smile. "Yes, indeed."

The game progressed and the men played for another ten minutes.

Just as Marston was getting ready to deal the newly cut deck, the basement door burst open.

Chapter 16

On the L'Eure River
Just south of Chartres, France
18 August, 0335 Hours

Just as Dunn's patience was wearing thin, the Germans simultaneously flicked their cigarettes into the water. The driver reached into his shirt pocket as if to get the pack out again, but the passenger evidently said something as he vigorously gestured toward the city, clearly wanting to get going. The driver raised his hand palm outwards, presumably to calm the man down.

The driver mounted the motorcycle and started it, then the passenger climbed into the side car. The driver, who was apparently irritated with his passenger, popped the clutch and the rear tire screeched as the machine tore off toward the west. A few moments later the engine sounds died away.

"Let's go," said Dunn.

The men holding onto the tree limbs let go, and then used their paddles to push off the bank. The men settled quickly into a smooth rhythm and before too long, Dunn's boat slid under the bridge where the two Germans had taken their smoke break.

As previously planned, Dunn slowed his boat as they approached the next bridge, only another three hundred yards downstream. This was so Saunders' crew could catch up, closing the gap to a few yards.

The bridge passed overhead, just a few feet away. Dunn looked over his shoulder at Cross and pointed toward the east bank. Cross nodded and shifted his paddle. The men on the starboard side briefly stopped rowing and the boat quickly moved close to the east bank. This was because the river split into two channels that flowed two-thirds of a mile, almost through the entire city, before merging back into one channel. The merge point was just a few yards south of the target bridge at the northern part of the city.

Dunn knew the next part might be tricky. Cross had told Dunn that the west channel was likely to be the main one, and the current would try to keep them there. They would have to make a sharp right turn out of the main west channel and fight their way into the east channel. He also warned about eddies that could suddenly push or pull a boat sideways. A miss by either boat could jeopardize the mission because there were twice as many bridges across the west channel and this increased the possibility that a German sentry could spot them floating by underneath.

In Saunders' boat, Chadwick was the boating expert, also the son of a fisherman. It was Chadwick who had piloted the stolen German patrol boat used in the commandos' escape after destroying submarines at the Wilhelmshaven sub pens.

Dunn's boat hugged the right bank. The east channel opening was ten yards away. Cross shifted the paddle so it was on the far left of the stern. He paddled toward the starboard side with each stroke by the other men to keep the stern left and the bow right. The boat slipped across the water. An invisible eddy caught the bow and moved it suddenly to the left, almost pointing toward the west channel. The men worked to correct course and the boat snapped through the eddy and lurched into the east channel.

Dunn gave a sigh of relief. One down. He stared past Cross at Saunders' boat. It seemed to be following exactly in the same path as Dunn's boat. When it also jumped sideways, Chadwick and the other paddlers also reacted perfectly and soon the second boat was pulling up behind Dunn's.

The current in the east channel was even slower, and Dunn wanted to maintain a steady, but slow pace, so he gave a quiet order. Four of the paddlers stopped working, shipping their paddles from the water carefully.

The boats glided silently downstream. Buildings began appearing on the left bank, their pale edifices gleaming in the dim moonlight. The moon was now at a point placing it more or less over the men's right shoulder, high in the sky. If it were the sun, it would be about eleven o'clock sun time. This created the problem of putting the boats potentially in the moon glare off the water. Dunn intended to stay as far to the right as possible until they reached the landing zones. The east bank was covered by vegetation and trees, with no buildings at all.

Dunn's chief worry was whether there would be sentries on the bridges. According to maps of Chartres and the recon photos, there were five bridges to pass underneath before reaching the landing zones. Two appeared to be foot bridges, probably wooden, and the other three narrow, stone bridges for vehicles. The first one was a vehicle bridge.

Dunn scanned the bridge quickly, and saw no one on it. A few moments later, the boats slid through the small arched opening. There was little room to spare and the men all instinctively ducked as the stones passed by just a couple of feet over their heads.

Four more to go, thought Dunn. Across the narrow river, the buildings took on more form and it was easier to see them. Each structure was built right next to the water, and it made Dunn think of the photos he'd seen of Venice, Italy. One building had a large deck with a white wooden railing. Several overflowing flower pots were hanging above the railing, but in the moonlight, there was no perceptible color. No lights were on anywhere; no surprise there, although Dunn wondered where the bakery was. They would be getting up soon to fire up the ovens.

There was no sound anywhere, no birds, no insects. Nothing. The total silence would be unnerving to some men, but not to the combat veterans stealing quietly through a sleeping city.

The boats continued on their slow, but steady path downstream. As they approached each bridge, Dunn would stare intently trying to make out any movement, any shape that did not belong. Nothing. Had the Germans already started pulling back? Had they declared the city open, which would mean they would not fight in the city? There was no way to know. For that matter, there was no way to know for sure whether the target bridge was under guard and wired for explosives. However, it was more than prudent to assume so.

Up ahead, the east channel turned to the northwest to merge with the main channel. Right at the bend was the last bridge, a footbridge. When Dunn was certain it was unoccupied, he gave a whispered order. All paddlers stopped, with Cross guiding the boat. When the boat slid under the bridge, Dunn stuck out his right hand and grabbed onto one of the wooden supports. Jonesy grabbed another beam and the boat came to a halt. Saunders' boat glided past, just inches off the port beam. Saunders raised a hand to Dunn, who nodded.

Fifty feet downstream, Saunders' boat came to a stop on the northeast bank, just before the point where the channels merged. Dunn and Jonesy let go of the bridge and the boat moved ahead a short distance, almost clear of the bridge. Cross shipped his own rudder and grabbed a support post to halt the boat again. Dunn's squad would lay back and provide supporting fire, if necessary, while Saunders' squad exited their boat.

As Dunn watched, Saunders and his squad climbed out of the boat. Chadwick tied off the stern line to a small tree to keep the empty boat from wandering off downstream, not that there'd be a need for it again. The British Commandos gathered all of their gear and the extra weapons, and disappeared into the black of the trees.

Dunn waved his hand at Cross, who let go of the support beam. The boat floated free and then the men began paddling toward the main channel. Dunn's landing zone was on the west bank, seventy-five yards away. This was the most perilous point because they were crossing the river, and would be in view of anyone on the bridge. Dunn intended to pause just before entering the main channel and scout the bridge for sentries as he had done the whole trip through the city.

The vagaries of fluid dynamics caught up with Dunn, however. Another hidden and stronger eddy grabbed the boat, and slammed it to the west, directly into the main channel before he could scout the bridge. Before the men could react, including the experienced Cross, the circular motion of the huge eddy whipped the stern around until the boat was going downstream assbackwards.

Hampered by the need for silence, all the men could do was look at Dunn, who in turn was looking at Cross for guidance. Cross used hand signals to indicate what he wanted and Dunn relayed them as quick as possible. The men on port side began paddling hard forward, or upstream, and the men on the starboard side paddled in the opposite direction like a tank rotating in place. Cross paddled sideways to help push the stern to the port side.

Even though the boat was starting to rotate clockwise, it was now smack dab in the center of the main channel and rushing under the target bridge.

There was no way to hit the landing zone.

Chapter 17

French Resistance meeting place
Paris
18 August, 0341 Hours

A red-haired woman with tucked under a black watch cap ran into the basement room. She leveled her 9mm Luger at the men. She stayed by the door, kicking it shut with her foot.

Each of the men lifted his hands above his head. Marston, who was facing away from the door, started to turn around, but the woman snapped, "Hands up!"

Marston carefully laid the deck of cards on the table and raised his hands. He had time to think, *bloody hell*.

"Take your weapons out of the holsters and drop them on the floor."

The men did so, very slowly and carefully, including Marston.

"Clasp your hands behind your heads. If you lower them, I will shoot you."

Quickly, the men had their hands behind their heads.

The woman moved to her left so she could see Marston's face.

He regarded her quietly. He recognized Madeline immediately, but he kept this knowledge to himself, and his expression gave away nothing, including his surprise at seeing her here in Paris.

"One of you is a spy."

This confused Marston for a brief moment. He *was* a spy, after all, but he realized she meant one of the other men, for she surely recognized him, too.

Two of the men looked at each other, then at Marston and Marston's partner, the cigarette man. Marston's partner looked only at Marston. His eyes narrowed.

Madeline squeezed the trigger and the weapon fired, incredibly loud in the basement room. Marston's partner gained a red hole in his right temple and slid off his chair with a thump. The other two Frenchmen stared in shock.

"You may put your hands down, gentlemen. Pack up and get out. Go to your personal safe house and wait for word from your cell leader." Madeline moved closer to the table, now that the traitor had been dispatched. To Marston, she said curtly, "You. Pack up your transmitter and come with me."

Marston nodded, taking her cue and refraining from talking to her. The two Frenchmen finished packing, picked up their weapons, and left.

Marston retrieved his own weapon, and then put the radio equipment into its suitcase and faced the French Resistance leader.

"It's nice to see you again, Neil."

"You, too, Madeline."

"Time to go. The Nazis will be here soon." She tipped her head toward the dead man. "We just found out for sure he was tipping them off. Came to rescue you."

"Thanks."

Madeline didn't reply, but nodded as she went to the door, and opened it carefully, just a sliver.

She listened, then peeked out through the slender gap toward the front of the building, the way she'd come down the stairs. She pulled the door open a little farther and looked the other way down the hallway. She slid through and Marston followed her toward the back of the building. They moved fast, feet sliding carefully across the concrete floor of the hallway. They made it into the alley behind the building just before they heard the sounds of a big truck screeching to a halt on the street in front of the building.

Madeline didn't hesitate as she ran across the alley and opened the back door of the building opposite. She flung it open and waved Marston inside. She darted in and closed the door. She moved past the spy, leading the way down the dimly lit hallway, and out the front door, two streets away from the Germans.

The darkened street was empty in both directions, except for a lone car parked a few spaces down to their left. Madeline walked toward it and said, "Get in."

After they both climbed in the 1935 Renault Vivasport, Madeline started the engine and drove off, being cautious with the engine speed so as not to screech the tires. At the end of the block, she turned right, away from the Germans' location. The street they were on had more vehicles, cars and small delivery trucks, parked here and there. After traveling only three blocks, she slowed, and then turned left. They entered a narrow street with a sidewalk on the left side only. Marston shrank back from the window, certain the car was going to slide into the buildings they were passing.

Chapter 18

East bank L'Eure River
Chartres
18 August, 0342 Hours

Unaware of Dunn's serious problem, Saunders gathered his men as soon as they disembarked from the boat. They were in a wooded area on the channel's east bank. The woods were thick and moonlight sifted through the leaves.

Saunders pointed with a camouflage-blackened hand at four men. He nodded, and jerked his thumb over his shoulder in a "take off" motion.

The scouts moved away in pairs. William Endicott and George Mills went slowly directly north, moving parallel to the main channel. Staying about two yards apart, they stepped carefully through the underbrush, testing each footstep. They carried their Sten submachineguns with one hand and used the other to fend off low hanging branches, being careful not to snap off one. Their job was to locate the east end of the bridge, and begin looking for evidence of explosives. According to the map, their boat landed about seventy-five yards from the bridge.

Geoffrey Kopp and James Pickering headed off to the northeast. The road that crossed the bridge made a sweeping, gentle right turn toward the south and they were responsible for locating German sentries. Saunders and Dunn, during the mission briefing, had said they expected to find a number of machinegun emplacements around the bridge. On the east side, they expected one or more to be located just off the road on either side of the bridge stone works, facing west, and or along a straight line extending from the bridge into the wooded area on the outside of the road curvature. This would give that machinegun crew a line of sight straight down the pike for several hundred yards.

When the bridge came into view, Endicott and Mills were only about twenty yards away. The roadway was about ten feet above them. They stopped and knelt, listening for human sounds. After listening for a full minute, they crept closer.

Kopp and Pickering reached the edge of the woods and stopped. The road was a few yards away directly in front of them. The pavement stretching left to right acted as a kind of no man's land. If they stepped out onto it, they would be exposed and visible in moonlight. The woods on the opposite side were less dense, but so far, neither man could see any Germans.

Suddenly, from their left and across the road, came the soft sound of a cough, then some gruff words in German. Someone getting chewed out. Kopp touched Pickering lightly on the shoulder and looked into his shaded eyes. Pickering nodded indicating, yes, I heard it. Both men examined the problem. They had to find out who was there. It was definitely two men, minimum, but what weapons did they have? Was this the machinegun Dunn and Saunders thought would be set up to fire straight down the pike? How could they cross the road without being seen?

The Germans were more likely to be watching the bridge, not the road to the south, but if someone just happened to glance their way, all would be lost.

Looking to the south, Pickering spotted a building, the only one on the west side of the road, just ten yards away. He thought through what he had in mind, then decision made, tapped Kopp on the shoulder. He gave hand signals for what he was planning, and what he wanted Kopp to do. The other commando nodded and then knelt, raising his Sten to his shoulder, aiming at the spot where the German sounds had come from.

Pickering slid back a few steps into the woods and made his way to the north side of the building. It appeared to be some sort of shop. A long porch ran the length of the building. A sign was hanging sideways above the porch, but it was too dark to read, even if Pickering understood French. Making his way downhill to the back of the shop, he moved carefully to the south side and back up the incline to the front. Once there, he took off his Brody helmet and tucked it underneath a shrub next to the shop. He put his Sten gun next to it. Last, he removed his gun belt and holster for the Webley .455 he carried and put it down. It was a last-ditch weapon and the enormous round would sound like a bomb going off in the still of the early French morning. Armed only with his commando knife, he stood straight, smoothed his hair and his shirt front.

He sauntered out onto the road as if he belonged there and headed south. No shouts of alarms came, although the hairs on the back of his neck were standing up. When he reckoned he was far enough to be out of sight of anyone in the woods where the sounds had come from, he crossed the road and into the woods on that side. Turning back to the north, he moved as quickly as possible while maintaining silence.

When he reached the point directly across the road from where Kopp was kneeling, Pickering stepped closer to the road. He was relieved when he couldn't see Kopp, which meant his partner was properly concealed. Getting back on his path toward the Germans, he continued northward.

Endicott was first to reach the bridge's east support pillar. He put a hand on the cool stone to steady himself as he listened. No sounds anywhere. He examined the pillar above him. The stone looked white in the pale moonlight. Wires that would lead to explosives would appear as black lines. He doubted the Germans would bother trying to hide them. There weren't any in sight. Next, he dropped to a knee and felt around the base at ground level, but found nothing there, either. Rising, he looked up, toward the road to the east. The embankment going up to the road was steep, and covered by shrubs and grass. It would be difficult to negotiate and remain silent.

Turning his attention to the river flowing by, he saw a narrow strip of earth between the base of the bridge pillar and the water's edge. If he followed that, he could get to the north side of the bridge and check for wires and explosives.

Facing Mills, he pointed at himself, and then in the direction under the bridge. Mills gave him a thumbs up.

Endicott took two steps along the narrow and, as it turned out, muddy and slippery, ground. He nearly lost his footing when, out of the corner of his eye, motion on the river caught his attention. Putting a hand on the wall to steady himself, he looked toward the source of the movement.

To his disbelief, Dunn's boat was sliding downstream sideways past the bridge.

Chapter 19

Paris
18 August, 0344 Hours

At the end of the block, Madeline slowed the car before edging it into the intersection. Satisfied it was clear of Germans, she turned onto the wider street. Ten meters down, she turned right into a large multicar garage built between two apartment buildings. She wound her way through the garage and parked as far from the street as possible.

She turned off the engine and turned slightly to face Marston.

"Things are heating up. The Americans are very close. You will be staying at a different location and only myself and one other person will know you are there. He's the only man I can trust completely."

"Who is that?" Marston asked, speaking in French as he had been since his recent arrival to Paris.

Madeline smiled as she replied to Marston's question. "My uncle, Remi Laurent. You remember him?"

"Sure I do."

Two months ago, Laurent and Madeline had provided critical assistance to Sergeant Dunn's squad, and Marston, because the spy was along for the ride. Unfortunately the ride, in the form of one C-47 Goonie Bird, had been shot down and everyone still alive had parachuted out, landing in a field near Saverne, France.

Taking refuge in the hay loft of a farmer's barn, Dunn and his men, plus Marston, and the defecting top scientist from the Nazi atomic bomb lab that Dunn's men had destroyed, had to rely on the local French Resistance leader for help.

When a local policeman, who was a Gestapo stooge, called in the secret police, Dunn and his men gained a tactical advantage and surprise, and annihilated the German squad that appeared on the farm. The head Gestapo agent, Luc, was a traitor to the French Resistance and he had earlier compromised a mission by Dunn that caused the death of one of Dunn's men, Timothy Oldham.

Madeline had vowed to track him down and kill him. After the ambush at the farm, only Luc temporarily survived. Dunn had shot him as the agent ran toward the farmer's wife and daughter, clearly intent on killing them both. In the aftermath, Madeline and Laurent had loaded the dead German soldiers into a truck for disposal, and Madeline took special care with her prize, the traitor.

"You and your uncle really helped us, back on that farm."

"We were glad to do it."

"How is your uncle?"

"He's well."

"Is the farmer's daughter doing okay? Killing that policeman must have been difficult to recover from."

"Claire is fine. She wanted to join the Resistance, but I talked her out of it."

Marston raised an eyebrow. "Why?"

"She's young. Did you know her fiancé was killed by the Gestapo?"

"No. Dear God."

"I told her to live through the war, find a man to love and have a happy life. I don't want this life for her." Madeline turned her head away from Marston, who waited, saying nothing.

"Anyway, she's fine and so are the rest of her family." Madeline swallowed hard, then was able to face Marston again.

"Tell me how you escaped. We never heard what happened exactly. I mean we did find out that two German airplanes and a fuel truck were blown to bits at the airfield, and that several Germans at the airfield were killed. But that's all we know."

Marston regarded the lovely young woman before him. Her eyes, whose color Marston couldn't make out in the dim light, seemed to sparkle with something unique. Her lips, although unadorned by lipstick, were full and inviting. Marston felt a sudden urge to kiss her, and only just managed to hold still and not lean in closer.

If Madeline sensed what he almost did, she gave no sign of it.

Marston suddenly felt nervous under the gorgeous French woman's steady gaze and he cleared his throat.

"Well, uh, you have the facts right. Dunn's squad did all of that."

Madeline's breath caught slightly at the mention of the Ranger's name, but Marston didn't notice.

"He had to destroy the Me109s because a flight of B-17s were right above them as they took on fuel. There was a German transport, one of those trimotor things, a Junkers fifty-something or other. Our pilot was able to fly us home in it."

Madeline shook her head as if coming out of a memory. "That's good news. So everyone made it home safely?"

Marston couldn't help but think, *I just said that*. Out loud he said, "Yes, that's right."

Madeline suddenly fidgeted in her seat. After a few moments she could stand it no longer. "How is Sergeant Dunn these days?"

Marston noted the hopeful inflection in her voice and everything suddenly fit for him. He wondered how to break the news.

Madeline picked up in his hesitation and nearly shouted, "He's dead isn't he?"

"Oh, no, no. Nothing like that." He wanted to reach out and touch her arm to comfort her, or maybe it was more of just wanting to touch her. "He's fine. The last I heard, he um, he uh, got married."

To Madeline's surprise, she nodded and grinned. "But he's okay, right?"

"Yes, I believe so."

Madeline was all smiles now. "Oh, I'm so relieved."

"I thought you might be upset at the news he'd gotten married."

"What? Oh, no, no. Well, I do have a spot in my heart for him, but when I last saw him I knew he was going to marry Pamela, the English girl. I'm just so happy he actually went through with it." She lowered her voice and leaned close to Marston, unaware of her effect on the spy. "I was worried he'd try to get out of it because of the war and wanting to wait and see what happened. You know, whether he'd make it."

Marston nodded, which was all he could do at the moment. *Lord, what is the matter with me?*

"Come on. Let's get you inside to safety."

Marston managed to say, "Okay."

They got out of the car and walked toward the stairs leading into the building next door.

Marston trailed Madeline slightly, and noticed how white her skin seemed on the back of her long, slim neck. He raised his hand and just in time pulled it back.

Madeline turned suddenly to look over her shoulder at him. She smiled.

Bloody hell, does she have eyes in the back of her head? he wondered.

Chapter 20

On the L'Eure River
Chartres
18 August, 0345 Hours

Cross and the other eight men with paddles were working hard to get the water craft turned around.

Dunn watched helplessly as they were swept past their landing zone and under the bridge. The boat was being pushed sideways down river as the men struggled to get the bow around. Dunn glanced back over the tops of the men's heads at the east pillar where he saw movement; a black figure was standing under the bridge. Alarmed, he started to raise his weapon, although he was unsure of whether he should take the shot. Deciding not to because he realized it might be one of Saunders' men, he was rewarded for the decision when the black form raised an arm in a British salute. In spite of the situation, Dunn grinned and waved back.

Cross and the men finished getting the boat turned the full one hundred eighty degrees and the correct end of boat was headed in the right direction. Dunn pointed toward an opening on the west bank and the men, even though tired from the sudden expenditure of paddling effort, set to work to get the boat grounded where their boss wanted it to go.

A few minutes later, the bottom of the boat scraped against the muddy embankment. Lindstrom, who was on the port side, jumped ashore and grabbed the stern line from Cross, and tied it off on a tree. The men climbed out and began to sort their weapons and equipment. Dunn and Cross put their heads together and took stock of their situation.

They'd landed about forty yards north of the bridge, a good hundred yards past their planned point. The area around them was partly wooded, and the buildings on the road crossing the bridge were easily visible as dark hulks.

Even though they were a long way from the bridge, Dunn whispered to Cross. "Get Jonesy and Lindstrom on their way. Make sure they know where they're going."

"Okay."

Cross moved away and grabbed the two men, the sniper and his spotter. After ensuring they knew where they were and where they were headed, he patted them on the shoulders. The men walked away quietly, Jonesy with his 1903 Springfield A4, with a new attachment on the front: a suppressor, which added another foot to the length, making the weapon appear somehow even more evil than usual. Jonesy had the rifle slung over his shoulder and carried his suppressed Sten gun in his hands. Lindstrom was also carrying a Sten gun. Both men carried the all-important 1911 Colt .45.

While Cross sent Jonesy and Lindstrom on their way, Dunn gathered his two pairs of scouts. Dunn pulled Al Martelli and Stan Wickham close and said softly, "You still have the south side of the bridge. See if you can squeeze along the water's edge. Report back as soon as you determine whether there's a machinegun there."

The two men nodded and stepped toward the bridge watching their boot placement carefully.

Dunn grabbed Clarence Waters and Bob Schneider next. "You're on for the north side of the bridge. Bob, you go first. Waters, pay attention to where Bob puts his big feet. He'll find the best path."

Cross rejoined Dunn as the other men moved away. The rest of the squad gathered around the sergeants. Dunn motioned for everyone to kneel with him, and once they'd done that, he said quietly, "Now we wait. Bailey, you and Goerdt step into the woods that way," Dunn raised a dark hand toward the west. "Watch and listen for anything out of place."

"Yes, Sarge," they replied softly.

The men moved off into the darkness, leaving Dunn and Cross to wait nervously.

Jonesy found the northeast corner of a three-story stone building where he expected it to be. It was about twenty yards from the bridge. There was a cleared path about a yard wide following the building's wall that ran west a good thirty yards, a sizable structure. Jonesy took off up the hill with Lindstrom a few steps behind him. Soon he reached the end of the wall. He put his back to it and edged closer until he could see around the corner. There was another building about ten yards away. To his left about twenty feet away was the back of yet another building forming a U-shaped open area. The two seemed to be interconnected. Looking up, he tried to make out the windows. They appeared as rectangular spots darker than the stone wall. There were no lights on.

Moving quickly, the men traversed the open area and continued along the wall. A few steps farther along, Jonesy found what he was looking for: a door. It was a wooden door with a pair of small windows set about chest high. He tried the knob and, to his relief, it turned freely. He gently pulled on the door, praying that it didn't squeak. He got it open just far enough with no alarming noise and slipped inside. Lindstrom darted inside and carefully closed the door behind him.

The space they were in was completely dark. Looking out through the windows in the door, the moonlight seemed ultra-bright on the trees. The next part was going to carry some risk, but Dunn had given Jonesy permission. He pulled a small flashlight off his belt. During mission preparation, the men had applied black electrician's tape across the lens leaving a gap an eighth of an inch wide. Holding the light so it pointed straight down, Jonesy switched it on. He moved it around slightly, never quite tilting it to horizontal.

They were in a storeroom, which had a few metal buckets on the floor and a pair of wooden saw horses leaning against one wall. Directly ahead were the stairs. Jonesy navigated up the stairs and found a hallway leading to the front of the building, which faced south. At the far end of the narrow space, a single window shined with moonlight, which landed on the hallway floor. Jonesy turned off the flashlight and hooked it back on his belt.

Moving quickly and silently the men advanced on the window. They passed several doors that were opposite of each other. Apartments, thought Jonesy. About ten feet from the window, Jonesy stopped. The moonlight shining on the floor was cast at an angle to his left. The hallway turned a corner and ran off to the right. Sliding to the right, keeping away from the light, he moved to the corner of the hallway and glanced down the hall. Windows on the left, doors on the right. Perfect.

He crossed the east-west hallway and stood to the side of the first window. Looking out toward the left, he could clearly see the west end of the bridge. Motion caught his eye on the south side of the bridge. Staring at the spot for a moment, he was able to make out a man's shape. The top of the shape had the distinctive German helmet. The man shifted slightly and moonlight glinted off a metal tube. Jonesy was certain it was a machinegun barrel. Probably the dreaded MG42, he thought. This was nicknamed Hitler's buzzsaw because of the rasping, tearing sound it made. It was capable of firing twelve hundred rounds a minute.

If there was a matching gun on the north side of the bridge, Jonesy couldn't see it from his vantage point because the building blocked the view. He wished he could let Dunn know what he'd seen, but he was confident the scouts would find a way to attack the gun emplacements.

Turning his attention to the hallway, he gauged the distance to the far end to be about thirty yards. There were four windows to get past without being seen. The two men moved off down the left side of hallway. When they reached a window, they got down and crawled under the moonlight, then rose again to move to the next.

A few minutes later they arrived at the last window. While Jonesy knelt to the left of it, Lindstrom crawled under and moved to the other side. Jonesy examined the window; it was unlocked. He put a hand under the handle and lifted carefully. The window rose, making a soft shushing sound. After he got it open twelve inches, he stopped.

Outside, he could see the road that crossed the bridge. As it ran farther west a few yards from the building, it split into a Y. About seventy yards farther away, both forks crossed a north-south road. Inside the triangle lay what had to be a green space. His visibility extended almost a hundred yards. At these distances, his shots would be easy. Jonesy settled in to wait, getting his Springfield ready.

Chapter 21

On the east bank of the L'Eure River
Chartres
18 August, 0358 Hours

Saunders was already starting to get impatient when Pickering and Kopp suddenly reappeared.

"Found one MG42. It's just under seventy-five yards from the bridge, tucked in among the trees on a straight line from the bridge. About where we expected." Pickering went on to explain how he'd crossed the road undetected. "So I have a way that'll take us straight to the jump off point I used." He pointed directly east. "It's actually straight up there."

"Right. Good job, lads," replied Saunders.

Saunders started to move away, but Pickering held up his hand.

"There are four men there. I think the other pair might be the explosives engineers. They were sitting on the north side of the gun, maybe five yards away. I couldn't see the trigger."

Saunders nodded. This was crucial information. That changed the primary target from the gunner and his assistant to the engineers. They would undoubtedly have the trigger that Pickering mentioned, a plunger style dynamo used to send the spark of electricity down the wire to the detonators.

Saunders recognized the irony of being in the position of trying to stop a bridge from coming down when only a couple of weeks ago, Saunders and squad had been on the demolition side of things in Italy. It had gone their way and the bridge had collapsed with a German supply train on it, although the price had been high with the loss of Neville Owens. Would it go their way this time?

He needed to know whether Endicott and Mills had found the explosives and the wires leading to them. Using the moonlight, Saunders checked his watch for the hundredth time and then looked toward the bridge. He thought he discerned a slight movement of a shrub about ten yards away. A moment later, Endicott popped into view with Mills right behind him.

When Endicott got closer, Saunders looked at him expectantly.

In a whisper, with urgency in his voice, Endicott said, "Sarge! Dunn's boat missed their landing spot."

"How far?"

"They're maybe fifty yards downstream. They got out okay."

"On the right side of the river?"

"Yes."

"Right. I think they'll be fine. Any luck on the explosives?"

Endicott shook his head. "Nothing on the south side, too dark underneath and on the north side. Just need more light."

Saunders turned back to Pickering. "Can we maneuver to the east of the four men you saw undetected?"

"Yes, it's all wooded."

"How close can we get?"

"Ten yards, maybe."

Saunders thought about the problem, examining his mental map of where the bridge, the road's curve, and the machine gun were located relative to each other. He ran an attack sequence, like a little movie, in his head, with certain men in particular places. He did this three times making minor adjustments each time, and when he was satisfied, gathered his men and gave them their instructions.

A few minutes later, two groups of deadly British Commandos split apart and moved silently through woods.

On the west bank of the L'Eure River
Chartres
18 August, 0402 Hours

Martelli left Wickham behind, just down the hill from the machinegun they'd found on the south side. He made his way back to Dunn and the others. Waters had already returned, leaving the big man, Schneider, behind.

Dunn had a plan prepared, making the assumption there would be two machineguns, one on the north side and one on the south of the bridge. Martelli and Waters had verified his expectations.

Martelli filled in Dunn. "We have a problem. There's only room for one guy to shoot and if our guys on the north are too high on their side, they could be hit by our fire."

"No way to squeeze in with Wickham?"

"Not really. We'd have to push into a big shrub to make room and that might alert the krauts."

Dunn adjusted his plan. "Okay, here's what we'll do then." He quickly gave his orders, including the timetable. He and Saunders had been forced to set a timetable that could not change because they would be on opposite sides of the river and out of communications with each other. First shots would go off at precisely 0415 hours.

Surprise had so much value on the battlefield that in some ways it made your attacking force seem larger, and definitely more effective. While well trained and combat veteran soldiers would react quickly, the sheer firepower of the attacker could completely negate that reaction. It was tough to react if you were already dead or wounded in the first three seconds of an ambush firefight. Dunn and Saunders had pulled one off in Italy, totally destroying a platoon of elite SS troops having only half the strength of the Germans. It had all been over within a few minutes.

Dunn expected this attack to play out in a far shorter time frame. Ten seconds would be on the long side of things. Provided, of course, things went according to plan. It was always the unexpected that fucked up things. How you responded to those things determined whether your men lived or died.

"Everyone ready?"

The Rangers all nodded.

"Let's get in position."

Apartment building
Chartres
18 August, 0414 Hours

Sergeant Dave Jones checked his view to the west again. Nothing was moving. He slung the Springfield over his shoulder and got down on his hands and knees. He quickly changed places with Lindstrom, who would watch the west side. Raising the weapon, and keeping the suppressor just inside the window, he sighted on a German manning the south machinegun. He would not be taking the first shot, but if something went wrong, he would help.

"Time?"

Anticipating the question, Lindstrom already had his watch up so he could see the second hand marching around the face. "Thirty seconds."

"Okay. Back off to the other window." Jonesy wanted Lindstrom to move away from the window so the muzzle blast wouldn't be right in his face. Aside from just flat out being dangerous, it would ruin Lindstrom's night vision at the crucial moment.

Lindstrom went to the next window east, crawled under it, and took up a position where he could still see to the west. He raised his watch. He held up five fingers for Jonesy.

Four, three . . .

The bridge, east side
Chartres
18 August, 0415 Hours

From just ten yards away, Saunders took aim at the center of a German's back and pulled the trigger. The Sten chuffed three times. The man fell sideways. Next to Saunders, Garner fired at the other man they suspected to be near the detonator. That man collapsed.

Two steps to the south, Pickering and Mills fired exactly at the same moment as Saunders. Their targets were the gunner and his assistant. The Germans died not having any idea what had happened. Both pairs of commandos ran forward.

Garner found the detonator and dropped to his knees next to it. He set about disconnecting the wires.

Pickering and Mills shoved the dead Germans aside, and took up positions to man the MG42. Like all commandos and rangers, each man knew exactly how to operate the weapon, both as the gunner and the assistant.

Fifteen seconds had transpired.

The bridge, west side
Chartres
18 August, 0415 Hours

Wickham stood right behind Martelli on the south side of the bridge. They were a few feet below the road level, waiting.

Schneider and Waters took aim at the two men manning the north machinegun and fired, killing the Germans with three shots each. As soon as they finished firing, the two men dropped down to get out of the line of fire from Wickham's and Martelli's weapons.

Wickham heard the metallic sounds of the Sten guns' bolts kicking back for each shot. He took two quick steps uphill. Martelli joined him, shoving himself into the big shrub, making a soft rasping sound. As Dunn had expected, the two Germans on the south side had popped up like prairie dogs and looked the other way across the bridge to see what was happening.

Wickham and Martelli fired, then immediately ran toward the gun. A few moments later, U.S. Army Rangers were positioned to protect the bridge from the west, while the British Commandos guarded the east.

Chapter 22

German Bio-weapon Facility, Building 6
Insel Riems Island, Germany
18 August, 0428 Hours

The first test subject fatality, a male in his thirties, occurred near midnight the night before, just over seventy-two hours after exposure. The second one died an hour ago, the young woman who had gotten up from bed to get a glass of water only hours after exposure.

Dr. Gebhard Teichmann and his two assistants, Major Egert and Dr. Baer, all wearing protective gear, walked into the room, having passed through the two airlocks. Egert flipped a switch with a gloved hand and the overhead light came on. The six sleeping subjects, who appeared to be healthy, woke up rubbing their eyes in the bright lights.

The three scientists walked amongst the survivors carrying clipboards. Teichmann stopped next to the cot of a male.

"Good morning. How are you feeling today?" he asked the fully awake man.

Teichmann had asked the exact same question each morning since the test began.

"Hungry. I'm very hungry."

Teichmann patted the man on the shoulder. "I know, I'm sorry we haven't been able to feed you well."

Teichmann had determined that the subjects who'd received the vaccine prior to the test would have to live on the amount of food German soldiers might be taking in daily in order to truly measure the vaccine's effectiveness. Hungry, nearly starving perhaps, German soldiers might have weakened immune systems. He had to know whether the vaccine would still be effective.

"When can I leave?"

"Oh, not much longer, perhaps a day or two."

"I still don't understand why we're in this room," complained the man. "You haven't answered me yet." In his late twenties, the man had longish hair that fell onto his forehead. His light brown eyes looked at the doctor with accusation in them. Who could blame him?

"Of course. I can tell you now that we have received your blood test results. It was necessary to inject you with antibiotics. You were exposed to some very nasty bacteria at your . . . retraining center. We want to make sure you're quite healthy before sending you on to your new life in Berlin."

"What kind of bacteria?" the man frowned, clearly worried.

"Well, typhus is one of them. You've no doubt heard of it?"

The man recoiled in fear. Yes, he'd heard of it. It had killed millions in Europe alone since the Great War.

"Did it work? Am I safe?"

"I believe so. We're just keeping you here a little longer to make sure you are all healthy."

"What about the others? We started with twelve people, but there are only six of us in here."

"You must be a kind person to raise concerns over others." Teichmann gave the man a warm smile. "We have the other group of six in another room like this. It was just to make sure there was a comfortable place for all."

While Teichmann was lying to the young man in front of him, Egert and Baer were taking temperatures of the others.

Teichmann patted the man's shoulder once more and moved on around the room talking with each of the temporarily fortunate survivors.

When all the needed information was gathered and the doctor was through talking, the three men left through the airlock leading into the large test area.

Egert turned on the lights. Four dying subjects, two men and two women lay on cots. None opened their eyes in response to the bright lights.

The three men traveled the distance to the far end. The subjects were all naked, although they were unaware of their nudity. Teichmann and Baer examined the victims carefully, noting the discolorations on their skin, a red, ugly blotching. In some places blisters leaked putrid smelling pus. The skin was hot to the touch, and wet with a sheen of sweat from the fever, which unabated had hit one hundred and five the evening before. There were no nurses to comfort the subjects. What was the point?

Egert and Baer spent several minutes working as a team to take the temperatures rectally, not an easy feat with the sweaty bodies. Teichmann walked around, writing notes on his clipboard, and drawing some of the blotches and blisters for future reference.

"The temperatures are at one-oh-six," Baer told Teichmann.

"Not much longer, then."

"No, sir. Sometime today. Maybe near noon."

Teichmann nodded. "Yes, I'd say so."

The men left the comatose subjects and entered the west airlock, which acted as the decontamination room. They carefully removed their outer gear and disposed of them in special containers. Next they took long hot disinfectant showers in a small shower area. After toweling off, they dressed in their daily garb and exited the room.

Ten minutes later they were seated in Teichmann's office in Building 1, which was located just north of Building 6, the test building. The office faced north over the Baltic Sea inlet. Faint light was growing near the horizon to the northeast. The windows were slightly open and the comforting sounds of the wind driven waves hitting the shore came through clearly.

The office was sparsely decorated with pictures of Hitler, Himmler, and Göring on the wall. A bookshelf dominated one wall, and was filled with medical books and journals, including some prewar copies of the prestigious *New England Journal of Medicine*, which had been published since 1812 by the Massachusetts Medical Society. Teichmann wished there was some way to get the latest issues, but he hadn't been able to work anything out. He was almost able to get them sent to him through Lisbon, Portugal, the infamously "neutral" spy haven, but the courier he'd been in contact with had mysteriously disappeared one night after a party at the German Embassy. Whether at the hands of the British, Americans, or Russians was never discovered. Or perhaps he'd just been caught dallying with another man's wife once too often, and had messed with the wrong wife.

From memory, because he couldn't take the possibly contaminated clipboard out of Building 6 until the cleaning crew had indeed decontaminated the papers, Teichmann described the blotches and blisters. Even though Egert and Baer had seen them with their own eyes, the exercise was merely to get confirmation from them.

"That's what I saw," Baer said.

"I agree," Egert said.

"The devices work exactly as we'd hoped. I'm going to contact our supplier for more after I give *Reichsführer* Himmler the good news. He's most anxious to hear about our results. I must say this is a message I'm happy to send," Teichmann said, beaming.

"I'm sure he'll welcome the news," Egert said, smiling in return.

Teichmann got up and moved to a wide credenza behind his desk. He poured some schnapps into three fluted glasses. He handed one to each man across from him and raised his in a toast. "To the Fatherland, to our success, and may it continue!"

The men clinked their glasses together and drank their schnapps in silence, savoring both the flavor and the success they'd achieved for the Fatherland.

When they finished, Teichmann gathered the glasses and set them back on the credenza.

"To wrap up the test, when the ill subjects expire, have the team take them to be burned. Be sure to remind them of the dangers."

Baer nodded. This would be his responsibility.

To Major Egert, Teichmann said, "Have the other six shot tomorrow at noon. For fun, make them think they are going to the train station. Get them excited to leave." Teichmann grinned.

"Absolutely, sir."

Chapter 23

West edge of Amilly, France, 4 ½ miles west of Chartres
18 August, 0620 Hours

Sergeant Mike Lynch's tank was one of five in the platoon assigned to help clear the village of Amilly, which was the last town on the road to Chartres. The *Ghost Devil* and her crew were the most senior in the platoon and therefore were tasked with leading in the tanks and the infantry. As the Sherman rumbled and advanced, an infantry squad walked right behind, hiding in the protective cone of the tank's armor. Five men trailed each tread. The next Sherman in line was fifteen yards back. The pace was painfully slow. Squads followed each tank, creating an infantry force slightly larger than a platoon. At the tail end of the column, three deuce and a half trucks followed, staying back about fifty yards.

The French sky was brightening in the east, entering the morning twilight time. Visibility was more than sufficient. Lynch rode with his shoulders and head above the hatch. He knew this was an exposed position, being the only soft target, but he needed to see more than he could from his periscope.

The road was typically French: narrow, and it formed a sweeping 'S' curve as it approached the city. The houses and other low buildings lay close to it and six-foot-tall walls and hedges along both sides created a tunnel. Lynch felt like he was back in the bocage country, where you couldn't see the enemy even when you could hear him.

"Ted, stop when we're almost at the first crossroads up ahead," Lynch ordered.

"Roger."

The intersection was about fifty yards ahead.

Lynch saw no movement. He doubted very many of the villagers would still be there, and those who were, should still be sleeping.

The *Ghost Devil* reached the appointed spot and Ted Ritter brought the thirty-three ton vehicle to a stop. Lynch lifted binoculars to his eyes and swept them across the houses and road in front of him. Nothing. He scanned right, to the south. Finding nothing, he said, "Edge out into the crossroad."

The tank crawled forward until it was in the middle of the intersection. Lynch carefully scanned the road to the north. It was clear and he said, "Forward, Ted. Tank two, take a left. Tank three, go right, the rest, follow me."

Lynch received confirmations from each of the other four tank commanders. Those tanks would follow their assigned road until they reached a turn that would again have them moving eastward. They would all eventually rendezvous at an intersection half way through the village. The tanks would provide cover as the infantry squads entered any suspicious houses.

Ritter gave some throttle to the *Ghost Devil* and she growled in response. As she advanced at a crawl along the main road, Lynch kept watch. When the tank reached a point that was half way through the road's left-hand curve, about one hundred yards ahead on the left stood a three story building. It was at the intersection where all of the tanks would rendezvous. One of the third floor's windows was open. Lynch's question to himself was whether there was a sniper or machinegun hiding up there, just waiting for a shot at the men behind his tank.

"Stop, Ted."

"We're barely moving, Sarge."

"Stop!" snapped Lynch.

The tank stopped.

Lynch turned and located the squad leader who, anticipating something happening when the beast came to a stop, was looking straight at Lynch.

Lynch gave a "come here" wave with one hand, then quickly turned back to the front of the tank. His lifted his binoculars and scanned the road ahead. As he rotated his view to the left, he was careful to raise the angle of the binoculars only enough so the third floor windows were just inside his field of view. If there was a machinegun or sniper up there, he didn't want to alert the enemy that he suspected anything.

The two tanks and squads trailing Lynch both stopped, maintaining their interval.

The squad leader climbed up on the tank and crawled around to squat behind Lynch's open cupola.

The squad leader, a young staff sergeant with a narrow, bearded face asked in a slow deep-south drawl, "What's up?"

Lynch spoke without turning to face the infantryman. "Don't look up, but there could be a sniper or machinegun ahead and left. Three story building."

The squad leader kept his face pointed toward Lynch and gazed over the tank commander's shoulder.

"Thanks."

"Rick, get ready to traverse left and up. Third floor. As soon as I come inside."

"Roger." To the loader, Gordon said, "Load HE."

The squad leader jumped off the back of the tank. He gave a quick hand signal, and the men behind the left tread squatted and duck walked over behind the right tread, joining their squad mates there to keep the tank's armor plating between them and the potential threat.

Simultaneously, Lynch dropped straight down, pulling the hatch cover with him and Gordon moved the turret, raising the barrel.

From the corner window of the third floor, an MG42 cut loose, spewing bullets at the men behind the tank at twelve hundred rounds a minute. The weapon sent tracers that snapped and pinged over the soldiers' heads. Some of the rounds hit the top of the tank and went whining off in the distance, lead missiles misshapen from the ricochet.

Gordon acquired the flash of the machinegun and centered it in his crosshairs. The two-man team must have decided it was time to move as the weapon stopped firing.

Gordon stomped on the floor trigger and hollered, "Away!"

The *Ghost Devil's* gun fired. The corner of the building erupted in flame and flying stone. As Gordon watched, a single human was flung high in the sky, before tumbling back toward earth. The distinctive German helmet flew off the dead man's head.

"Got 'em!"

"Good shooting, Gordy," Lynch said.

Gordon was already traversing the gun back to the front. In his view screen, he watched for any telltale signs of Germans.

"Let's move, Ted," Lynch said as he popped the hatch and rose to a standing position. He glanced over his shoulder and the squad leader gave him a thumbs up with a grim smile. Lynch had saved the lives of all of his men.

Lynch nodded.

The tank jolted into motion and the squad advanced along with it, still staying behind the right tread. The tank was moving at about three miles an hour, a moderate walking speed. Soon it was at the building Gordon had fired into.

"Stop at the intersection."

Ritter advanced the tank a few more yards and it ground to a halt.

The squad leader moved around to the front of the tank and examined the intersection, the single story houses near it, and the three-story building where the machinegun nest had been located. He glanced up at Lynch and signaled his plan. Lynch nodded and grabbed the handles of his .50 caliber machinegun. With his right hand, he charged the weapon and aimed at the building.

The squad leader rejoined his men and gave a quick order. The squad darted out from behind the tank, running low. Soon, they were at the structure's back door.

As the infantrymen were moving toward the building, Lynch saw tank three make the turn onto the north-south road and head toward him. "Gordy, Murray, stay alert. Johnson's tank is coming our way."

He got a pair of "rogers" from his gunner and the co-driver, who was manning a .30 caliber coaxial Browning machinegun on the tank's front right side.

About the same time as Johnson's tank reached the intersection and stopped, the squad leader stuck his head out of a third floor window near the tank. "All clear!" he shouted down to Lynch. Lynch raised a hand to acknowledge the information.

The squad leader turned away from the window facing the Sherman and grabbed one of his soldiers. Together, they walked out of the empty bedroom into a hallway. Following the hallway, they made their way to an apartment on the east side of the building. The squad leader opened the door and strode across the living room to stand a few feet back from a window. He took a knee and brought binoculars to his eyes. He examined his field of view for several minutes, finding nothing. No Germans moving about, none advancing or retreating. He changed his focus of attention to the eastern outskirts of the village, a mere five hundred yards distant.

He was about to lower his field glasses when he spotted slight movement. He zoomed in and refocused. He dropped his glasses and ran from the room and down the stairs.

Chapter 24

On the west bank of the L'Eure River
Chartres
18 August, 0645 Hours

Having secured the only bridge in the city that could bear the weight of armor, Dunn's next goal was to defend it long enough for Patton's units to arrive and begin to cross over it. This meant extending his defensive perimeter by at least a hundred yards. With the sun rising, two questions were foremost in his mind: would the tanks arrive on time, and would daylight bring German troops his way?

Dunn pictured his squad's deployment on the map in his head. The road leading west from the bridge split into two lanes, each nearly twenty feet wide and fifty yards long. The two lanes formed a right triangle as they intersected and ended with the north-south street a hundred yards from the bridge. A grassy area lay within the triangle.

About thirty yards beyond the building where Jones and Lindstrom were keeping watch were two other buildings housing a flower shop and a café. Dunn had stationed Rob Goerdt and

RONN MUNSTERMAN

Leonard Bailey behind the building farthest from Jones with one of the special weapons Dunn had requested.

Cross and Waters were on the third floor of the building across the street from Jones. They manned a .30 caliber Browning machinegun giving them a crucial crossfire on the streets as well as providing a clear line of fire down the road that ran away to the north.

Cross had asked Dunn to assign Waters to him because he'd heard rumblings of the new man's smart mouth and wanted to keep an eye on him.

The rest of the squad was at the bridge: Wickham and Martelli manned the German MG42 on the south side of the bridge, while Schneider was stationed below and to the north of the bridge to guard against German surprise from that direction.

Dunn and Saunders sat on their haunches behind the abandoned MG42 on north side of the bridge comparing notes.

"Where the hell is everyone?" asked Saunders. No city inhabitants had stirred outside so far even with the rising sun.

"They must feel something's about to happen. I don't understand why we aren't seeing more German resistance."

"You complaining, Tom?"

"Nope. Just an observation. You heard about the rout through the Falaise Pocket?"

"I did. I heard it was incredible."

The Germans had been retreating, simply trying to avoid being surrounded by Allied forces. The aerial and artillery bombardments, and the armor and troops on the ground caused over ten thousand casualties, and another fifty thousand were captured.

During the previous hour, a few men from each squad had removed all of the explosives from under the bridge and had ensured there were no other nasty surprises lurking there. On Saunders' side, his men had set up their own .30 caliber Browning, facing to the south.

"Endicott told me you made a nice recovery job with the boat. He thought you guys were going to end up in the drink," Saunders said.

"That was all Dave. I had no fucking idea what to do." Dunn shook his head. "I'm gonna go check on Jonesy. See if I can see anything from his vantage point," Dunn said. "You want to come with me?"

"Nah. I'm heading back across the bridge."

"Okay. Be careful."

"Aye, you, too."

As Saunders took off across the bridge, running low, Dunn moved quickly around the back side of the building and entered through the same door as Jones. A few minutes later, he made it to the second floor. Jones was situated on the left of a window facing southwest and Lindstrom, ever protecting his sniper's back, was on the right side facing Dunn's way. The two men had bonded on a mission to France, which was the first time Lindstrom had acted as Jones' spotter and protector.

The previous month, Jones had set up in a position about six hundred yards from an airfield. The aircraft the squad was tasked to stop was carrying a new weapon created by Nazi scientists, an electromagnetic pulse weapon, which would have changed the battlefield in the Nazis' favor. Jones had killed the pilot and copilot as they were walking to the plane, then dropped several German troops while Dunn and the rest of the squad attacked from the rear. The plane and weapon were soon destroyed completely in a ball of fire.

Lindstrom spotted Dunn and gave a small wave. He spoke quietly to Jones, who didn't take his eyes off the street below, but replied equally softly that he understood.

Dunn waved back as he advanced on his men.

"See anything, Jonesy?"

"Not a thing, Sarge," replied the sniper without looking at Dunn.

"Stay sharp. Both of you."

"Yes, Sarge," replied both men.

Dunn walked farther down the hallway and peered out another window, being careful not to stand in front of it. Movement caught his eye. On the far side of the green space, on the west side of the street, two people were walking. Civilians. An older man and a little boy, who Dunn guessed to be about five years old. He was wearing shorts and a white shirt. On his head was a small black beret. The man, the grandfather, Dunn thought, had on a dark suit and also a black beret. They were holding hands. They turned right to cross the street, stepping onto the pavement after the grandfather had looked both ways for traffic out of habit. Just as they were about to step onto the sidewalk on the east side, they both snapped their heads to the left.

Although they were too far away for Dunn to make out their expressions, it was clear they were in panic mode for the grandfather grabbed the little boy up into his arms. The boy put his hands around his grandfather's neck, his spindly legs wrapped around the man's waist, and he tucked his face into grandpa's neck. The man ran as fast as he could toward the building where Dunn and his men were located. As they got closer, Dunn could see the man's expression, which was a mix of terror and determination.

Dunn jumped into action. He gave a low whistle and pointed toward the west. Jones and Lindstrom immediately changed position to get the best angle possible.

There was a window that was smaller than the others at the very end of the hallway, facing west. Dunn ran to it and looked out.

"Here we go, men," Dunn said.

A Tiger tank advanced into the city from the north. About three hundred yards away, it rolled slowly, but steadily down the main road.

Dunn had hoped this wouldn't occur, but being thorough during the planning of the mission, he'd accounted for the eventuality. The Tiger tank was the most dangerous ground weapon in the world and all Dunn had was one piece of equipment. If it didn't kill the tank, the mission would be a failure.

Dunn raised his binoculars to his eyes. The tank commander, wearing the black uniform of the SS, stood proudly, arrogantly, in his open hatch. The driver's hatch was also open and the man's head and shoulders were visible.

Judging the tank's speed, which was a little faster than a man walking, against the distance it had to cover, Dunn guessed he had about two minutes to act.

Dunn sprinted back to his men.

As he ran past Jones and Lindstrom, he ordered, "Tiger. Jonesy, be ready to kill the tank driver, and then the commander at zero yards!" Knocking off the driver first was key, as the alternate driver would have to pull the man's body out of the way, and get seated himself. In the meantime, the tank would have come to a halt. By the time the tank commander realized he had a problem, Jonesy's second bullet would be on its way to his head.

"Roger, Sarge."

Dunn stood in front of a window and waved his hands a few times to attract Cross's or Waters' attention. Across the street on the third floor, Cross rose to his feet and returned the wave. Dunn gave a couple of quick hand gestures and Cross signaled his understanding of the message: Tiger coming. Hold fire.

Dunn turned and sprinted down the stairs two at a time, and then darted left when he got outside in the cool morning air. As he ran to join Goerdt and Bailey, he could clearly hear the dreaded Tiger's clanking and rumbling, deep-throated engine sounds. A predator in search of prey.

Dunn spotted his men exactly where they were supposed to be, kneeling and keeping watch on their field of fire. They were positioned a few feet back from the corner of the building to stay out of sight. They had obviously heard the tank's sounds because Goerdt had the special weapon, an M9 bazooka, on his shoulder.

Bailey slid an armor-piercing round into the ass end of the rocket launcher and tapped Goerdt on the helmet.

When Dunn got within a few yards, he said, "Dunn here, men."

Neither man looked at him, staying focused on their job. Goerdt did say, "Sounds like a Tiger, Sarge. Is that right?"

"Yep. One all by itself." Dunn took a knee behind Bailey.

The M9 bazooka on Goerdt's shoulder was four and a half feet long, and the rockets in the ammo case by Bailey's right knee were the new M6A3, which were supposed to be capable of penetrating four inches of German armor. If this was the standard Tiger, Dunn knew the side armor was just over three inches. According to General Patton, the bazooka was most effective at thirty yards or less. Dunn was more than happy to take that advice.

Goerdt would have to stay out of sight, and resist the temptation to peek to prevent exposure to the deadly coaxial machinegun on the Tiger's right front.

"Goerdt, if the tank turns left toward the bridge, you'll fire into it broadside the second it comes into view."

The rocket would be completely useless against the frontal, angled and very thick glacis armor, even with a pointblank shot. Goerdt would have to make his shot against the side armor, just below where the turret met the hull.

"You guys keep firing until it's destroyed or you run out of ammo. If it goes straight, to the south, you'll have to run out behind it and shoot it in the ass. We'll provide cover and Jonesy will take out the driver and commander. Any questions?"

"None, Sarge," Goerdt replied.

"Nope," Bailey said.

"Good men."

Dunn slapped Bailey on the back and rose, taking off at a run toward the building just to the east. He made his way around the entire structure, ending up at a corner just off the street that was the hypotenuse of the triangle. He knelt and peered around the edge of the flower shop. He was forty yards from the intersection the Tiger would cross. From here, he would be able to see the action, whichever way it went. He backed up and turned toward the bridge. He could almost see its west end. To see the bridge fully, he'd have to step out into the street, not something he was interested in doing.

The grinding sounds of the Tiger's treads grew louder and louder.

Dunn took off his helmet and set it on the ground, then he got down into a prone position. He scooted forward just enough to check on the tank.

Suddenly it came into view at the intersection. Without slowing, it turned left onto the street toward the bridge. The monster advanced a few more yards and came to a stop, short of Goerdt's position and firing angle.

"Fuck," Dunn muttered to himself.

The tank commander had both hands on the rim of his hatch, looking like a preacher at the lectern. He wore a headset to communicate with the other four men in the crew. He raised a pair of binoculars and studied the road ahead and the bridge.

Dunn was thankful he'd told Wickham and Martelli to don German helmets and gray battlefield jackets while they manned the MG42 on the south side of the bridge.

The commander seemed satisfied with what he saw and must have said something because the Tiger advanced.

Dunn knew that above and to the east, Jones was lining up a shot on the tank driver. Jones would fire the moment the Tiger cleared Goerdt's position, zero yards. The shot for Jones would be sixty yards, spitting distance for his Springfield.

"Get ready," Goerdt said.

Bailey slid closer to Goerdt's back and slightly to the left, to avoid being roasted by the rocket's flame about to shoot out the bazooka's ass. He put his right hand on Goerdt's back, like a home plate umpire does with the catcher when taking his position.

"Ready," Bailey said.

The Tiger rolled into the engagement zone.

"Bonjour, Américain!"

Dunn nearly jumped out of his skin. He spun around to see the little boy staring at him with a friendly, open face, his black beret still on his small head.

Chapter 25

Center of Amilly, France, 4 ½ miles west of Chartres
18 August, 0650 Hours

When the squad leader arrived at the Sherman, he clambered up and knelt by Lynch.

"Five hundred yards, a Tiger is parked just off the road, behind some low buildings. Just past the east edge of town. "

"You sure there's only one?"

"Yes, I'm sure. There's no place for another one to hide."

"Okay," replied Lynch, accepting the sergeant's word. "Which way is the turret pointed?"

"Straight down the main road, toward us."

"Of course, it is," Lynch muttered. "What's the layout at that end of the village?"

The sergeant described in sharp detail exactly what lay ahead.

Lynch nodded, thinking. The question was how to kill a Tiger without getting his crew or any of the other twenty tankers killed in the process.

Some knucklehead in the Third Army had calculated that it takes five Shermans to kill a Tiger. Fortunately, that was exactly how many Lynch had.

After giving precise instructions to the other tanks, and being as clear yet as cryptic as possible in case the Nazis picked up their radio transmissions, Lynch waited for the other four Shermans to get in position. He had moved his tank so it was just short of crossing the road that led to the Tiger. At five hundred yards, the Tiger gunner would be shooting fish in a barrel.

He glanced up at the third floor window, where the squad leader also waited, watching for any Tiger activity. Lynch had finally asked the sergeant his name: Johnny Lewis from Mississippi. From his vantage point, Lewis was also keeping track of the advancing Shermans and relaying that information to Lynch by way of prearranged hand signals.

When the moment came, Lynch gave the order to move.

As the Sherman crept forward, Gordon began to turn the turret to the east. When the tank cleared the last house and entered the intersection, Gordon acquired the Tiger and stomped the firing pedal. "On the way!"

The Sherman's round clanged off the Tiger's glacis armor.

At the same time, Ritter gunned the engine and the Sherman rocketed, as much as a huge lump of steel could, through the crossing and out of the Tiger gunner's sight. A split second later, the building where Lewis had been stationed, but had abandoned just in time, exploded, sending bricks, glass, and wood flying into the street. It caught fire and flames jetted upward.

"Stop!" shouted Lynch. He knew they were out of sight, but a good gunner would guess where they'd be and fire.

The German gunner was indeed good. Two seconds later, a small house thirty yards ahead disintegrated in the flash of another armor piercing round.

While the Tiger's attention was focused on the Sherman that had crossed from left to right, the two Shermans taking the southern path through the village rounded the corner of the last house in town. The two tanks roared out into the open field with ten yards separating them. They were just over one hundred fifty yards away from the Tiger, whose vulnerable flank was exposed.

The Tiger's commander, who had his hatch open, saw the Shermans and screamed an order to his gunner.

The Tiger's turret rotated, the deadly 88mm barrel arcing toward the Shermans.

Advancing at twenty miles an hour, both Shermans fired.

As soon as the rounds were away, the Shermans turned right at a forty-five degree angle to make it harder for the enemy gunner to track them.

One 76mm armor piercing round struck the Tiger just below the bottom of the hull, almost on the German black and white cross. The other tank's shell hit the front drive wheel and blew the tread off in chunks. When the first round went off inside the tank, the commander shot into the sky like a bottle rocket, flames included.

From the north, two more Shermans thundered across the field and fired from less than one hundred yards. The shells screamed past the side of the building partially hiding the Tiger. The force of those two rounds' explosions tilted the turret off its track. The Tiger lay in ruins, flames and smoke shooting into the French sky.

At the sound of the Tiger's death and cheers coming across the inter-tank radio, Lynch directed Ritter back onto the eastbound road. Sergeant Lewis and his squad formed up and followed right behind.

As the tank advanced, Lynch thought, *one more village freed.* Then he wondered how many more he'd see.

By the time they reached the east edge of the village, it was obvious that the Germans were gone, having left only the Tiger to wreak havoc upon the Americans. Something it had failed to do and its crew was dead in a smoking funeral pyre of a hulk.

All five of the Shermans gathered in a group along the road to Chartres. The infantry squads all showed up, as did the three trucks.

Lynch turned around in his commander's hatch and waved at Sergeant Lewis, who was standing nearby.

"You may as well load up. We need to get moving to make it to Chartres as soon as possible. It's less than five miles, so we might make it in there in about fifteen minutes."

Lewis nodded and gave a quick order. A few minutes later, the trucks were full.

Lynch said, "Let's go, Ted."

The *Ghost Devil's* driver goosed the engine and the Sherman got up to speed quickly.

The other four Shermans followed, then came the trucks.

Chapter 26

Three things happened at once: Dunn scooped up the little French boy and ran along the east side of the building, Jones fired his first shot, the driver's head huge in his Unertl scope at the ultra-short range, and Goerdt triggered the bazooka's rocket.

Jones' supersonic bullet hit its mark before the bazooka's rocket, and the driver's head exploded. Before the tank commander was even aware he had a problem, the rocket struck the thinner armor plating just behind the German cross. Its armor-piercing nose burned through, entered the Tiger's hull compartment, and found the stored stacked of 88mm rounds, and then went off. The turret erupted in a ball of fire and pieces of molten metal flew in all directions.

When Dunn reached the end of the building, he darted around the corner and knelt. He hugged the little boy close, putting his own body between the blast and the boy.

Goerdt and Bailey had ducked back a few yards from the corner of the building. When a huge piece of the turret slammed into the same corner and blew out a giant chunk of stone, Goerdt hollered, "Shit!" as he and Bailey dove to the ground, faces in the dirt. Somehow, Goerdt kept a grip on the bazooka.

More pieces of red hot shrapnel peppered the building and the street area around the tank. Glass shattered along the fronts of several shops including the flower shop and the café.

There was no doubt all aboard the Tiger were dead, either blown to pieces or burned beyond recognition.

Jones surveyed the streets below him without using his scope, watching for German soldiers daring enough to poke their heads out to see what had just happened. No one stirred.

Cross and Waters examined the road from the north looking for German troops and other tanks. The road was clear. The Tiger had been traveling alone trying to escape Patton's Third Army.

Dunn stood up slowly, still hugging the little boy. He knew where the boy had come from, but wondered how he'd gotten out of the grandfather's sight. He knew kids just did stuff without thinking about the consequences; he'd done plenty himself. His memory took over and brought to mind one event.

One Sunday when he was four, he had awakened before his parents. The sun was shining, and he quite naturally wanted to go out and play. He had dressed himself, including shoes on the wrong feet, and ran outside. He walked around the entire block looking for his friends. Why weren't they outside playing? By the time he returned home a half hour later, his mom and dad were out in the front yard, frantically looking for him. To little boy Tommy, they seemed scared. He walked up to them calmly and said, "Hi MommyDaddy." All one word, which was kind of how Tommy saw them anyway.

When the parents saw him they both cried out in relief. Mr. Dunn picked up Tommy and held him tight while Mrs. Dunn turned it into a family hug. Tommy thought all was okay until they got inside the house. Mr. Dunn set Tommy on the living room sofa and then stood up, putting his hands on his hips. Now he looked sort of angry and scared.

"You are not to leave the house by yourself ever again!"

"Okay," Tommy nodded, still unsure of why he was in trouble.

"What if something had happened to you?" Mrs. Dunn asked, stifling a cry.

But nothing did, thought little Tommy. He didn't say anything out loud. He knew that was sometimes not a very smart thing to do.

"You worried us. We thought you were lost, Tommy."

"I knew where I was," chirped little Tommy.

Mr. Dunn started to reply in anger, but thought better of it and turned away to face his wife. Mrs. Dunn refused to meet his eyes and seemed to be having trouble breathing as she kept making these little coughing sounds and her face turned red. She suddenly ran from the room, into the kitchen. Tommy thought he heard a laugh, but that didn't make sense.

Mr. Dunn took a knee and put a hand on Tommy's shoulder. Unknown to Tommy, Mr. Dunn was also having a terrible time repressing a laugh. He finally managed to say, "Even though you knew where you were, your mother and I did not. Promise me you will always ask permission before leaving the house."

Tommy shrugged. "Sure, okay, Daddy, I promise."

Mr. Dunn hugged his son tight for a long moment, then released him and said, "Go see if your mother needs help with breakfast. Are you hungry?"

Tommy nodded, then got up and ran into the kitchen.

Mr. Dunn buried his face in his hands and laughed as quietly as possible. *I knew where I was.* Good Lord, we are so in trouble, he thought.

Dunn peeked around the corner of the building and determined it was safe. Walking quickly, he made his way to the front of the building where Jones and Lindstrom were positioned. The boy's grandfather stepped out onto the street a few feet away from Dunn, a stricken look on his face, just like Dunn's parents those twenty years ago, then he spotted Dunn carrying his grandson and he broke into a wide smile, his eyes brimming with tears.

"Jean! Jean!"

The man ran the few steps and took the boy from Dunn's arm. *"Merci! Merci! Vous l'avez sauvé mon petit gars!"*

Dunn inferred the man was thanking him for saving the little boy and said, "You're welcome."

After the hand off of the boy, the grandfather stepped closer and leaned in. He kissed Dunn on both cheeks and patted his face gently. He stepped back and waved his hand in the general direction of the small antique shop where he'd come from, his intent clear. *Won't you come in?*

Dunn smiled, but shook his head, "No, I'm sorry." He turned slightly and pointed toward the burning Tiger.

The Frenchman nodded, and said, *"Merci beaucoup, mon ami."*

"You're welcome."

The man turned and reentered his shop, closing the door behind him.

Dunn retrieved his helmet and then headed toward Goerdt and Bailey at a run, going behind buildings to get there. Being on the street still wasn't prudent.

The two men had regained their position and were peering around the jagged corner of the building. Bailey had reloaded the rocket launcher and Goerdt was searching for new targets.

Dunn rejoined them.

"Hell of a shot, Rob. Great job. Both of you."

Goerdt glanced over his shoulder, surprised. His previous squad leader, Bagley, hadn't been known for giving compliments. "Thanks, Sarge."

Dunn looked up toward Cross's location. When they made eye contact across the wide street, Cross signaled the all clear for the road coming in from the north. Dunn nodded. Only Cross was visible, so Dunn guessed the assistant squad leader had directed Waters to check out the view to the south from another window.

Cross turned his head and said something to Waters, who was out of Dunn's view. Cross nodded and turned back to Dunn. He gave the all clear for the south.

Movement on the street to the right caught Dunn's attention. People were walking slowly toward the triangular grassy area in groups of two's and three's. They were all staring and some

138   RONN MUNSTERMAN

pointed at the smoldering Tiger tank. There were many cautious smiles.

Dunn turned to Bailey, "Leonard, Go get Schneider. Hurry."

The crowd advanced and crossed into the green triangular space, but kept their distance from the hot ruins of the German tank. The people, who appeared to be of all ages, from the same age as the little boy Dunn had picked up, to the elderly, were just milling about. Some gestured toward the tank and shouted something that sounded like a curse at the German tank. Dunn thought it was probably "Fuck you!"

Dunn tried to hang back from the corner, but a woman saw him and pointed, shouting, *"Américain!"*

The crowd gave an audible gasp and moved as one unit toward Dunn.

Dunn scanned the windows around the area, praying the Germans hadn't left a sniper or two behind to kill Americans, and perhaps French citizens. He knew that Jonesy would be also checking all open windows in sight for shooters.

Schneider showed up with Bailey. Both men had run straight down the street instead of the long way behind the buildings. From the antique shop, the grandfather came out carrying his grandson in one arm. He met the other civilians and began telling the story about Dunn rescuing the little boy. When he finished the story, the crowd turned together, as if choreographed, to look at Dunn. Then they surged toward him. In moments he was completely surrounded. Everyone was trying to touch him and those that did patted him everywhere, shoulders, helmet, and back. Several women grabbed him by the shirt in turn and planted kisses on both of his cheeks. Some of the younger women kissed him on the mouth.

From above and across the street, Cross hollered down. "Ask them if the Germans have left the city!"

Dunn couldn't quite make out what Cross said, but luckily, Schneider caught it all and began talking in earnest to a distinguished-looking gentleman of about seventy. After a few exchanges, Schneider shouted at Dunn, "This guy's the mayor. He said the Germans all left last night around midnight, except those around the bridge. He wanted to know what happened to them, so I told him we killed them."

Cross shouted down at Dunn again. This time he was pointing up the road to the north where the Tiger had entered the city.

"Tom!"

Dunn managed to disengage from the crowd as Schneider started explaining to the people what had happened. He trotted over to stand under Cross's window.

"What?"

"I can see the first of Patton's armor coming down the road. Maybe five hundred yards. Five Shermans, three trucks. Looks like a lot more farther down. They're moving fast, should be here any time."

"Okay, stay where you are. Stay focused along the road going south."

"You got it."

Cross disappeared from the window.

Dunn made his way through the crowd, which was now growing larger and larger by the minute, only by allowing everyone to touch him and or kiss him. He idly wondered what Pamela would think of all the French girls' kisses. He grabbed Bailey on the way.

Once he got to Goerdt, he said, "Rob, you and Bailey load your gear up and head back to the bridge. Bailey go on across the bridge and give Saunders an update on what's happening here."

"Yes, Sarge," replied both men as they set about getting the bazooka and the case of left over rockets ready to carry. They took off a minute later.

Dunn ran along the street until he got to the road coming from the north. Only a hundred yards away now, the Shermans were a sight for sore eyes. Dunn stepped out from the building and held up his hands, waving. The lead tank commander saw him and waved back.

When the tank reached Dunn's position, the tank commander gave an order and the Sherman stopped a few feet from Dunn. The Ranger scrambled up the tank and knelt beside the commander.

"Tom Dunn."

"Mike Lynch."

"We're glad to see you," Dunn tilted his head toward the crowd, "but not as much as they are, I'd say. The mayor's in there somewhere, a distinguished looking gent. He told us the Germans all left last night, except for those who were supposed to blow the bridge. We took care of them and the bridge is intact."

"That's swell. Thanks." Lynch leaned forward a bit and was able to see the ass end of the ruined Tiger.

"Huh. How'd you kill the Tiger? Bazooka?"

"Yeah, that's right. About a twenty yard shot. One of my guys."

"Great work." Lynch paused, looking back over his shoulder, then back to Dunn. "I've got five Shermans and a little more than a platoon of infantry. About ten minutes behind us is a tank company with their infantry. I'll spread my tanks out to secure both ends of the bridge and my infantry will secure the buildings along the road we want to use. You can withdraw anytime and wait for your rides."

"Okay. Good to meet you. Good luck." Dunn and Lynch shook hands. Dunn hopped off the tank and once again was forced to wind his way through the crowd. The people had heard the Sherman and now were headed over to it. It wasn't hard for Dunn to imagine the excitement and relief they must be feeling due to being liberated.

He was soon below Cross's window and he shouted to get his second in command's attention. Cross leaned out.

"We're relieved. Pack up. Let's go back to the bridge."

"Okay. Meet you there."

Saunders noticed Bailey running his way. He rose from a kneeling position to go meet Dunn's man who Saunders was sure had a message. His men were positioned in the woods behind him, some facing south down the road that Pickering had crossed nonchalantly earlier. Saunders stepped down onto the road and looked west across the bridge. He saw the huge crowd milling about, and then suddenly the beautiful sight of a Sherman's business end, the barrel, and then the distinctive sloped front poked itself into his view.

Saunders let out a sigh of relief. For once, the army had done what it promised it would do.

Before Saunders reached the bridge, he heard his name from behind. He turned around and saw Barltrop waving his arm for Saunders to come back. Now! Saunders bolted and ran back to join his second in command.

"What is it?"

Barltrop pointed to the south along the road they were guarding.

Coming straight toward them was a fully occupied German halftrack with a manned MG42 on top.

Chapter 27

Chartres
18 August, 0657 Hours

Saunders and Barltrop sprinted toward the woods, then ran through them to join Chadwick and Dickinson. Chadwick had stepped close to the road and knelt with a bazooka on his shoulder. His partner loaded it, then thwacked him on his Brody helmet.

The eight-ton Sonderkraftfahrzeug 251 rumbled toward the bridge. It looked to Saunders like there were eight or nine men in the back, with one of them manning the machinegun. Saunders was certain he'd been seen while running, but the gunner hadn't opened fire.

When the armored vehicle hit the fifty yard mark, Saunders could see into the driver's cab through the narrow slit windows. The driver and the other German in the passenger seat, likely the squad leader, were just new faces of an old enemy. The men appeared to be arguing; the passenger waving his hands in anger and then pointing toward the bridge.

Chadwick said, "Another ten yards and I'm firing."

Saunders was about to agree when the most peculiar thing happened.

The driver raised a pistol and shot the squad leader in the side of the head. The dead man slumped out of Saunders' view and the halftrack came to a halt. The men in the back carrier section all stood up together with their arms raised.

"Blimey! Hold fire, Chadwick."

One of the soldiers climbed over the edge of the carrier and jumped to the ground, where he immediately raised his hands again. He walked steadily toward the British Commandos.

"Hold steady, Chadwick. Steve, come with me."

The two men stepped out from the woods, making sure they didn't block Chadwick's line of fire.

Saunders raised his Sten and aimed at the man's forehead, just under the brim of the German helmet. "Wave him to hurry, Steve."

Barltrop waved his arm energetically at the German. The soldier responded by breaking into a jog, an awkward proposition what with his hands still in the air.

When the soldier reached the two commandos, he came to a stop. He had fear in his eyes, but Saunders noticed something else. Relief.

The German had no obvious weapon on him, but Barltrop stepped forward and frisked him carefully.

"He's clean, Sarge."

Saunders eyed the soldier carefully. The man was unshaven, perhaps a three-day growth, but his eyes were clear and focused intently on Saunders.

Saunders gave a low whistle and three of his men stepped out of the woods, weapons trained on the men in the halftrack.

"Do you understand English?"

The solider lowered one arm long enough to waggle a hand as he gave a half smile. "Some," he said.

"Tell your men to climb down one by one. You can put your arms down."

"Thank you."

Saunders noticed something about the accent. What part of Germany was he from?

The soldier turned and called out to the men. They immediately began to follow the order.

Saunders turned to Barltrop. "That's not German. Is it?"

Barltrop shook his head. "He sounds like those Polish pilots we met last year."

"Aye, he does." Saunders had picked up a few Polish words from the pilots who he'd grown to admire for their courage and spirit. They'd treated each and every enemy plane they shot down as a point of national pride and revenge.

"Polski?" he asked.

The soldier turned around with a big smile on his face. He grabbed his helmet and threw it into the woods, then he took off his uniform top and did the same thing.

"Tak, Polski!" He tapped his own chest and then pointed to the men running toward him with their hands in the air. *"Polski!"*

"We want to . . . surnder . . . ," he shook his head at the wrong word, "give up. Life good. England."

As the men from the German halftrack ran, helmets and uniform tops flew in all directions. The driver, who had killed the German handler, climbed down and followed his friends.

Saunders stuck his hand out to the Pole who grinned even wider as he shook it. Within seconds all of the Poles were jumping up and down and jockeying for position to shake Saunders' hand.

After everything settled down, Saunders said to the de facto leader, "We have to hold you here for a while. Do you understand? You wait here with us."

"Yes. I understand. We wait. We know."

Saunders gave a quick order. Mills, Pickering, and Redington came over and helped corral the Poles, then led them to an area in the woods where they would wait for the advancing Third Army.

Bailey, who had watched Saunders run away from him had followed the big British sergeant and witnessed the entire episode. He made his way to Saunders and got his attention.

"Sergeant Dunn said to tell you Third Army tanks and infantry are in the city."

"Good to know. What happened over there? We heard a big explosion."

"We killed a Tiger."

"Right. You can head back."

"See you." Bailey took off at a run.

Chapter 28

British Field Hospital, 3 miles west of Caen, France
18 August, 0705 Hours

The surgical tent was full with five doctors, twice as many nurses, and a number of orderlies working on men with various life-threatening wounds.

Pamela Dunn wiped the surgeon's brow with a clean white cloth. She then stepped around to stand on the opposite side of the patient. The doctor's hands were deep inside the solider lying on the table. He was trying to find the bleeder that had filled the man's chest cavity with bright red blood.

Attached by tubing to the patient was a transfusion bottle hanging from a metal pole near the head of the table. The bottle was already half empty. The last full one sat on the work table near the metal pole. It had been a busy night in the surgery.

"I'll go get a suction pump," Pamela said.

"Hurry."

Pamela ran over to grab a cart with the suction pump on it. As she rolled it toward her patient, she cried out, "Billy! Get over here!"

The young orderly moved as quickly as possible to join Pamela at the surgical table. Together they got one tube inserted into the patient's chest and the exit tube from the machine into a metal wash pan on the floor. Billy started cranking the old-style mechanical suction pump; all the other generator-powered devices were being used.

The blood level began to drop immediately.

"There you are, you bugger. Suture."

Pamela handed over the suture line and needle and the surgeon worked fast. By the time he was done, all of the excess blood had been drained from the chest cavity.

The surgeon raised his hands, holding them high and away from the patient's chest. He stared intently into the chest. After a minute or so, he gave a sigh of relief. "It's holding. Let's give it another minute and I'll close. Stop suction."

Billy stopped the crank.

"Yes, doctor." Pamela got some thicker, stitching sutures ready for the doctor after taking the needle he'd just used out of his hand and placing it carefully on a tray of used surgical implements. They would all have to be sterilized after everything was all over.

Another minute passed and the doctor seemed satisfied that the bleeder had been completely repaired. "Okay, get the suction tube out." He glanced at the transfusion bottle. "Give him the rest of that bottle and stop."

"Yes, doctor," replied Pamela.

She and Billy gently pulled the suction tube out of the patient's chest. Billy set about replacing the tube that had touched the patient with a fresh one.

While he did that the surgeon began sewing the incision closed.

Billy finished working with the tubing, then bent over and picked up the metal pan. The patient's blood sloshed around, but Billy was careful not to spill it. He walked slowly over to the door flap at the back of the tent. Once outside, he walked a few paces, then poured the blood into a short wooden barrel. This would later be burned in a hot oven-like furnace a few feet away. This was the same oven used to destroy amputated body parts.

The surgeon finished his task of closing the patient. "All yours, nurse."

"Thank you, doctor."

"I think he's the last one."

Pamela looked around the tent. All of the other doctors were in some stage or other of closing their own patients.

"Yes, I think so, too."

Without another word, the surgeon walked away, heading for the washing area. Pamela knew that as soon as he was done cleaning himself up, he would step outside and light up a cigar. Then he would go for a walk around the hospital grounds to unwind.

Pamela got some clean water and soap and began to wash the patient. After gently drying his skin, she pulled a clean sheet off a cart and flapped it open, then draped it over the patient from the shoulders down.

Billy returned from disposing the blood.

"He's ready to go, Billy. Will you cover him with a blanket, and check on his transfusion level in about five minutes?"

"I sure will, Mrs. Dunn."

"Thanks."

Pamela's job done, she also walked over to the cleanup area and scrubbed herself clean. When she stepped outside, she found her new friends Edith and Irene sitting on some old wooden chairs. They had cups of hot tea.

Pamela joined them, sitting down between them. The tea pot was on a round block of wood about two feet tall, part of a tree trunk.

After pouring herself a cup, she leaned back and took a sip. The warmth passed through her chest and into her stomach. She sighed at the welcome comfort.

"I lost two," Edith said.

"Four," Irene said.

"Four for me, too," Pamela said.

They'd all said their score for the day with remarkable ease. Just in the three days they'd been there, they'd come to accept the inevitable.

"I know we saved some who probably should have died, and lost some that should have lived," Pamela said. "I guess I'll never really understand that."

No one said anything for a bit, then Edith asked, "Do you believe it's a matter of luck?"

"I think it's fate," answered Irene. "It's what was meant to be."

"You really believe that?" Pamela asked.

"I do."

"So you think everything happens for a reason, too?"

"Yes. It's God's plan."

"What about free will?"

"What do you mean?"

"I mean God gave us free will. Why would he then step in and change things?"

"Don't you pray to Him?"

"Every day."

"Aren't you being hypocritical to pray if you don't believe in His plan?"

Pamela looked away for a long moment. She and the girls had had similar conversations recently. She enjoyed them and appreciated Edith's and Irene's sharp intellect.

"Perhaps it is. But perhaps I'm just helping guide His plan."

Edith laughed lightly. "I think Pamela won this one, Irene."

Irene gave a pseudo huff of indignation, then took another sip of her tea. "I concede she may have a point."

Pamela reached over and patted Irene on the shoulder.

"Don't pat me, I'm not a dog!"

"Yes, I see that, although you are wagging your tail!" Pamela said with a twinkle in her eye.

"Ah, good one," said Edith.

Irene shook her head, but smiled widely. Then her expression turned mischievous. "So what's handsome doctor like? How come you're the only who works with him?"

Pamela grinned. "He's unusually compassionate for a surgeon. He sees the patients as people, not just problems to solve."

"Did you say 'passionate?' " Edith smirked.

"Oi, you two. I am married, you know?" She held up her left hand and waggled her fingers.

"Oh, so we hear. Still, what's he like?" Edith pressed.

Pamela raised her hand again and pointed off behind Edith. "Why don't you just go ask him?"

Edith said, "Huh?" She turned around and spotted the doctor in question walking by only ten feet away. Had he heard her talking about him? He suddenly looked straight at her and smiled. Edith's face turned red and she turned around quickly, and raised a hand to her mouth.

"Oh."

The doctor made his way around the nurses and stopped in front of them. Irene and Pamela shared a look, then turned to the doctor and smiled. Edith, whose face was still pink, wouldn't meet his eyes. The doctor wore his light brown hair parted on the left side. His eyes, which appeared to be green in the morning light, seemed to sparkle with friendliness.

He was indeed handsome, thought Edith.

The doctor raised the hand holding the burning cigar as a wave. "Ladies. I hear the breakfast line is open. Be sure to get some food while it's hot." He glanced at Edith. "Perhaps you'll all join me?"

Pamela decided she would be the spokeswoman for the group, especially since Edith looked like a rabbit under the gaze of a predator.

"Well, then, doctor, we'd love to join you." Pamela gave Irene a look, which Irene understood.

The nurses all rose.

Irene and Pamela started to move to join the doctor, but at the last moment, hesitated and sidestepped. This put Edith, who had been effectively faked out, right next to the doctor. When she realized what her friends had done, she looked at them over her shoulder and gave them a "what for" look.

Pamela and Irene just grinned.

Chapter 29

Hitler's Office, The Chancellery
Berlin, Germany
18 August, 0708 Hours

Heinrich Himmler, who held the rank of *Reichsführer-SS*, smiled at his idol, Adolf Hitler. "It's so good to see you again, *Mein Führer*! Are you well?"

The Nazi *Führer* returned the smile. Himmler was one of his oldest believers and possessed a puppy's loyalty, a killer puppy perhaps, but still a puppy. These were traits Hitler valued.

"I am well."

Himmler nodded, truly pleased to hear the man he worshiped was indeed well.

Raised a Catholic by his teacher father, and mother, Himmler turned his back on the religion, focusing his attention and beliefs on the occult and antisemitism. Himmler first joined the Nazi party in August 1923 at the age of twenty-three, and participated in the Beer Hall Putsch. He soon grew in importance to the party and traveled all over Bavaria as a rabble-rouser giving speeches and handing out Nazi literature.

He took over the *Schutzstaffel*, the SS, in 1929, and then the next year, convinced Hitler to let him run it separately from the

Sturmabteilung, Ernst Röhm's brownshirted SA. The SS had grown from around three thousand to a massive fifty-two thousand, specially selected members of the Aryan master race, by 1933. Hitler, and others, noted early in Himmler's Nazi career that he was an outstanding organizer. He successfully planned and conducted the Night of the Long Knives, the killing of Ernst Röhm and nearly two hundred other SA members. Within weeks of the demise of the SA, the SS was answerable only to Himmler and Hitler. Himmler was rewarded with the title of *Reichsführer-SS*, the equivalent to the army's field marshal.

It was in October 1943, at Poznan, Poland, that Himmler's antisemitism gave rise to the official Nazi declaration of a plan to exterminate the Jews. Hitler had given his approval for Himmler to give the speech at a secret meeting with top leaders of the SS and of the Reich. Himmler had always suspected, but had never asked for confirmation, that the reason the *Führer* had agreed to the speech was to ensure that the leaders were aware and that they wouldn't later be able to deny knowledge of the plan. This was a well-known technique to share the guilt.

Another of Himmler's traits that Hitler valued was the SS leader's problem solving skills. He had proved to be extraordinarily efficient with the Jewish question, changing methods until he had arrived at the most viable solution, the poison gas Zyklon B.

Himmler was a small man, well under two meters in height and a bit plump. He wore round-framed glasses behind which beady eyes peered out at the world. With a small, dark moustache, he had an odd passing resemblance to the Japanese Prime Minister, Hideki Tojo.

"It pleases me to hear you are well, *Mein Führer.*"

Hitler merely nodded, accustomed to Himmler's sycophant ways.

The early morning meeting was unusual because Hitler was more of a late night rat. He'd agreed to this meeting only because Himmler had promised something worthwhile, some good news.

Himmler opened a black leather satchel he held in his lap. A silver SS Death's Head-shaped clasp faced Hitler, just a small way of showing Himmler's devotion. Himmler undid the clasp, reaching over the top of the satchel. He removed a single sheet of paper, then closed the satchel, and placed it by his right foot. He lifted the paper at an angle.

Himmler was about to speak, but Hitler held up a hand.

"Is that a report on the Jews?"

"No, sir."

"Well, I want to hear about the camps first. What is the progress like at Auschwitz, Birkenau in particular?"

Birkenau was the largest of the extermination camps and was one of the many facilities at Auschwitz. It could house ninety thousand prisoners.

"We are running at top speed, and are exceeding our original goals. The gas chambers and ovens are far more efficient than we first thought. I can show you the exact figures if you would like to do that now."

Hitler waved his hand dismissively.

"I'll move on, then. I have wonderful news from Doctor Teichmann at Insel Riems to share with you." He leaned forward indicating he wanted to lay the paper on Hitler's desk, and asked, "May I?"

Hitler nodded, his eyes taking on a dark, excited appearance.

Himmler rose to lay the paper on the broad desk, turning it around so the *Führer* could read it. He waited while Hitler read the short summary he'd written especially for the *Führer*. Hitler was not interested in details, only results, so Himmler had taken Teichmann's fifty-page account of the recently conducted tests and summarized them into three simple paragraphs. The lead paragraph told Hitler the most important piece of information: the mortality rate of the virus: 100%. The second paragraph noted how much of the virus was already available: twelve canisters, and the final paragraph explained the speed at which the virus could be prepared and quantity: ten days per batch, and fifty batches at a time.

Hitler's expression grew more and more excited as he read the paper. When he lifted his face to look at Himmler, his eyes were ablaze with exhilaration.

When Himmler saw the expression, he knew he would be allowed to do anything he wanted with the virus. He also knew that Hitler would likely follow any suggestions Himmler might have, and he certainly had one.

"I know how you feel about Paris."

Hitler had mentioned his loathing for the city many times since his one and only visit to the city in June, 1940. His tour had taken only a few hours and he had gotten out of the car exactly once. That he had no interest in ever returning was well known at the highest levels. Field Marshal Göring on the other hand, had made many, many trips there to bolster his art collection.

"Yes?"

"I believe we could deploy this virus in the city just prior to our departure."

If Hitler was angry about Himmler's suggestion that the army would not be able to hold Paris, he hid it, although truth be told, Hitler wasn't known for holding back anger.

Encouraged, Himmler went on, "It would be the most efficient method to depopulate the city."

"I've already given Choltitz an order to destroy the important buildings."

"Yes, *Mein Führer*." Although Himmler had not heard of the order until now, he was not surprised by such an order. It was a typical reaction from Hitler. He decided to take advantage of the order. "Then by depopulating the city, it would in essence cease to exist. Imagine a world with no Paris and no history of it left."

Hitler turned his head to look out the gigantic floor-to-ceiling windows on his left. Himmler waited patiently, although he was pretty sure what the decision would be.

A few minutes passed, then Hitler said, without looking at his SS leader, "Yes. It is so ordered." He then turned to Himmler. "When can it be deployed?"

"The transportation of the canisters will take the longest. I've already worked out a plan and a backup plan to ensure that the canisters arrive in Paris. I could have them in the city within a week. I'll assign my most faithful men to accompany them and set them off. I will grant mercy on my men, and allow them to use timers so that they may at least attempt to return to the Fatherland. However, they would of course lay down their lives for you to accomplish their mission."

Hitler nodded. Of course they would.

Himmler started to say something, but stopped and Hitler said, "What is it?"

"I'm reluctant to ask such an impertinent question."

"Go ahead."

"Yes, *Mein Führer*. I was wondering if the army has provided a date they believe the enemy will arrive in the city." To indicate not once, but twice, that the *Führer's* army would fail in its mission was dangerous ground. The first had been forgiven. Would the second?

As expected, Hitler's eyes narrowed and his brows furrowed. Then they returned to normal. "Most likely, departure of the army will be near the end of next week. The enemy will parade themselves like stupid peacocks down the *Champs-Élysées*."

Himmler thought for a moment. This is exactly what he'd foreseen. "That will be the perfect time to release the weapon, *Mein Führer*. Massive crowds. Cheering Parisians. Lining the streets of Paris. Exposed. Many thousands jammed all together. Perfect conditions for a virus to be deployed."

Hitler smiled wide and his eyes sparkled.

To Himmler he looked like his old self; the strong, virulent *Führer* he so admired. He'd lost some of that following the twentieth July assassination attempt at Wolf's lair. Well, thought Himmler, if I can help return him to his old self, then I have served the Fatherland and *Mein Führer*.

"What are the next steps?"

"I'll contact Dr. Teichmann at Insel Reims, the head of the project, and give him the order to begin shipment to Paris immediately. I will, of course, coordinate the shipment's plans through my office and staff. I won't leave anything to error. I can assure you, *Mein Führer*, that the shipment will arrive in time for deployment when the crowds are cheering the so-called victors."

"Good. Do you require anything from me?"

"No, sir, you have already given me approval, that is all I need."

The two Nazis regarded each other briefly, relishing the thought of the destruction of Paris, in terms of both humans and property. They nodded to each other and Himmler rose to stand at attention in front of his beloved leader. He shot out his right arm at the exactly correct angle. *"Heil Hitler!"* he cried.

Hitler returned the salute, this time in his excitement, much more formally than his usual wrist flap.

Chapter 30

The French grandfather and grandson walked slowly toward Dunn, who was facing away, standing next to one of the German MG42s on the west side of the bridge.

"Bonne jour."

Dunn turned around and when he saw who had spoken broke into a wide grin.

"Hello." Dunn looked over at Schneider across the road. "Hey, Bob. Come here will ya?"

Schneider joined the group and said hello in French to the grandfather.

The man smiled and held out a half-bushel basket filled to the brim with various fruits, cheese, and bread. "This is for your men," said the grandfather, looking directly at Dunn.

Dunn hesitated. The last thing he wanted to do was take from civilians. "There's really no need."

Schneider translated.

The man simply lifted the basket toward Dunn to emphasize he was giving it to him and he wouldn't take "no" for an answer.

Dunn dipped his chin in acceptance and took the basket, which he handed off to Schneider. "Thank you very much. My men haven't had breakfast." He sent a smile to the little boy, and then knelt down to be at the child's eye level.

"Hello, Jean."

The boy seemed surprised that Dunn remembered his name from his earlier brush with danger.

"Hello."

"Do you like chocolate?"

Jean shrugged.

Dunn realized the boy might not have ever seen or tasted chocolate.

Dunn dug into his shirt pocket and pulled out a big bar. He unwrapped it a little bit so Jean could see it, then held it out. This made Dunn think of the little Italian girl, Marie, who he'd met after the action at Ville di Murlo. How many more will there be, he wondered.

Jean glanced at his grandfather, who nodded. The boy took the candy. He held it close to his nose and sniffed. A wide smile appeared and he chomped a big bite out of it, chewing and melting the chocolate as fast as possible. When he was done with the first bite, he remembered his manners and said, "Thank you, sir."

Dunn ruffled the boy's hair and stood up. "You're very welcome."

The grandfather asked, "What is your name?"

"I'm Tom Dunn and this is Bob Schneider."

"Lafleur." The man offered his hand. "I'm very grateful to you, Mr. Dunn. For saving Jean, and for saving the city." He stepped forward and kissed Dunn on both cheeks, then repeated the courtesy to Schneider.

"We can never repay you for what you've done, but please know we will be eternally grateful. Do you have a minute for a little story? I just heard about it yesterday."

Dunn looked around at his men, who were gathering closer, due to the length of Dunn's interaction with the civilian. He eyed the Sherman tanks, two on the east side and three on the west side, guarding the area until the rest of the Third Army showed up. From the sounds coming from off in the distance, it wouldn't be much longer now.

"One moment, Mr. Lafleur." Dunn turned toward his men and said, "Jonesy, take the basket and make sure everyone gets some, then take it over to Saunders."

Jones stepped forward, hunger in his eyes at the sight of the bountiful basket. He took it from Schneider and set it down. He carefully portioned out items.

"Go ahead, sir," Dunn said to Lafleur.

"Do you know a Colonel Welborn Griffith?"

"No, afraid not."

"Do you see the cathedral spires over there?" The man pointed off to the southwest where two differently shaped spires appeared over the buildings.

"Yes."

"That's the Cathedral of Our Lady of Chartres. It's over seven hundred years old. You should go see it. The stained glass is beyond words. Your Colonel Griffith saved that sacred cathedral from American artillery two days ago.

"You see, he knew orders had been given to bombard it because your people thought Germans were up at the top either as snipers or observers. He drove through the German lines and climbed all the way to the top, and then when he learned there were no Germans there, he rescinded the order.

"He is a hero to this city and our country for doing that. The mayor is already planning to submit his name for a medal from the French government.

"So do you see why our people are meeting you in throngs? Living under the Nazis for four years has been hell and you helped rescue us."

Dunn was about to say they were just doing their jobs, but thought better of it. That wouldn't sound right at all. The French freedom meant much more than that.

"We're honored to be of service to your country, sir."

The man's eyes welled up, and he said, "There's one more very sad part to the story: Colonel Griffith was killed that very same afternoon just north of Lèves, a short distance from here. His medal will tragically be awarded posthumously."

"Oh . . . I see." Dunn thought he would have liked meeting the man.

"I leave you now. I wish you safety as you continue across the continent. Hitler and his kind must be eradicated from the face of the earth."

Lafleur reached into his jacket pocket and pulled out a gold pocket watch. He handed it to Dunn. "Please take this. It belonged to my father. It is a Bonard, made in Paris in 1862. I want it to belong to an American soldier."

"No, I—"

"No, no. You must. Please."

Dunn held out his hand and Lafleur placed it gently, lovingly there. "Open it."

Dunn pressed the button and the gold lid popped open with a light swishing sound. The watch had a bright white face, elegant slim hands, and Roman numerals. A separate movement inside its own circle below the center contained the seconds with a small hand that ticked over each second, rather than sweeping across the face.

Dunn closed the lid. "Thank you, Mr. Lafleur. I'll treasure this always."

"Perhaps someday you'll be able to hand that down to your own son."

Dunn's eyes teared up, and he just nodded.

Lafleur nodded in return, grasped Jean's little hand, and left to join the celebration in the streets.

Dunn slipped the watch into his pocket.

From the north came the loud rumbling clanking sounds of many tanks.

The nearby throng of French villagers suddenly cheered and waved their arms as they looked to the north.

"Well, Bob, it sounds like Patton's bunch is here. Get hold of Colonel Edwards. Let's see what he wants us to do now."

"Will do, Sarge." Schneider stepped away and got busy on the radio set he had left sitting by the MG42.

Dave Cross had watched the exchange between Dunn and the Frenchman. He sidled up next to Dunn and said, "Can I see your watch?"

Dunn pulled out the watch and handed it to his friend. "Sure, here."

Cross examined the outside briefly. "That's beautiful." He popped the lid and held it to his ear. He closed the lid and lowered his hand. "Where do you think we're headed next?"

Dunn shook his head. "No idea."

"Maybe we'll make it to Paris."

"Could be, yeah."

"Hey, Sarge," called Schneider.

Dunn looked his way.

"I have the colonel."

Dunn nodded and walked over to take the handset. "Dunn here, Colonel."

Cross and the other men crowded in to hear what Dunn was saying.

"I hear congratulations are in order."

"Thank you, sir. Things went pretty well. No casualties."

"Great. Your next assignment is to attach yourself to a tank platoon. Have you met any tankers yet?"

"Yes, sir, a tank commander named Mike Lynch. He has five tanks."

"Okay. Wait one."

Dunn heard papers rustling in the background.

"I have him. His company commander is Captain Chambers. I'll contact him and let him know you're being added to his TO and E temporarily. His orders are to make way to Rambouillet. You know where it is?"

"Yes, sir. About twenty miles northeast."

"Correct. In any case, tell Lynch you'll be joining him on my order."

"Will do, Colonel."

"Is Sergeant Saunders nearby?"

"I can send someone to get him if you can wait a couple of minutes."

"Go ahead and get him, but I have to go now. Call me back."

"Sure thing, sir."

"Once again, congratulations on securing that bridge. I'll make sure General Patton is aware, and I'll contact your Colonel Kenton, too."

"Thank you, sir."

Dunn gave the handset back to Schneider, who put it away. To Bailey, he said, "Go get Saunders. Tell him Colonel Edwards wants him on the radio."

"Yes, Sarge." Bailey turned and ran off over the bridge.

Dunn gave his men the new orders, and each of the Rangers nodded their understanding.

"Let's get our gear together."

"What about the machineguns?" Rob Goerdt asked.

"Well take them with us if I can talk the tankers into letting us store them on the tank."

"Okay, Sarge."

"Dave, let's go find Sergeant Lynch."

As the men began the tasks of getting the gear and weapons together, Dunn and Cross walked toward the Sherman tank *Ghost Devil*.

After a few steps, Dunn held out his hand.

Cross looked at it and smiled innocently. "What?"

Dunn snapped his fingers twice.

"Fine." Cross pulled out the pocket watch he'd snuck into his trousers pocket and laid it in his friend's hand. "Worth a try, anyway."

"Yup."

After working out the details of joining Sergeant Lynch's platoon with the tank commander, Dunn and Cross made their way back to the bridge, which was now supporting vehicle after vehicle of Patton's Third Army. The crowd had grown to epic size and people were now lining the road on both sides waving and cheering.

Saunders was finishing up his conversation with Colonel Edwards as Dunn walked up to join him.

After Saunders signed off, Dunn asked, "You captured a truckload of Polish soldiers?"

"Aye. Well, sort of. I think they were ready to give up at the first sight of an allied group of soldiers. One of them shot their German handler."

"Huh. So what are your orders?"

"It seems Monty is in need of our special skills. We're to meet him in Belgium."

"You're going to meet with Monty? Himself?"

Saunders shrugged. "Could be. Orders specified his headquarters. I figured we'd get a good meal out of it anyway."

Dunn grinned and hit Saunders on the shoulder. "Be careful."

"Aye. Now that I have someone waiting for me, I plan to. Not that I wasn't before. It just matters more now, I guess."

"I remember some advice you gave me a couple of months ago, before Devil's Fire. Do you remember?"

"I do."

"Okay, then. Follow your own advice. Tuck Sadie away and stay focused."

"As I always do, mate."

Saunders offered his hand and the two friends shook. "You stay alert, too."

"Will do."

Saunders turned away and whistled. His men, who were mingling with Dunn's men to say goodbye, looked his way, then said their final farewells. The squad of commandos quickly loaded into a deuce and a half idling nearby. A few moments later, the truck roared away taking the now vehicle-cluttered road to the north.

Chapter 31

Bletchley Park, Hut 3
18 August, 0820 Hours, London time

When Reggie Shepston arrived at work, he'd had a small breakfast with hot tea before leaving his flat. As he opened the door to Hut 3, a couple of other analysts came up behind him, and Shepston held the door open for them.

"Morning, Shepston," said one.

"Bancroft, Henley, good morning to you."

And that was the extent of the conversation. Shepston walked over to his desk ignoring the men. Part of what made him a good analyst great was his ability to focus on the job at hand, and having no interest in extended conversations with coworkers. Even when Shepston was off the clock, he was thinking about something he'd worked on, especially if it seemed critical, and even after passing on his analysis.

He pulled his stack of messages closer and examined the first one. He handled about ten messages in the first hour and discovered he was thinking about the series of mysterious messages to and from Insel Riems. Eileen Lansford had continued bringing him all messages related in any way to that location, or to the men noted at the beginning of all of this: Dr. Teichmann and Himmler.

In spite of his focus on the work, Shepston had begun to look forward to her sudden appearances during the day. He found her presence to be comforting and pleasant. And to be honest, quite exciting. She was absolutely the most beautiful girl he'd ever met. Which in his mind meant she must already have someone.

A few messages later, he heard the door open and looked toward it, a happy anticipation suddenly rising. Sure enough, in stepped the lovely Eileen. Shepston felt his pulse rise, but then he noticed she was lacking her usual smile. This made him think, *uh oh*.

Eileen went directly to Shepston's desk and, without waiting to be asked, sat down, lifting her always-with-her satchel onto the desk.

"Good morning, Mr. Shepston."

Taking the young woman's cue, given since there were others in the office, Shepston replied, "Hello, Miss Lansford. What do you have for me today?"

Eileen frowned as she pulled a stack of papers out and handed them over.

"As bad as all that?" His voice, which he'd meant to come out sounding light, seemed to carry dread instead.

"Yes. I think so."

Shepston laid the messages out. There were only four, but they were lengthy, more text than usual, reaching almost a page each. Eileen's custom now was to order the messages from most to least important. By the time he finished reading the first one, his heart, which had slowed back down to normal, was pounding so hard he could feel it. For a split second he thought he was going to pass out.

He gathered himself and then pulled a calendar close, the kind where you flip a page to see the next day, and which had a miniature of the whole month printed in a little box next to today's number. A week. He only had a week. He checked his watch; Finch would be in his office by now.

He picked up the phone and dialed. When Finch finally came on the line, Shepston said, "It's happening, Finch. It's worse than we feared. I'm heading your way."

"Worse?"

"Yes."

"Quickly."

"Yes. As fast as I can."

Shepston hung up the phone, rising to his feet at the same time. He looked at Eileen, whose expression was filled with fear. Knowing there was nothing he could say to make her feel better, he said, "You're coming with me."

"What? Where?"

"Ten Downing Street."

Eileen's mouth dropped open, and under other circumstances, Shepston might have chuckled.

"I . . . wait. Me? What for?"

"I want Finch to meet you."

"But why?"

Instead of answering, Shepston unlocked and opened his large desk drawer. Reaching inside he withdrew two large accordion-style folders that contained all of the previous Insel Riems messages. He handed them to her.

"You can help me carry these."

"But I have to tell my supervisor."

Shepston picked up the phone again and dialed. When it was answered, he said, "Shepston here, Miss Woodhouse. Miss Lansford is going with me to Ten Downing Street on a matter of extreme urgency."

"That's most irregular, Mr. Shepston. I should think we would need a higher authority's approval."

Shepston could see Miss Woodhouse's expression. Pinched lips, frowny face.

"No time. I'll clear it with someone when we return. If anyone asks, we're to see Mr. Finch."

"I see. Yes, after you return then."

"Thank you."

Shepston started to move the phone away from his ear, but Miss Woodhouse had a parting shot, "Don't forget to do that."

"Certainly not. Good bye."

This time, he did hang up the phone even though there was still another comment coming his way.

"Let's go, Miss Lansford." He glanced at her, and saw her face was still in a state of confusion. He let his eyes drift downward to her neck. "You have your ID on your blouse, I see. Good girl." Her ID was hanging from a clip attached to her collar. He walked around the desk. "Come on. We have to go right now."

Eileen got up, gathered the messages and slipped them back into her case. She picked up the folders and turned to Shepston.

Without another word, he led the way to the car, which was parked near the hut entrance. It wasn't his car, belonging to the group as a whole. The key was in the ignition.

After Shepston and Eileen presented their identification to the guards, the walk through the door of 10 Downing Street caused Eileen to go wide eyed.

As they continued down a short hallway, Shepston said, "That's the Prime Minister's office." He pointed off to his right. The door was closed.

"Have you ever met him?"

"No. I've seen him here, practically running from one place to another, but I haven't ever talked to him."

"And your friend, this Alan Finch?"

On the drive, Shepston had told Eileen what little he knew: how Finch had been hired away from MI5 directly by the Prime Minster himself following some work on a top secret mission, the details of which he quite understandably did not know. He'd never asked Finch for the information, knowing it would cross the line.

They ascended a large curving staircase. At the top, Eileen suddenly gripped Shepston's left bicep tightly and they stopped walking, turning slightly to face each other at an angle.

"Why am I here? Exactly?"

"I want Finch to meet you." Shepston smiled, although her touch seemed to light his arm on fire.

"You said. But why?"

"Didn't I say?" Shepston's eyes twinkled.

Eileen suddenly saw the little boy underneath everything. The terribly ornery boy. "No. You haven't done," she replied testily.

"Oh, well. Right." He started walking and she had no choice but to take two quick steps to catch up.

"You'll soon see."

Eileen gave an exasperated sigh. "Fine."

"Finch, may I introduce Miss Eileen Lansford?"

Finch came around from behind his desk to take Eileen's hand. "A pleasure, Miss Lansford."

"Pleasure, sir."

"Please, be seated," Finch waved in the direction of the two chairs in front of his desk as he went back around to sit down himself.

Once everyone was settled, Finch got right to the point. "Tell me."

And Shepston did.

After five minutes, he concluded, "There's no question in my mind. They are going to release this new virus in Paris next week."

Finch had not interrupted Shepston, instead just listening intently.

"This is airborne. How do you think they plan to disperse it?"

"I see them placing these canister devices out in the public, out of doors."

"But wouldn't it be self-limiting?"

Eileen, who had been silent as Shepston told the story, spoke up after clearing her throat first. "They would pick locations where there are large crowds."

"Such as?" asked Finch.

Shepston suddenly understood what she was thinking. Unexpectedly, he felt proud of her and waited for her to continue.

"When we liberate Paris there will be crowds of unbelievable size, sir." She stopped for a moment to shudder at the thought of poisoning so many people. Then her analytical mind took over. "All they'd have to do is know which way the wind would be blowing. They could spread them out along the most occupied streets with the devices upwind so they can cover the largest portion of the crowds?"

Shepston noticed she'd ended her comment with the rising inflection of a question mark. He'd observed this among women he'd worked with, even when he was in college. He'd asked a friend studying psychology what that was about. His friend had explained it may have to do with the fact that women, through no fault of their own, were uncertain whether their comments would be taken seriously and to counteract possible conflict fell into the sing-song question mark ending. Shepston's own thought was to suggest to Eileen that she stop doing that. She was good at her job. Very good.

This comment was met with a long silence as the men imagined what she'd described. It made Eileen begin to wonder whether she'd overstepped her bounds. She started to say something to deflect her comments, but Finch spoke first, to Shepston.

"I see why you brought Miss Lansford with you."

Shepston nodded. "We can use all the help we can get."

Eileen looked slightly embarrassed by the attention. It wasn't something she craved or even needed. "I'm glad to help."

Finch smiled at her, then said, "I see two problems, Shepston: first and foremost, stopping the release of this bioweapon, and secondly, preventing the Germans from manufacturing more of it. Is there any way to determine where in Paris they're taking it?"

Shepston nodded at Eileen, and she answered the question, "We know when it's leaving Insel Riems, and that it's expected to be in Paris by the end of next week, but we don't know yet where. I would expect more detailed information to come out today or tomorrow. The plane is supposed to leave this Sunday, but will make security stops along the way. They're worried about it getting shot down."

"The moment you get that information, get it to Shepston here so he can call me."

"Yes, sir."

"What about after we know where it's going?" asked Shepston.

"I have a couple of ideas."

Shepston asked, "Are you ready to share those ideas?"

"Sure." Finch told them.

Afterwards, Shepston shook his head. "I had no idea we had units like that."

"We do."

"Let's say these guys find and destroy the canisters."

"Wait. We don't know how to destroy them, sir." Eileen said.

Shepston ran a hand through his hair, then rubbed his face. "No, we don't know." To Finch he said, "Know any biologists? Or bioweaponists? Is that even a word?"

Finch shrugged, keeping his face blank.

Shepston understood immediately and changed his next question to, "How will you take care of the manufacturing plant?"

"I'm not permitted to say anything on that matter."

This didn't surprise Shepston. He was perfectly capable of figuring out that the only way to destroy a manufacturing facility would be through the use of Bomber Command or the Eighth Air Force. He pictured the dolphin-shaped island of Insel Riems in flames from the dolphin's nose to the tail.

Shepston stood up, knowing the meeting had reached its conclusion. "Thanks, Finch."

Finch rose and shook Shepston's proffered hand, then Eileen's.

To the young woman he said, "You've done excellent work."

"Thank you, sir."

Finch smiled, but it was just a polite one, that didn't quite reach his eyes. "Don't thank me, Miss Lansford. I'll just be expecting more of the same from you."

Eileen swallowed the nervous lump suddenly rising in her throat, and then was able to speak. "I understand perfectly, Mr. Finch."

The moment after his old friend and the bright young woman left his office, Finch jumped up and ran over to the door, which he pushed shut. The heavy wooden barrier clicked into place. Back at his desk, he opened a small black leather phone book; its pages and cover were bound by gold rings set along the spine. On the front cover were the initials ACF in gold. Alan Charles Finch.

Finch paused a moment to just look at it. His late wife had given it to him when he'd learned he was going to work for MI5, in 1938, before the war started. She had died only two years later in the blitz, taking their unborn child with her. Finch smiled at the memory of the gift, then flipped open the book.

He made two calls in quick succession and arranged a meeting for the next morning with Colonels Kenton and Jenkins. They were happy to come to London.

After the calls, he wrote a note to himself in big letters.

CONTACT MARSTON TONIGHT!

Chapter 32

British Field Hospital, 3 miles west of Caen, France
18 August, 0725 Hours, Paris time

Pamela's sixth patient in a row died on the operating table. He was the last British soldier to be on the table, for the time being at least. The doctor handed her his instrument and called the time of death. He walked away shaking his head.

Pamela removed the items used during the surgery: the clamps, the forceps, the sutures and needle. She dropped the clamps, forceps and suture needle into a metal pan she would use to carry them to be sterilized. The unused exposed sutures would be tossed.

She pulled the sheet up over the young man's face, glancing only briefly at his youthful, sleeplike countenance. She refused to allow her mind to go to that horrible place, the one where she would see Dunn's face on every dead man. If she didn't keep that under control she'd be useless, something she would never let happen. She'd agreed to come to work for the Queen Alexandra's Nursing Service, and she intended to learn, and to do her very best every moment.

Someone else from graves would come and dress the body for burial and take it away. Reaching above the body, she turned off the surgical lamp, and left the tented arena, and the dead man in darkness.

She tended to the instruments by putting them carefully in a hot, ready, and empty autoclave. She took off her surgical clothing and dumped the articles in a special hamper. As she washed her hands for several minutes at a sink nearby, scrubbing thoroughly, especially under her nails, which were kept short for this very reason, other nurses came and went without conversation.

At last, finished with everything, she left the main surgical tent and stepped into the fresh air of the out of doors. As usual, the camp was buzzing with activity. Walking fast, Pamela wound her way along the "streets" of the hospital grounds. Eventually, she broke through to the side where there was a large copse of trees which stood as both a barrier and a reminder of the rest of the world. She found the path she was seeking and began strolling through the woods. It had become her place to unwind, to forget the horrors of surgery. She had expected this assignment to be difficult, but if she was honest, it was worse than she'd imagined.

She walked to the other side of the woods, then turned around and headed back. On the return trip, she began to feel better, stronger again, as usual. When she had made her way about half way back to her habitat tent, she saw her supervisor, Agnes, the same young woman who'd picked her and the others up at the airfield. Was that only two days ago, she wondered.

Agnes saw her, smiled and waved, then beckoned to Pamela, who got the impression the woman had been searching for her.

Agnes wore her nursing uniform and cap. She was a little shorter than Pamela, and stockier. Her black hair was carefully brushed into place under the cap. Her smile was infectious, and Pamela smiled when she neared her supervisor.

Agnes was only thirty-two, ten years older than Pamela, but her experience made her a terrific nurse, and her personality made her a natural leader.

"Hi, Pamela."

Agnes put a hand on the younger woman's shoulder and turned her so Pamela was on Agnes's right side. "Let's walk together."

The women started toward the side of camp opposite the trees. "I heard you had a rough go of it today."

Pamela glanced at Agnes sidelong, wondering how she'd already found that out.

"Yes. We lost six patients in a row at the end."

Agnes nodded. "Yes. Yes, that can be terribly hard to bear." She turned to look at Pamela.

Pamela felt the gaze and turned. What she saw in Agnes's eyes was compassion.

Agnes turned away to see where they were walking. After a few more steps, she asked, "How many successful surgeries did you have today?"

Pamela was caught off guard by the question. "What?"

"How many did you save today?"

Pamela started to say the word 'well,' but stopped with her mouth open on the unfinished 'w.' Her eyes moved to look skyward, as she tried to think of the number. "I don't know."

"Eleven. That's how many you and doctor saved today."

"Oh, right. Eleven."

"I want you to start writing down the number you save every day. Do you keep a journal?"

"Sometimes."

"Every day. Each day, add the previous total. Keep a running score. Then any time you have a day like today, you go to that journal and read the numbers."

"I know what you're trying to do, and I appreciate that, but I'm fine, really."

"No, you are not fine. I can see it all over your face. You don't think it's there, but I recognize it. I've worn that same expression many days of my life, believe me. Do yourself a kindness and listen to an old woman's advice."

"You're not old!" protested Pamela.

"No? I feel old."

Pamela glanced over. Agnes's smile had disappeared.

"You don't look a day over thirty-two."

This caused Agnes to chuckle lightly. "You're funny. Thanks for nothing."

"You're welcome."

"I have news to share with you. I'll be telling the others shortly, but since I have you."

They turned a corner and Pamela realized Agnes had directed their walk toward Pamela's tent. They stopped outside it and Agnes turned to face Pamela.

"We're advancing the hospital. The front line has moved much farther to the east and we need to get closer."

"When?"

"Sometime next week. It's a gigantic proposition, as you may imagine, so we need to get started on the organizing of it well ahead. You're going to be responsible for all of the surgical equipment."

"I see. I'm glad to do whatever you need me to do. Where are we going?"

"Paris."

Chapter 33

The apartment building where Marston was currently staying was located was on the east-west *Rue d'Auteuil*. It was about one and a half miles southwest of the Eiffel Tower and a few blocks northwest of and across the Seine River, which flowed northeast to southwest in this part of the city.

Instead of the basement, he was on the top floor, the fourth. Madeline had pointed out the escape route, which would be across the rooftops of the neighboring buildings, then down to the *Rue Chardon Lagache*. The particular apartment he was in had once belonged to a Jew and his family. The man had been a shopkeeper on the street below, antiques, in particular ancient Rome and Greece. He'd been arrested and deported several years ago to where no one knew. Everyone knew though, by now that he was never coming back. Shortly after his disappearance, a wealthy non-Jew purchased the apartment. He never moved in. Instead, he'd allowed his thirty-year-old son, Mortimer Fontenot, to move in. The owner, himself in his late fifties, ran a newspaper, one that was friendly to the Germans for the sake of survival.

The son was a cell leader of the French Resistance. Fontenot had been responsible, either directly at his hands, or through his leadership, for the deaths of dozens of Germans, particularly officers, around the city. His group also had quite a lot of expertise in explosives, and had destroyed numerous rail lines and warehouses throughout the city.

Fontenot rarely made an appearance at the apartment, and certainly never during daylight. Tonight, though, he was there in the room with Marston, and Madeline was there, too. Madeline's uncle Remi was sleeping in another apartment. Remi had introduced Madeline to Fontenot, and the two had both felt an immediate chemistry that had nothing to do with the Resistance.

The trio sat at the dining room table. A single lamp was shining brightly from its place on a large walnut buffet table set against the wall. The apartment had high ceilings, typical of turn of the century architecture. The air was thick and warm. No windows were open, which would have let the cooler night air in, because it would also let light escape out onto the street. That could lead to German curiosity, which could lead to German questions. Questions that would be difficult to answer, like, why do you have a radio set? A British radio set.

Madeline, wearing a beige shirt and black shorts sat to Marston's right. Fontenot sat across from the British spy. The young leader wore a dark blue suit, with the jacket hung over the back of his chair, and a neatly pressed white shirt and blue tie. He wore horn-rimmed glasses and his dark hair was combed carefully, parted on the right. A small moustache adorned his upper lip. He was attractive, but not movie-star handsome. To Marston, he looked more like an Oxford professor than a proficient killer.

Each was nursing a cup of hot coffee, a hard-to-come-by treat. In front of Marston sat his Morse code key and transmitter. The transmitter was turned on in preparation of his sending the daily report. Next to it were his notepad, a couple of knife-sharpened pencils, and the code book.

The conversation in progress shifted from Marston's reports that he would be sending within the hour.

"Over half of the railroad workers are on strike. The city is at a standstill," Fontenot said.

"I heard that all the policemen have refused to report, too," Madeline said.

"Yes. There were several anti-German demonstrations, the largest one near the Eiffel Tower. The Germans made no attempt to stop them." Fontenot leaned forward, placing his folded hands on the table. "Today, we plan to take over as many police stations, town halls, ministry offices, and newspaper buildings as possible."

"Including your father's?" asked Madeline.

"Yes, we can't let the Germans know how much support he's given us."

Madeline nodded.

"What about Choltitz?" Marston asked. "Is he still at Le Hotel Meurice?"

"Yes," replied Madeline. "Checked myself today. Yesterday, I mean."

Hotel Le Meurice was located a mile and a half northeast of the Eiffel Tower. Relative to the apartment in which Marston found himself, the hotel was a little over three miles away on a line through the Eiffel Tower.

Marston knew the Le Meurice. He'd made a trip to Paris in 1938 with the intention of taking a holiday. It had turned into a working holiday when he discovered he could get access to some seventeenth century French documents. While he couldn't possibly afford to stay there on his professor's salary, he'd had occasion to walk past the hotel many times.

"You know of Raoul Nordling?" Fontenot asked Marston.

"Sure. The Swedish counsel general to Paris."

"Correct. We're going ask him to meet with Choltitz and convince the general to declare a truce."

"Do you think Choltitz will go for that?"

"He's got twenty thousand men defending the outskirts of the city. We estimate that leaves around five thousand within the city itself. If we have a truce, he won't have to worry about us as much, although we will keep up the pressure by continuing the strikes. We don't have enough weapons for lengthy battles with the Germans."

While Fontenot was speaking, Marston happened to glance at Madeline. She was looking only at Fontenot. From what he understood about people, it was 'the look.' Her eyes were bright and shiny and in spite of the circumstances, her lips formed a small smile. Marston was immediately grateful that he hadn't acted on his impulses. He couldn't know how long she'd had feelings for Fontenot, but it was brand new since they'd only just met. Madeline seemed to feel his gaze and turned to him. He nodded and gave her a gentle smile, and she returned it, then looked at Fontenot again.

Fontenot seemed unaware of the silent message between the other two people at the table.

Marston asked, "If Nordling agrees to meet Choltitz, when do you hope to have that meeting?"

"Today. Tonight at the latest."

"Good luck."

"Thank you. Will you be staying through the liberation?"

"As far as I know.

"I believe you'll be safe here. We don't expect there to be another breach like the one at your previous location."

Marston glanced at Madeline, who had singlehandedly saved him from the clutches of the Gestapo. "Thanks, once again."

Madeline raised her coffee cup in a salute. "You're welcome."

"Do you know how the breach occurred?"

"Yes, and it's been rectified." Fontenot raised his hand in a pistol shape and pulled the trigger.

"Good." Marston was about to say something additional, but the radio beeped out its hello from England. He glanced at his wristwatch. "They're early."

He pulled the notepad closer and opened it to a blank page. He keyed out a pre-coded response.

After the first line of the message came through, the beeping stopped, so he began the decoding process. When he was done, he looked up at the two French Resistance members. "My apologies. I have to be alone for the message."

"Top secret, hm?" said Fontenot with a grim smile.

"Something like that." Although it was virtually impossible for either of the two people at the table with him to figure out the message based on what came over the receiver, Marston had to follow the rules.

"We'll be across the hall. Come get us when you're done, or if you need anything."

"Thank you."

Fontenot and Madeline departed, and Marston heard the apartment's hallway door snick closed.

Marston sent his reply and waited. Only a few seconds had passed when he received the beginning of the message stating that he was talking directly with Alan Finch.

As time and the message decoding progressed, Marston's insides grew increasingly knotted, and his brow carried a sheen of sweat. Half way through the message, he had to change pencils.

Twenty minutes later, a stunned Marston sat back from the table.

Chapter 34

Rambouillet, France
19 August, 0642 Hours

The morning still carried the nighttime cool, but the sky was a bright blue and the sun would warm things soon.

The day's beauty was lost on all members of the Sherman tank, the *Ghost Devil*. The Sherman had advanced to within fifty yards of Rambouillet's buildings and stopped. Their attention was necessarily focused on watching for things that could kill you. The city was just over twenty-five miles southwest of downtown Paris and about fifteen from Versailles. The tank commander, Sergeant Mike Lynch, cast a wary eye along the street in front of him. Contrary to Chartres, the narrow street was quiet, no civilians were moving anywhere, a stark indicator that the city wasn't free yet. It was clear of rubble, the city having not been bombarded either by air or artillery. Lynch hoped it could stay that way. Several cars were sprinkled along the curbs, and farther down a small truck sat in front of a furniture shop.

Everyone else in the tank was buttoned up, but Lynch crouched in his open commander's cupola, with just his neck and head exposed. He knew he was an easy target for someone close or for an elevated sniper. His chief concern, however, was whether a German soldier lay in wait inside one of the many dark windows up and down the street with a panzerfaust.

Behind Lynch's tank was the rest of the armored platoon and the infantry bodyguards, including Dunn and his men. Dunn's men were gathered directly behind the engine of the Sherman, whose heat radiated toward them like a sauna.

When the tank came to a halt, Dunn immediately jumped into action and ran around the left side, then climbed up to kneel behind Lynch. Dunn looked past Lynch and saw the same thing the commander had: nothing.

"You need us to go ahead now," Dunn said, not a question.

"I'm afraid so."

Dunn patted Lynch on the helmet. "Stay put."

"Absolutely."

Dunn jumped off the tank and rejoined his men. He explained quickly what they were going to do, although this was no surprise to anyone.

Tanks were at their most vulnerable not just against the German armor, but against the German foot soldier. The Americans had learned by trial and much error that the Shermans needed protection from the German infantry. Advancing toward the enemy always ended up exposing the weaker flank of the Sherman. The only way to protect the flanks was to send American infantry ahead to root out Germans who had antitank weapons like the panzerfaust. This was especially true when moving through wooded areas and otherwise confined passageways like the street that lay ahead of them now.

After talking with his men, Dunn signaled to the squad leader next in the line to bring his men forward. It was going to take a lot of men to clear the buildings.

When the other squad arrived, the leader asked, "We clearing the buildings?"

He spoke with a southern accent, evidence of his Atlanta, Georgia roots. Corporal Mac Rhoades was about Dunn's age, about four inches shorter and twenty pounds lighter. He wore tortoise shell spectacles and had an open friendly face. He carried a Garand M-1 with the barrel down, and a holstered 1911 Colt .45.

Rhoades had come ashore late in the afternoon on D-Day and had fought his way through the horrible French hedgerows, then across the flat fields and forests of western France. He and two others were the only remaining survivors of the original squad. The first squad leader had died on D-Day plus two when a German MG42 machinegun opened up on them. Four others had died at the same time. That made Rhoades the squad leader. The replacements had arrived the next day, and somehow they'd all made it this far together. No small part of that was Rhoades' smarts.

"Yep. We'll take the north side."

Rhoades had talked with Dunn on their trip to this spot, and liked what he saw. Dunn reciprocated the feelings and the two struck up a quick friendship, the kind where you immediately feel comfortable with someone.

"Okay. How far ahead are we going?"

"Two blocks at a time."

"Got it. See you later." Rhoades waved a hand and walked toward his men.

Both squad leaders got their men lined up in the order they wanted. Dunn had point and right behind was Schneider. Next in line came Rob Goerdt, the squad's other Iowan. The rest of the squad fell in line with Cross taking the last spot.

Dunn glanced across the street at Rhoades and nodded. The corporal gave a small wave and both squads began to run forward in the distinct hunched-back gait of a solider advancing into enemy territory. A stand of trees stood about ten yards from the first building on Dunn's side, paralleling the street. Dunn ducked in amongst the trees and eyed the building from behind a white birch. The windows on the west side were all closed and dark. The building was three floors tall. Constructed of stone, there was a single entryway door facing the street with symmetrical windows on either side. Awnings protected the windows from the sun, which would shine directly in otherwise. Dunn guessed it held apartments.

Dunn checked the windows in the building just across the street and while some were open, he saw nothing behind them. Rhoades had reached the corner of that building and he glanced at Dunn, then up at the building on Dunn's side.

They gave each other an all-clear sign.

Dunn took off at a run toward the nearest corner of the building. Once he arrived there he took a quick glance down the street and then across the street again, looking for shooters in the windows. All clear, so far. He gave a quick wave and a line of Rangers darted across the short gap to join him.

"The windows are down to shoulder height, so stay low," he warned his men.

Dunn ducked and glided forward until he reached the front door alcove, which was recessed a few feet. His men were strung out behind him either crouched or kneeling when Dunn had stopped. He leaned forward slightly, just enough to peek into the doorway. The front door was dark wood with a large rectangular window from top to bottom. A narrow window the same height stood on the right of the door. Through the glass, Dunn could see a small foyer, and just beyond, a half-flight set of stairs that led to a landing. The foyer and landing were empty.

Dunn moved in front of the door, and put his hand on the brass knob. He nodded at Goerdt. Dunn pushed the door open and Goerdt dashed through and stopping at the bottom of the stairs. He waited until Clarence Waters joined him, and then he started up the short set of stairs. He kept his back against the wall on his left as he moved up one step at a time. His focus was on the set of stairs going to the second floor.

When they reached the landing, Goerdt was surprised to find the doors to the two first floor apartments open, as if inviting them inside. The doors were opposite each other and located a few feet from the stairs. Brass-colored numerals identified the left as number one and the right as number two. The air felt still, the way a house does when no one is home. Goerdt waved at Dunn and indicated that the doors were open. Dunn replied to wait. A moment later, Wickham and Bailey ran through the front door, followed by Cross and Lindstrom.

Goerdt checked the next set of stairs. Still no movement. He nodded at Waters who ran the rest of the way up from the foyer. At the same time, Goerdt slowly edged toward the bottom of the next set of stairs, and Waters took a quick glance into the apartment on his left to make sure the living room was empty, which it was.

When Goerdt was able to see that the next landing was clear, he moved to stand between the bottom of the stairs and the open doorway of apartment two. He nodded and Waters crossed over to stand on the left side of the doorway. Wickham and Bailey moved up to positions outside apartment number one.

Cross and Lindstrom set up at the top of the stairs.

Goerdt held up three fingers and did a countdown. When he hit zero both teams entered their respective apartments.

Cross turned to Dunn, who was watching intently, and signaled that entry had been made. Dunn nodded. A couple of minutes passed and then Goerdt and Waters exited apartment two. Goerdt gave Cross a thumbs up. Just after that, Wickham did the same thing. Goerdt made his way to Cross.

Whispering, he said, "It's one apartment on each side running all the way to the back. The back door leads to an alleyway, but it was locked."

"Only two more floors and a roof to go," Cross replied.

It took another five minutes to do just that.

Dunn could hear his men coming down the stairs. One down. Blocks to go. He turned toward the street and saw Rhoades coming out of his building. The men exchanged thumbs up signs again.

It was the eighth building where everything went to hell.

Chapter 35

French Resistance safe house, Paris
19 August, 0703 Hours

Neil Marston's mind was still reeling from Finch's news. As he had once feared for England's survival, he felt terror at the threat to Paris, and perhaps all of France. The conversation by Morse code with Finch had grown worse and worse by the minute.

Another problem facing Marston was how much of the truth he could tell Madeline and Fontenot. Finch had told him to use his own discretion. Marston's first thought was to hold back the complete truth, however, sitting directly across from the French duo, Marston made a decision he hoped wouldn't create a city-wide panic. Looking from one to the other, he said, "We have intelligence that the Germans have a new kind of weapon. You're familiar with the gas during the Great War?"

"Yes," replied Madeline. Fontenot nodded. Dread appeared in both of their expressions.

"They have created a biological weapon and Hitler intends to release it here, in Paris."

Fontenot buried his face in his hands.

"Dear God," said Madeline, her pale face even whiter. "When?"

"The exact target date is unknown, but it's suspected that the timing is meant to coincide with the eventual liberation of Paris."

Fontenot lowered his hands and looked at Marston. "The crowds will be enormous!"

Marston nodded. "I know. It's barbaric to think that anyone could release a weapon of this kind, but Hitler is not just anyone."

"What can we do to help?" asked Madeline. Her lips compressed, and her expression changed from despair to resolute.

"The bioweapon is supposed to be coming by air from northeast Germany. There are three airfields in and around Paris. It could be going to any of them. My contact said they're working on getting the destination, but . . ." Marston shrugged and frowned.

"You want to watch all of the airfields, and not just for a few hours, but for days," Fontenot said.

"I know it seems an impossible task."

"We're in the midst of a concerted effort to get rid of the Germans once and for all. Why can't the bastards just leave? They are beaten."

Marston understood the man's frustration and anger, as well as the need to blow off steam. "I don't disagree with you. But this has to have top priority."

"How sound is the intelligence? What if it's just a diversion the Germans want us to expend our energy on?" Madeline asked.

Marston drummed his fingers on the table. As far as he was concerned, the source was unimpeachable. He didn't know what the original source of the intelligence was, but he had complete confidence in Finch.

"My contact is at the highest level. If he says this is what the Germans are doing, I'm certain it's from a viable source. This person does not jump to conclusions."

Madeline closed her eyes and pinched the bridge of her nose. She was still for a while, almost as if she was posing for an artist. Finally, she lowered her hand.

"We only need twelve people, two per airfield, twelve hour shifts each. Male and female pairs, where possible, to blend in as much as possible. Three radios, handed off by each pair. A command center with four people, two on, two off all day. Three cars or trucks."

Marston admired the woman's ability to think under pressure. He understood her thought process as well as the detail of using men and women together to reduce attracting attention.

"How soon can you get people in place?"

Madeline blew out a breath and looked at Fontenot. "Two hours?"

The Frenchman nodded. "Yes." He turned to Marston. "How exactly can we tell if an airplane coming in is the right one? The Germans could just be flying in supplies. For that matter, they could ship the weapon on a regular flight with other supplies."

"That's true. We can only hope that we'll learn which airfield and the arrival date and time. Until then, we have to know everything we can about any flights arriving." Marston had a sudden thought. "What if the Germans bring it in, we see it, but then they load it on a truck and leave the airfield? How can we handle that possibility?"

"We would have no choice but to follow the truck to its destination," Fontenot offered.

Marston mulled the suggestion over and could find no better alternative. The idea carried many risks, up to and including losing sight of the truck at some point. The British operative was accustomed to facing mission risks, but this one in particular carried risks higher than ever. He knew he'd have to get more information from Finch. But for now, Fontenot's suggestion was as good as anything else.

"Let's plan on that then," Marston said, at last.

Chapter 36

Rambouillet, France
19 August, 0748 Hours

Dunn traded places with Cross and prepared to enter the eighth building. Dunn estimated they were about half done with clearing the village's main street. This particular building housed a small clothing shop on the east half, and an apartment on the other side. There appeared to be one or more apartments on the second floor, the top floor. There had still been no sightings or sounds of either Germans or villagers. Dunn had to assume the villagers had evacuated some time ago.

The entryway had two doors at an angle to each other, one leading to the store and the other the apartment. Since he could clearly see in the store, and no one was there, unless they were in the back, he elected to breach the apartment door first. Unlike the other buildings, which all had doors with glass in them leading to the foyers, this door was solid wood. Dunn figured it must lead directly into the apartment. The windows facing the street were closed with the curtains also pulled closed, so there was no way to view the interior.

　　　　RONN MUNSTERMAN

Dunn motioned to Lindstrom to cover the door from the sidewalk. Once Lindstrom was in place, Dunn took a step closer to the door, then crashed his right boot against the door just to the side of the doorknob. Subtlety was not required. The door shattered at the lock and flew open to Dunn's left. He slid to the right to see into the room. His eyes widened. He raised a finger to his lips in a shushing motion.

To Lindstrom, Dunn said, "Civilians to the left."

Lindstrom peered in to the right and said, "Clear on the right."

Dunn advanced into the apartment's living room and knelt beside a young, dark-haired woman who was holding a little girl on her lap. The girl began to cry and both females' eyes were wide with fear. The woman pulled the girl's face into her neck and patted her on the back.

"Do you speak English?"

There was no recognition in the woman's eyes. Dunn went back to the door and got Schneider's and Cross's attention. "Bob, come in here. Dave, help Lindstrom clear the rest of this apartment."

Cross darted in, and he and Lindstrom carefully set about moving throughout the apartment, which went all the way to the back of the building.

Schneider joined Dunn. With the big man translating, Dunn began questioning the woman.

"My name is Tom. What's your name?"

"Margo."

Dunn nodded to the little girl, who he guessed was three years old. "Your daughter?"

"Yes, Yvonne."

"Is anyone else in the apartment?"

The woman shook her head, but her eyes flew upwards.

"Someone is upstairs?"

Margo shook her head no, but her eyes kept going back to the ceiling.

"Are there Germans up there?"

She gave another little shake.

Dunn realized what was happening and dropped to a knee again. He leaned close so he could whisper. Following in suit,

Schneider whispered his translation, "Are there Germans upstairs holding someone hostage? Say 'no' very loud if I'm right."

The woman grasped what Dunn was doing right away and shouted, "No!"

The woman's expression was pleading and Dunn knew he had been right. He'd never heard of German soldiers holding civilians hostage in a situation like this, but they were doing it to keep the woman quiet about their presence. He assumed they were somehow listening to what was going on down here.

Still whispering he said, "How many Germans?"

The woman said "None," but she held up four fingers.

"How many hostages?"

"None," said loudly. One finger. "My husband," said quietly.

Dunn stood up and motioned to the woman to go out the door and turn right. "Run that way." He pointed to the west where he knew she would be safe. He raised his finger to his lips again.

"Thank you, Ma'am," he said loudly.

"You're welcome," she replied.

"Cross? There's no one here. Get your asses out." Cross and Lindstrom came running back into the living room. Cross's expression showed surprise. Dunn pointed upstairs. Cross nodded.

"How do we get upstairs?" Dunn asked the woman.

The woman pointed to the back, and whispered, "Go outside to the back door. Stairs are there."

"Is the door locked?"

"No."

Dunn nodded and said, "Okay, go. Now."

The woman was crying hard now, fearing for her husband's safety, but she got to her feet and ran out the door carrying her daughter, then to the west as instructed.

"Everyone out. Check out the shop next door."

Dunn went last and when he got back out on the street, he looked east. A narrow alleyway opened just to the far side of the shop. He understood that rescuing the Frenchman was going to be very risky, but it had to be done. The Germans had to be killed or captured.

After Cross and Lindstrom exited the shop, declaring it free of Germans, Dunn moved his men to the alleyway. He laid out his plan to the entire squad, who were arranged in a semicircle in front of him, their backs to the alleyway.

Dunn gave a nod and the squad split into two groups, Cross took Martelli, Goerdt, Wickham, and Waters to the front of the next building. Instead of entering, they waited outside.

Dunn's group included Bailey, Lindstrom, Jonesy, and Schneider. With Dunn in the lead, they ran quietly north through the alley. They had to avoid a number of tin trash cans that were strewn about as well as some empty wooden fruit crates. Fortunately, there were no cats or dogs who might give them away by barking or screeching. As they advanced, Dunn eyed the second floor, wondering whether the Germans posted anyone overlooking the alley. Too late now.

Dunn stopped at the building's edge, and peeked around the corner. Behind the building was a paved area big enough for about three cars to park. A small backyard extended to the north where a line of three small houses ran east-west. If they were occupied by Germans, things could go very badly very quickly. Nevertheless, he had to clear the building; it was his first priority.

Dunn backed away from the corner and turned to Schneider, who was waiting right behind him. "Stay here a couple of minutes. Keep an eye on the three houses to the north. Anyone shows up there, shoot them. Once we're inside, you follow."

"Roger, Sarge."

Dunn pointed at Jonesy, who was carrying just the Sten submachinegun; his Springfield was lashed to the *Ghost Devil* on the back right, on top of the tread plate cover; all the guys had done the same with their gear for extra freedom of movement. Jonesy moved up to stand beside Dunn, while the other two Rangers, Bailey and Lindstrom, followed.

Dunn led the way around the corner, staying close to the side of the building. His nose suddenly wrinkled at a pungent burning smell. He spotted the culprit about ten yards ahead: a smoldering trash can, wisps of smoke trailing into the air and into the slight westerly breeze. He wondered who had bothered to take out the trash.

A few steps farther took him to the recessed back door. He examined the door. It was just a plain wooden door, no glass, no frills of design. He took two quick steps toward the door, and put his hand on the knob. He waited a couple of seconds for his men to get in place behind him. Gently, he turned the knob. When it reached its stopping point he pulled on the door. The woman had been right, for the unlocked door swung open. He got it open wide enough to peek around. Straight ahead were a set of stairs and a wooden railing on the right side.

Dunn knelt so he could see the top of the staircase. It was empty. There was only one door at the top; thankfully he wouldn't have to choose between two. Moving forward he placed his right boot lightly on the first step, close to the baseboard and underneath the railing. This was in the hope that the step wouldn't creak close to its support point. He put weight on his foot. No creak. Carefully, he proceeded up the stairs. He couldn't get his left foot as close to the edge, but no sounds came when he put weight on it.

When he got far enough to see the second floor, he paused. He tried to see under the door, where a sliver of light shone through, but the gap was too thin. Just as he was about to take the next step up, the light flickered and part of it went dark. Someone was moving. Without looking, he briefly held out his left hand behind him as a stop sign, then returned it to its position on the Sten's fore stock. He raised the nine millimeter weapon and stared at the door knob.

It rotated, and then the door opened slowly.

Chapter 37

Hotel Le Meurice was already bustling with Germans who were members of General Dietrich von Choltitz's staff.

Opened in 1835, the hotel was the greatest of them all in Paris, and was originally built by Charles-Augustin Meurice for British travelers. It provided an English speaking staff and easy currency exchange. Upon their arrival in 1940 the Germans had commandeered the hotel for their headquarters.

It was about six blocks northwest of the Louvre, and was a perfect example of a palatial hotel. At seven stories tall, it covered two full blocks and was directly across from the astonishingly beautiful Tuileries Garden, which itself was nearly a quarter mile by a half mile in size. On the far side of the garden, the Seine flowed past. It was no surprise that the Nazis had selected it for their headquarters.

Choltitz had taken over the hotel manager's office, an opulent and spacious room on the mezzanine. The general's desk was to the right of the office's double doors. Straight ahead were knee-to-ceiling windows framed by burgundy drapes which were pulled back to let in the morning sunlight. A variety of comfortable stuffed chairs were arranged around the office, including a couple of matching wing chairs in front of the desk.

The desk was an eighteenth century Louis XV Kingwood and Ormolu Bureau measuring two meters in width and a little more than a meter in depth. The surface trim was inlaid wood that surrounded the black matt work surface. The Ormolu gold was gilded along the desk edges, down the finely curved legs, and formed the handles on the three drawers.

The general was seated at the desk. One thin stack of papers lay in front of him: the day's orders ready for his signature. He read the top one and signed it quickly, then set it aside, upside down.

A light tap on the door caused him to look up. "Come."

One of the double doors opened and his aide stepped through, a colonel who had been with him for two years ever since the siege of Sevastopol, which ended in a Russian defeat on the fourth of July, 1942.

The colonel was carrying a piece of paper which Choltitz recognized as a cable. The aide walked over to the desk and held out the paper. "This just arrived, sir."

Choltitz took the proffered message. The words TOP SECRET had been stamped across the top of the paper in bright red ink. He spotted Hitler's name in the "from" section. He sighed deeply; what had arrived from the insane leader this time? He leaned forward, put his elbow on the desk, and rested his chin and cheek on the palm of his hand. The message subject line said: FINAL ORDERS RE PARIS.

The body of the cable contained just two instructions:

```
1 - The city must not fall into the enemy's
hands except lying in complete rubble.
2 - Colonel Doctor Gebhard Teichmann arriving
soonest and you are to afford all he requires
to accomplish his mission.
```

Choltitz shook his head and let the paper slip from his grasp. It fluttered to the desk. He looked up.

"Prepare orders to begin laying charges on all bridges. We'll start with that."

"Yes, sir. Do you know who this Colonel Teichmann is?"

Choltitz shrugged his shoulders. "Find out."

"Yes, sir. I'll also have the orders prepared within five minutes."

"Fine." Choltitz glanced down at the other orders awaiting his approval. "Anything in here worth looking at?"

"Not really."

Choltitz quickly signed them without bothering to read any.

"Take them with you."

The aide leaned over to pick up the papers. "Yes, sir."

He turned and left the office, closing the door gently behind him.

The general got up and walked across the carpeted floor to the windows. He stood there with his hands behind his back. The Seine River flowed past not far from the hotel. He tried to imagine all of the bridges ceasing to exist in one moment. Well, he'd done it before in Rotterdam and Sevastopol. Orders were orders.

He went back to his desk and sat down. He lifted the receiver from the gold phone. Someone answered immediately.

"I'll have my breakfast."

Chapter 38

Rambouillet, France
19 August, 0801 Hours

Dunn tensed his legs in preparation of a run up the stairs.

The door opened fully and a German soldier stepped through carrying a Mauser. The soldier's mouth opened when he saw Dunn and they locked eyes.

Dunn fired twice, striking the soldier in the center chest. The soldier crumpled and his Mauser clattered to the floor.

Dunn ran up the stairs and entered the room. His men were right behind him.

In a split second Dunn took in everything in the room. Two soldiers were facing the windows that looked out onto the street, and were turning toward the sound of Dunn's footsteps. A civilian was sitting on the sofa staring at Dunn with fear in his eyes. He had bruises on his face and a bloody nose. He wore a white shirt and black slacks held up by black suspenders; Margo's husband. Seated next to the Frenchman, a third soldier reached for his Mauser, which he'd leaned against the sofa while he smoked a cigarette.

RONN MUNSTERMAN

Dunn felt Bailey slide into position next to him. He knew Lindstrom was doing the same. Three on three, with surprise on their side.

Dunn pointed his Sten at the sitting soldier and shouted, "Halt!"

The two soldiers at the window completed their turn and raised their Mausers.

Bailey and Lindstrom fired a short burst, Bailey into the soldier on the right, Lindstrom the soldier on the left.

The seated soldier continued his motion and got a hand on the Mauser.

Dunn fired twice and the soldier slumped back, two holes in his chest.

Dunn heard someone pounding up the stairs and turned toward the door, weapon raised. Schneider burst into the room with his Sten gun at the ready.

Bailey and Lindstrom ran over to the soldiers they had dropped and kicked the weapons away. It was obvious the soldiers were dead. Dunn knew his target was dead, so he turned his attention to the civilian, who was still trying to make sense of what had just happened. It all seemed to click suddenly and the man shot to his feet and hugged Dunn, and kissed him on both cheeks. He began talking rapid-fire French and Schneider started translating for Dunn.

"Thank you! You saved my life." With a frightened, despaired expression he asked, "Do you know where my wife and daughter are?"

"They are safe."

The man hugged Dunn again and asked, "Where?"

Dunn pointed toward the west. "They're down the street."

The civilian started to leave, but Dunn held up a hand. "Please. Wait. I have questions for you."

"Yes?"

"Do you know of any other Germans in the village?"

"These four were the last. They got left behind and were angry. All the rest left in the middle of the night."

"They beat you, and then threatened to kill you if your wife told us anything?"

"Yes, one of them understood English and he was listening by the heat vent." The man pointed to a foot-square metal grate in the wall by the sofa.

"Where is everyone else? We haven't found any people here."

"Probably at the church at the east end of the village. We were about to leave when these soldiers suddenly showed up."

"I see." Dunn looked toward the door at the lifeless body there. "Why did that one come to the door?" Dunn pointed.

"They were hungry. I think he was going to my apartment to get food. There isn't any up here." The man's expression changed to sadness. "They were just boys. Stupid little boys with guns."

"What? What do you mean?" Dunn glanced over at the dead soldier on the couch. Dunn frowned. He *did* look awfully young.

"They are from the Hitler Youth SS Division."

Dunn knew of the Hitler Youth, the only legally permitted youth organization in Nazi Germany, but he'd never heard of them being in combat.

Dunn patted the man on the shoulder. "Thank you. Go find your family."

"*Merci!*" The man turned and ran down the stairs.

Dunn leaned down and started going through the pockets of the dead soldier on the sofa. In the third pocket he found an identification book. He flipped it open and saw the birth date: 5 März 1930. "Fourteen." He slammed the book down in disgust. "Fourteen fucking years old. Fucking Nazis. Using boys."

Dunn shook his head, his lips thin in anger, furious that he'd been forced to kill a boy just a few years younger than his sister, Gertrude.

Bailey and Lindstrom stared at the boys lying dead on the floor. The Rangers' expressions matched Dunn's: anger and disgust.

"Damn it." Dunn took off his helmet and ran a hand over his forehead and through his hair. "Damn it," he repeated. Replacing his steel pot, he stared at the three boys for a while, saying nothing. Finally, shaking his head at the utter stupidity of it, he turned and walked away.

"Let's go," was all he said.

Dunn passed the word quickly that the village was clear. A half hour later, the armored column and the flanking infantry guards were through the village and on the way to Versailles. Next stop, Paris.

Chapter 39

10 Downing Street
London
19 August, 0915 Hours, London time

The problem at hand seemed insurmountable.

Alan Finch pulled a handkerchief from his pocket and wiped his brow for the second time in a few minutes. Even though it was still early in the day, sweat seemed to be pouring out of his skin. The last time he'd felt like this was during Operation Devil's Fire, the mission to destroy the Nazi's atomic bomb facility near Stuttgart. He recalled the long night's wait in the radio room in Number 10's dungeon-like lower levels. He had been with the Prime Minister and Howard Lawson of the OSS. While waiting for word of success or failure, the Prime Minister had ordered a full English breakfast at three a.m. Churchill had been able to eat with gusto, while Finch and Lawson picked at the food.

Finch's phone rang and he answered, "Finch."

He listened briefly, then said, "Yes, send them in, please."

RONN MUNSTERMAN

He opened a black leather notebook, removed two sheets of paper, closed the notebook, and then placed the papers on top of it.

His office door opened and Colonel Rupert Jenkins stepped through with Colonel Mark Kenton right behind him. After the pleasantries, Finch asked the two men to be seated.

The colonels had worked with Finch before and knew he wouldn't ask them to drive to London on a whim, so they waited to learn what Finch needed from them.

The wait was short. Finch in return knew these men were busy commanding special mission forces, and sometimes had several squads out at the same time.

"We have a problem and need a couple of your teams to solve it." He picked up the top paper and handed it to Jenkins, and then handed the other one to Kenton. "These are the necessary orders. You can see the approval comes from the top."

The men read the cryptic top secret orders quickly and noted the signature at the bottom: Dwight D. Eisenhower.

"You'll no doubt have noticed the lack of specifics. I will give those to you, but first I must know for certain you have teams available." Finch looked at each man in turn, an expectant look on his face.

"I see that the problem is in Paris. Tom Dunn is somewhere west of there," Kenton said.

"Saunders is in Belgium with Monty, but doesn't have an assignment yet. He can be back and ready to go today," Jenkins said.

"Here are the details of what we know. Intelligence indicate that the Germans have the means to infect the entire population of Paris with a new biological weapon. Based on what we know, we're certain they are capable of unleashing this horrific death on France, if for no other reason, spite.

"The method of delivery is a cylinder about four inches in diameter by twenty inches tall. That makes it about the same size as an 88mm shell casing. There are probably a dozen of these, we hope to get a firm number soon. We suspect the biological agent will be deployed through an aerosol mist. We know nothing about the agent itself, but have seen the reported results, which shows a mortality rate of one hundred percent." Finch paused.

"Even though the sampling of test subjects was small, that's still going to be far higher than the Black Death of the Middle Ages."

Kenton's face blanched and Jenkins looked like he was about to throw up.

Finch looked at Kenton and said, "We need Dunn to get his men to Paris quickly. We don't have a delivery date yet, and we're working on that, but it is an imminent threat. You remember Neil Marston?"

"Sure, I do. He did an incredible job during Operation Devil's Fire."

"He's in Paris, working with the Resistance. He's coordinating with them to watch the airfields for the weapon's arrival. We will have open communication with him throughout this."

Jenkins raised an eyebrow. "Won't that expose him to the Germans? Being on the radio that often?"

"It's a risk, yes, but we hope the Germans are going to be too busy worrying about the workers' strikes and the trouble the Resistance will be causing throughout the city."

Jenkins nodded. "Saunders is going to the manufacturing facility?"

"Yes, sir. It's on a small island called Insel Riems on the Baltic Sea. It's about one hundred and twenty miles north of Berlin."

"Transport by submarine?"

"Yes, sir. They'll have to leave right away. I'm coordinating with the Eighth Air Force. We're going to bomb the place; level it. But he has to go in and capture or kill the lead scientist and any other scientists he can find. And be off the island before the bombs fall."

"Are there plans for holding off the bombers if for some reason Saunders can't get off the island in time?"

Finch glanced down at his hands. He knew Saunders, and liked the big Commando. He realized he might be sending the man to his death on this mission, and obviously, so did Jenkins. "No sir. We can't take the risk holding the bombers over Germany."

"No. Of course not. I understand."

Jenkins looked decidedly unhappy and Kenton noticed. This was a first. Jenkins had always been so implacable, abrasive, and seemingly self-centered. Kenton found himself reappraising the British colonel. Maybe there *was* a feeling human underneath all of the other bullshit.

"Our command center will be the Cabinet Room downstairs. You're welcome to attend, but of course, it's not required."

Jenkins glanced at Kenton, who stared right back. They nodded to each other.

"We'll be here," Kenton said.

Finch nodded. He pulled another pair of papers from his notebook and handed them across to the men. "These are additional orders."

Jenkins and Kenton read the orders. When they looked up at Finch, their expressions were stoic. They understood the need for the orders. They put the two sheets of paper together and folded them carefully, then placed them in an inside breast pocket.

"Any questions, gentlemen?" Finch asked.

Both colonels replied no, and rose.

Finch rose, also. "Would you please call me after you have relayed the orders to your men? I'll need to complete coordination with Paris and the Eighth Air Force."

"Absolutely," Kenton replied.

"I will," Jenkins said.

Finch shook hands with each man. "Thank you both."

The colonels nodded and left.

Finch sat back down and rubbed his face. He'd slept poorly after his lengthy message exchange with Marston in the early hours of the day. He picked up a mug of coffee he'd poured some time ago and smelled it. He debated drinking the bit that was left even though it was stone dead cold. He decided against it and got to his feet.

He glanced at the sole photo on his desk. His late wife smiled at him from five years ago. Before the blitz attack that killed her and their unborn baby. He could look at her picture without bursting into tears, but there had been plenty of times when that was all he could do. They'd been married three years, having wed in the time before the war. He'd been working for MI5 for a couple of years when she died.

Living for his work, Finch never did anything unrelated to his job. As far as he was concerned, killing Germans and ending the war was his purpose in life. He reasoned that after the war he could strike up a balance and maybe try living again.

Following Operation Devil's Fire, at Churchill's request, he'd been transferred to the Prime Minister's staff. He handled all manner of "problems" for Churchill. He met with the Minister on a daily basis, and had received the signed orders for Jenkins and Kenton just after seven a.m.

Next on his to-do list was the call to the commander of the Eighth Air Force, Lieutenant General Jimmy Doolittle. The conversation was brief, and Doolittle was immediately on board with the plan. Finch promised to messenger over the orders signed by Eisenhower right away.

The second phone call was to the commander of a British photo reconnaissance unit. He quickly gave the map coordinates he needed and when he told the commander when he needed the photos, the commander chuckled.

"You're bloody joking, right?"

The question was met by silence.

"Yes, sir. We'll have them to you by noon tomorrow."

"Thank you, Colonel. We appreciate it."

The colonel knew exactly who "we" meant. The call was from bloody 10 Downing Street, after all.

The last call was to the commander of the Royal Navy submarine force. Details were ironed out and Finch rang off with a 'thank you.'

Finch sat back in his chair. Was there anything else to do? He racked his brain and could come up with nothing. He had set things in motion. It was up to those people who would execute the plan.

He snorted to himself as he thought perhaps his title should be changed to Coordinator Extraordinaire.

Chapter 40

Reginald Shepston and his new daily partner, Eileen Lansford, were across from each other at his desk. German messages, already decrypted by Hut 6, and translated by his own hut, lay in a huge stack between them.

They'd started by examining the messages quickly just to winnow out the ones that were of no use whatsoever. That had taken thirty minutes, but left them with a more manageable stack to read in more detail. They divided the remaining messages between them and started reading.

They'd both worked late the night before, until nearly one o'clock in the morning. Shepston had driven Eileen home and walked her to the door.

"See you in the morning, Reggie. Sleep well." Eileen reached up and touched him on the cheek. He leaned forward slightly and she brushed her lips along the same cheek. Then she turned and disappeared through the doorway, leaving Shepston standing there unable to move. His hand went to his cheek and he smiled. Then he drove home and fell into bed fully clothed.

When the alarm went off at five-thirty, he pounded it with a fist to shut it up and muttered, "Bugger."

He debated stripping and taking a shower, and was about to bypass the morning ritual in favor of an early start when he suddenly remembered who he would be seeing.

With fresh clothes, clean skin and hair, he pulled the car up right outside of Eileen's building. Before he could even get his door open, she came flying down the short sidewalk and hopped in the car.

She leaned over and kissed his cheek again. "Morning, Reggie."

"Morning, Eileen." Shepston didn't mean to, but he stared at her for a long moment. Her brown hair was up and away from her face as always, and her cheeks were rosy, probably by pinching them. Her eyes took on the green from her dress today.

Eileen smiled at him, perfectly aware of his scrutiny.

Reggie was torn, as he had been nearly since meeting her. He knew he was falling for this bright and beautiful young woman, but they had serious work to do and a relationship could well and truly muck up things. But he wanted both: to get the job done and to have a relationship with her.

"Eileen, I . . ."

"Yes, Reggie?"

"I, er, you look nice this morning."

"Thank you. So do you."

Shepston looked down at his clothes in surprise. He was wearing the exact same thing he always wore: dark suit, white shirt, more or less matching tie, and worn shoes. "Thanks."

He put the car in gear and pulled away from the curb.

His thoughts were running fast and there was so much he wanted to say. That he wanted to be with her. That he hoped she felt the same way. That maybe they could be together in spite of the work. That—

"Reggie?" Eileen interrupted his train of thought.

Shepston glanced over at her. "Yes?"

"What's the policy about coworkers dating?"

Shepston glanced over at her again, then back at the road. "It's kind of frowned on, but it's not against the regulations." He swallowed a rising lump in his throat. Had he waited too long? Was there someone else she liked? He felt like a schoolboy. "If you don't mind my asking, who are you thinking about?"

To his surprise, Eileen chuckled and put her hand on his arm. "Oh, my God, boys are so thick."

"You mean me?"

"Well, you're not a topnotch analyst for nothing."

"Oh." He laughed nervously. "Really?"

Eileen sighed. "Yes, really. If you're interested."

"I am. The truth is, I have been since I first met you."

"Me, too! Although I don't quite know what my parents will think."

"What do you mean?" Wariness crept into Shepston's voice.

"You're Cambridge. My parents are Oxford."

A relieved Shepston said, "Oh dear. That would be serious."

They arrived at Shepston's hut and walked in together. Shepston had to stop himself from taking Eileen's hand along the way.

"What do we need?" Shepston was speaking rhetorically, which Eileen already knew from their working so closely together recently, so she just waited. Shepston then held up his right hand and ticked off points with his fingers: "Airfield name, the aircraft identification, although that might not come until the last moment, who is expecting the crate and who, if anyone, is traveling with it. Can you think of anything else?"

Eileen thought for a moment, her brows furrowed deeply.

In spite of the problem they were working on, Shepston couldn't help himself and smiled at the sight of the beautiful woman with her face scrunched up, thinking it made her somehow, incredibly, . . . cuter. Eileen didn't notice the smile and Shepston got rid of it, worried she might not be exactly pleased by his thought.

Eileen snapped her fingers and said, "We need to check for communications between Berlin and commanders around Paris asking for troop support at an airfield."

Shepston stared at her openmouthed. "Bloody hell. It's practically obvious. Why didn't I think of that?"

"You are a Cambridge man, after all."

Shepston smiled. "Is this the way it's going to be?"

"You have no idea." She lowered he voice to a whisper, "Wait until you meet my mum and dad."

Shepston's eyebrows shot up and he looked alarmed. "Meet your mum and dad?"

"Don't worry, they won't bite . . . too badly anyway."

"Isn't it a bit early in our . . . relationship for me to meet them?"

"Not at all. I always bring them home as soon as possible."

"Them. Have there been a lot?"

"Oh, bunches. Kittens, puppies, a snake once, and possibly a goat. Not sure about that last one, I was only three."

Shepston snorted, then said, "You're a real confidence builder."

"My goal every day, don't you know. Sir."

Shepston shook his head. "Oh boy." He set aside the message he'd just read and they turned their attention back to the messages. Each took one and the hunt began.

An hour later, Eileen said with excitement in her voice, "Here's something, sir." She placed a message in front of Shepston, facing him.

Shepston read the message. It stated that a crate was to be picked up at Insel Riems and delivered to Paris. The pickup was scheduled for the twenty-third, four days away. The crate's identification number was NVH2351798, which was similar to those found within previous transportation messages relating to deliveries in the Nazi world. It didn't say which of the airfields around Paris would be the recipient. It did state contents were twelve containers.

"Okay, great, so we have the date and an identification number, and it will have a dozen containers in it." Shepston said.

Another half hour passed in silence, the only sound the rasping of one message against the other as they pulled them one by one in front of themselves.

"Uh oh," Shepston said.

"What is it?"

"Have an order with an identical crate number going to Warsaw. That would be about where the Russian front is currently."

"Why wouldn't they send it in another crate?" She looked at the ceiling briefly, then said, "Oh, I see. Disinformation. It's a decoy. What do you think?"

"That makes sense, provided we are right about Paris being the primary target."

"You think they would try to hit two places with the weapon?"

"I don't think we can rule it out just yet."

"Right."

Back to the stack they went.

Another half hour passed and they discovered two more sets of orders: one for Bologna, Italy, and the other for Brussels, Belgium.

"Four targets," Shepston muttered.

A glum Shepston spread the four messages out between them, sideways so they could both read. They glanced at the remaining messages. There were only perhaps twenty more.

"It's got to be in here," Shepston mumbled hopefully.

When Eileen was on her second from last message, she read it, read it again and then jumped up with a squeal of delight. "I've found him!"

The hut's other three analysts looked up from their own stacks of messages. One smiled, but the other two frowned and looked back down right away.

"Teichmann himself is going to Paris!"

"Oh, that is fantastic."

"There's more, Reggie." She'd forgotten their agreement on being formal.

Shepston either didn't notice or didn't care about formality anymore. He sat back in his chair and spread his arms wide. "Tell me."

"He leaves at seven in the morning, Insel Riems time, and is expected to land at an airfield in Paris. And guess what else?"

Shepston waved at her to continue.

"He and the weapons are flying in a Junkers 52, identification I, Z, A, R." She read a little more of the message. "Hm, this is interesting."

"What?"

"The pilot won't be given the exact flight plan until he boards the plane."

"They're probably afraid of someone being on the inside, either a traitor, maybe a leftover from the twentieth July assassination attempt on Hitler, or a plain old fashioned spy."

Shepston tapped a few bars of his jazz beat with his pencil eraser. "This is most of everything I need to move forward with Finch. We have the date, aircraft, the cargo, including Teichmann, and the airport. The only other useful thing we can look for is whether the army is going to support Teichmann once he arrives. Can you track down a picture of Teichmann?"

"Possibly from university year books; it shouldn't be hard to find out where he went."

Shepston gathered the relevant messages and put them in his satchel. He stood up. "You focus on Teichmann for the next hour or so. I'm going to go see Finch."

"Right."

Shepston picked up his phone and called Finch.

When Finch answered, Shepston said, "I have the details we need. I'm coming your way right now."

"Hurry. I need to get that out to the commanders right away."

"I will."

He hung up the phone and said, "Great job, Miss Lansford."

Eileen looked up and smiled.

He took a quick peek at the others in the hut. They were all head down with their work. He leaned forward and whispered, "I could just kiss you right now."

Eileen winked. "I'll be counting on that. Sir."

Chapter 41

After clearing Rambouillet, Dunn and the armored platoon had met with only light and sporadic German resistance as the enemy retreated pell-mell eastward.

The armored platoon joined up with other units of Patton's Third Army and they all were strung out in a miles-long column along the road south of the Palace of Versailles. The extended line of vehicles was moving slowly, not in small part so everyone could goggle at the palace of King Louis XIV. Dunn and his men were all sitting on the *Ghost Devil*, enjoying the view like everyone else.

From his position on the Sherman tank, Dunn could clearly see the massive palace, only a quarter mile away. He stood up to better see over the eight-foot-tall stone wall along the north side of the road. The gardens were in their summer riot-colored splendor and he wished he had a camera.

"Look at this, Dave."

Cross, who was flat on his back taking a nap, stirred and asked, "What?"

"The gardens."

"What gardens?"

Dunn glanced down at his friend, who had his helmet over his face to hide from the midday sun. Dunn kicked Cross's boot and when Cross lifted the helmet to scowl at his sergeant, Dunn grinned.

"You don't even know where we are, do you?"

The squad members laughed. They were used to Dunn and Cross needling each other in quiet moments.

Cross put his helmet on, the leather straps hanging alongside his cheeks, then he sat up on his elbows. "France. This is still France, right?"

"Nice. You've always had such great situational awareness."

"Yes, I know. Thanks."

Dunn held out a hand and Cross grabbed it and pulled himself to his feet. Dunn pointed, although it was pretty much unneeded, as Cross stared open mouthed at the gardens. "Holy shit. I wish my mom could see this."

Sergeant Lynch, the tank commander, was sitting in his hatch enjoying the Rangers' exchange. It reminded him of his crew. He suddenly pressed his hand against the left headset and said, "Repeat."

He listened and then said, "Roger." He twisted in place to see Dunn. "Hey, Dunn, just got word that Colonel Edwards wants to talk to you in person right away."

"How do I get to him?"

"He's in motion about two miles back and he's coming our way in a jeep. Should be here before too long. His driver will have to maneuver around the vehicles behind us."

"So I stay put with you?"

"Yeah. When he gets here, we'll stop long enough for you to change vehicles."

"Okay, thanks." Dunn turned to look westward for a fast moving jeep. A few minutes passed, and then he saw it. A jeep was indeed weaving around the slower moving tanks and trucks, passing on the left.

The jeep pulled up on the left of the tank and matched its speed. Colonel Edwards, Patton's chief operations and planning officer, waved at Dunn. Lynch noticed the jeep and gave the order for the tank to halt. At the same time, Edwards stood up in the jeep and faced the tank about ten yards behind. When he held up his hand the following tank driver saw him, and stopped the tank. The line began to accordion as it slowed, then stopped.

Dunn knew what the colonel intended and he hopped down and climbed in the jeep behind the colonel. Edwards gave the 'go' signal and all the vehicles started moving again. The jeep driver kept pace with the *Ghost Devil* for a little distance, then slowed, and ducked in behind it.

Edwards sat down and turned slightly to somewhat face Dunn. His face was grim, but he said, "Good to see you, Sergeant."

"You, too, sir."

"New orders for your squad from Colonel Kenton. Top priority. I just learned a little of the scope of some of your recent, uh, exploits, from Colonel Kenton. I knew you excelled at being a Ranger, but my God, I had no idea what you've done. So it should come as no surprise to you that the fucking Nazis have cooked up another secret weapon."

Dunn's face blanched. "Shit. Again?" Dunn looked up at his men on the tank in front of him. They had all sat up straight and were watching him intently. They knew something serious was coming their way. That's what they did, handle impossible problems. The only question was what is it this time?

Dunn glanced at the jeep driver, wondering whether he should be hearing this and realized he wasn't an enlisted man. It was Captain Alford, who had helped Dunn and Saunders procure the equipment for the mission to Chartres.

Edwards nodded. "They have a biologic weapon and are planning to release it in Paris very soon. Intelligence thinks they may be planning on doing it during the liberation celebrations that even the fucking Germans know is coming."

Dunn's mind reeled for a few seconds. Biologic. What does that mean? "Is it some kind of virus or something?"

"Unknown for certain, but intelligence believes so. Something that may be worse than the plague."

"Oh my God."

"The weapon will be in steel cylinders about two feet tall and four inches in diameter, with some sort of timer on the top. A dozen of them. They will all be in a large wooden crate. Here's the crate identification number." Edwards pulled a scrap of paper from his shirt pocket and handed it to Dunn.

Dunn read the numbers, which seemed to be random letters and numbers: NVH2351798. He memorized them and handed back the paper.

Edwards looked nonplussed. "Why don't you keep it?"

"No need, sir. I have it."

"Oh. Okay. You're sure?"

Dunn smiled. "Yes. Anything written, especially numbers stick permanently for me."

"I see. Well, we know where the weapon will be arriving in Paris: a German airfield north of central Paris. Not really that far from the Eiffel Tower. Naturally, I'm going to give you whatever support you need. What can I acquire for you?"

Dunn gave it some thought as they drove along. After a few minutes, he told the colonel what he wanted.

"Done," replied the colonel immediately. Then his expression changed suddenly, looking as if he'd just bitten into something bitter. "However, there's another critical facet to your orders."

Wary, Dunn said, "Yes?"

"This is not a destroy mission. You are to acquire the weapons by any means necessary. All twelve of them, but," Edwards held up a finger for emphasis, "any that cannot be captured are to be destroyed, in particular, by explosive fire."

Dunn stared at the colonel, considering what he'd just been told. Of course the Allies would want the weapon. If for nothing else to study it. Whether it might actually be used was up in the air. Perhaps it would be used as the stick in the carrot-stick method of negotiating with the Nazis. Maybe they would then finally see the futility of continuing the war.

"Yes, sir."

"You understand this is why I can't just send a battalion to that airfield. They would manage to stomp all over everywhere and destroy everything. Success rests with you. I know I don't need to emphasize how crucial it is to keep the Nazi fuckers from

214   RONN MUNSTERMAN

releasing the weapon. If they trigger just one of them, people will start dying within three days. Lots of people."

Dunn turned to look to his left. The Palace of Versailles had retreated in the distance. They were now entering the countryside. He looked eastward and spotted vehicles going off the road to the north and south, creating the new offensive line in preparation of the attack on the Germans in Paris.

"Your contact in Paris is a guy named Marston. He may be at the airfield, we're not sure. But if he is, he can provide some assistance."

Dunn looked at the colonel and raised an eyebrow. "Marston? Neil?"

"Yes, I believe so. You know him?"

"We worked together a couple of months ago. I thought he was working in England."

Edwards shrugged, in essence saying, things change.

"Thanks for the heads up."

"Sure. Any questions for me?"

"We're going to also need some Thompsons."

Captain Alford glanced over his shoulder. "I'll get those for you."

"Great, thanks, sir."

"You got it," the captain replied.

Dunn looked at his men on the tank and found Cross. Their eyes met and, as usual, an unspoken message passed between them. Cross understood the mission was high risk, and not just for the squad. Dunn understood that Cross would be ready for anything.

Chapter 42

In flight, 200 miles northwest of Insel Riems, Germany
20 August, 0712 Hours, Berlin time

Twenty-six-year-old Flight Lieutenant James Allender banked the de Havilland Mosquito PR Mk VIII slightly left to cross the Danish shore about ten miles north of the border with Germany. Flying at an altitude of thirty thousand feet would likely keep them out of trouble. The lithe, twin-engine reconnaissance aircraft shot through the clean air.

The Mosquito, known as the "Wooden Wonder" because it was almost completely constructed of laminated wood, had entered service in 1942 performing duties ranging from light bomber and fighter bomber to night fighter and photo recon. The Mark VIII had the distinction of being powered by the new two-stage, two-speed supercharged Rolls-Royce Merlin 61 engines, which generated 1,565 horsepower each. She had a maximum speed of 436 miles per hour and a range of 2,550 nautical miles. The cockpit sat forward along the front edge of the wings and the main camera array sat below and in the nose of the aircraft. Side-

and-down facing cameras were placed along the fuselage behind the wings. A rear-facing camera sat in the belly toward the tail.

Navigator Boyd Warmington said, "Stay on this course for eight and a half minutes." At their present speed of 350 miles per hour, they would only require that amount of time to cross the Danish peninsula. They would then be over the inlet from the Baltic Sea.

"When we clear land, come right to one-one-two."

"Roger, heading one-one-two." Allender replied.

The two men had worked together almost two years. Warmington had been just twenty years old when they first met. He grew up on a farm in central England, miles from anywhere. He'd joined the Royal Air Force in hopes of leaving the farm behind and seeing the world. He'd done just that, although just the European continent.

Allender had worked as a lorry driver in London when he signed up. The son of a successful and highly regarded barrister, he'd been a disappointment to the family because he had absolutely no interest in attending university for anything, especially law. However, after he'd earned his Pilot Officer rank, and he'd gone home for Christmas leave in 1942, he had been received as a hero, getting a rare hardy handshake from his father.

At just the right moment, Allender banked the aircraft to take the heading provided by his extraordinary navigator. "Time to target?"

As usual, Warmington already had the calculation ready. "Twenty-four minutes to descent." This point was one hundred forty miles away, and about twenty miles from Insel Riems. Allender would start his descent to ten thousand feet and Warmington would double-check the cameras. They would be just under four minutes from the target, coming in from just south of northwest.

"Thin clouds at about fifteen," Allender said. They would be no problem.

At the twenty-four minute point, Warmington said, "Mark."

"Roger. Descending to ten." The pilot nosed the aircraft over, carefully eyeing the airspeed indicator. It started to increase, so he reduced power. They flew right on path and angle.

They shot through the clouds. Allender spotted the dolphin-shaped strip of land jutting out into the bay leading to the Baltic Sea. "I see the target."

He brought the plane into a sweeping left curve to line up with the western point of the Insel Riems Island. He had been scanning the sky for German fighters the whole trip, and he continued to do that. Seeing nothing to worry about he focused on his flight path.

"Cameras ready," Warmington said.

"Roger." Allender put his finger on the camera trigger button. He gave the plane a little left rudder and the nose yawed that way. Satisfied, he leveled the plane's wings and pressed the button. The cameras began firing frame after frame as the Mosquito raced across the German facility at over four hundred miles an hour.

Neither crewman knew why they were taking pictures. It was too dangerous to tell them in case they got shot down. All they knew, and wanted to know, was when and where and how many pictures.

Allender clicked off the cameras when they crossed over the east end of the island. He let the aircraft cover several miles before he turned her around to head back for a second and final pass. He checked the airspace for Germans and saw none. It was rare for German fighters to even try to get to altitude and attempt to shoot them down due to the high speed of the Mosquito, but it did happen.

He lined up the aircraft and took another complete series of photos. As soon as they were done, he pulled back on the yoke. Soon they were climbing back toward thirty thousand feet and on a reciprocal heading toward home. They would be back on the ground in a little more than an hour and a half.

The photos landed on Finch's desk at five minutes to noon.

Chapter 43

German airfield, Paris
24 August, 1435 Hours

Dr. Gebhard Teichmann leaned close to the window of the trimotor Junkers 52 and took in the sight of Paris spread out beneath him. The plane was coming in from the northeast putting the Eiffel Tower just to the left of the plane's nose and barely in Teichmann's view. Farther to the left and closer, the *Arc de Triomphe de l'Étoile* rose skyward in its white stone beauty. It was a stark contrast to the Eiffel Tower's black iron.

The airfield was a few miles north of the Eiffel Tower. Only when the plane's altitude was almost zero did Teichmann pull back from the window.

The plane touched down with a puff of dirt and grass, then taxied off the north-south air strip. It made its way toward a row of wooden buildings situated along the east side of the airfield. The pilot carefully guided the plane along so it lined up parallel to the airstrip and the buildings. He left the engines running, just as his orders stated.

Teichmann was first out of the plane and he was soon standing on the summer-dried grass of the German airfield. Coming down the stairs of the Junkers were a half dozen black-uniformed SS troops. The leader gave a quick order and the men formed a cordon around the plane. A canvas-topped truck that was parked at the north end of the field lumbered alongside the air strip, coming to a stop about ten meters from Teichmann. The back gate dropped open and a dozen more SS troops jumped down. A lieutenant colonel stepped down from the cab and approached the doctor, who was wearing his SS uniform. He saluted and Teichmann returned it with a raised arm *Heil* Hitler salute.

"Welcome to Paris, Colonel Teichmann. I am Colonel Neubert. We are at your disposal, courtesy of General von Choltitz."

"How far away are the Americans?" Teichmann had been told by Himmler to ask this question in order to be able to determine whether the time table would need to be altered.

"The more important question is 'where are the French?' Leclerc's Second Armored Division is just a few miles away." Neubert pointed toward the southwest. "That way. All German units are starting to melt away. There is really nothing of consequence between them and us."

"What do you mean 'melting away?' "

"There's been a railroad strike here for days. Troops that were supposed to be taking trains east were stranded, so they just started making their way out of Paris the best way they could. We're actually under a truce with the Resistance."

Teichmann looked alarmed. "You mean the city has already been captured?" He was afraid he was too late for the French celebration with its massive crowds. His targets.

"No, no. But it's just a matter of days. Probably this weekend."

"Yes, that's perfect," Teichmann said, feeling relieved.

Teichmann was already moving ahead mentally. There was still much work to do.

Behind him, the airplane's rear door opened, the same one that paratroopers would have used, and a man wearing a suit leaned out. It was one of Teichmann's lab assistants. He called out to the doctor and Teichmann turned around. He nodded at the assistant. To the colonel, he said, "Have your men assist unloading the airplane."

"Yes, sir." The colonel saluted and waved at his men to move to the plane. They formed a line and several men on the airplane started handing down wooden crates.

Dense shrubs grew just east of a sparse tree line running along the western edge of the airfield. Neil Marston and Mortimer Fontenot were lying on their bellies between a pair of shrubs two hundred yards away. Each had stolen German binoculars to their eyes. They wore dark clothing, and dark plaid flat hats.

"That has to be Teichmann," whispered Marston. He had received a ton of information from Finch in the middle of the night, including which airfield the bioweapon was coming in on, the crate number, and a description of Teichmann. Fontenot had gone out to the airfield at two in the morning and verified it was where Finch said it was. It was all quiet, and no troops seemed to be about. All of this was reported right back to Finch.

It was during this second communication session that Marston learned that he could expect help to come in the form of one Sergeant Tom Dunn. Marston knew Dunn well and welcomed the news. Dunn had helped Marston get safely out of Germany after spying for four years. When their escape aircraft was shot down, through quick thinking, Dunn had gotten all the men home to England, including the German lead nuclear scientist, who was ready to defect. They'd stolen a German Junkers 52 right out from underneath the Germans' noses. The surviving C-47 pilot had flown them home.

The question now was when would Dunn arrive? The clock was ticking on the weapon and the truck was in the process of being loaded. Where were they headed? Fontenot had set up a perimeter of four cars along the streets that could be possible exits from the airfield. Risk was high that they might lose the truck, but there was nothing else to be done.

***

Suddenly, the unmistakable clanking sounds of tank treads reached his ears. They were coming from the west, behind him. He thought they must be German tanks rushing to escape the closing net of the French and American armies.

"I'll be right back," he whispered to Fontenot, who nodded and returned his attention to his binoculars and the Germans.

Marston wriggled backwards until he was out of the shrubs. He crawled around in a half circle so he could see toward the west. A large grassy open space ran away from him and uphill toward another tree line two hundred yards away. He raised his binoculars and swept them across the trees, which ran north to south for about three hundred yards. There was a gap almost in the exact middle of the tree stand. A Sherman suddenly popped into view, moving fast.

As if the sight of the American tank wasn't enough to surprise Marston, the Sherman veered to the right, and another iron beast roared into sight. Within seconds, Marston was facing five Shermans. And they were rumbling directly toward him.

"Shite!" No whisper this time. "Fontenot!" he called. "Get back here."

A slight rustling of the shrubs told Marston the Frenchman had heard. Fontenot crawled into position next to Marston.

"The bastards are going to ruin everything," Fontenot said, anger in his voice. "We have to stop them." He made to get up, perhaps to wave the tanks down.

The tanks were only fifty yards away, showing no signs of slowing down.

"Wait," Marston said, placing a hand on Fontenot's arm, while staring through the binoculars at the tank that had appeared first.

"There are American soldiers on board one of the tanks." He focused on one of them, who was kneeling next to the commander's hatch, with a hand on the rim to steady himself against the rocking and bouncing of the charging tank.

The soldier had his own binoculars to his face, which were sweeping the area in front of the tank, then they seemed to be staring right at Marston. The soldier lowered his glasses, peering at Marston from just thirty yards now. He raised his glasses again. Marston got up on his knees and lowered his glasses. The

RONN MUNSTERMAN

soldier dropped his binoculars. He grinned and raised a hand to lift up his helmet just enough for Marston to see who it was.

"Oh my God. That's Dunn," Marston said, with some reverence in his voice.

"The one your man in London said was coming to help?"

"Indeed. That one."

Chapter 44

On deck – British Submarine *HMS Spark*
Laying off Insel Riems Island
24 August, 1435 Hours

The submarine *HMS Spark* sat still in the water, one hundred yards from the northern shore of the island Insel Riems, lying parallel to the shoreline. The Baltic Sea lapped at the sub's outer skin. The trip had taken most of three days and nights, much like the voyage to Wilhelmshaven, Germany when Saunders and his squad had destroyed the submarine pens.

Saunders thought this was probably the most unusual mission he'd ever had. Just as he and his men had arrived in Belgium to get their assignment with Montgomery, the British general's chief of operations had given Saunders new orders. Back to England where additional new orders for a mission would be awaiting him. Colonel Jenkins would meet him at the airfield near London. Following a very brief meeting with Jenkins, Saunders and his men had been trucked straight to the London docks where they'd boarded the submarine. The sub departed within ten minutes of their arrival. All the gear they would need was already on board.

Saunders' orders seemed simple: find a Nazi doctor named Teichmann, capture or kill him, and capture or kill any scientists, absolutely do not attempt to recover anything from the lab, especially any steel, cylindrical containers. Exposure to any mist-like substance would be fatal. Failure to meet the extraction deadline of 1530 hours would also be fatal to his men due to the B-17s coming in to level the facility's structures. Right, Saunders had thought, no bloody problems here. His men had been stoic when he relayed the orders on the sub. Barltrop had given him a serious look, but that was all.

While on the way to the target, when the sub came up for air and to recharge the batteries at night, Saunders had contact with Finch. Finch gave Saunders everything he had on the island, from the recon photos, and excellent, detailed descriptions of the layout. Saunders knew which building was most probably the laboratory, and which could be housing for the staff. Finch had insisted they hit the island during daylight, so they would be more likely to find the scientists in one place, the laboratory. It was unknown whether there would be any appreciable size, if any, of a guarding force on the island as nothing useful had appeared in the recent photos. There were no docks or boat slips, which struck Saunders as odd, although an, at the time of the photo recon, empty airfield was located about a half mile from the western tip of the island.

Saunders' men were loading the two black rubber dinghies they would row to shore. Each man carried a Sten submachinegun, unsuppressed to double the weapon's effective range to a hundred yards. Saunders had binoculars to his eyes. He scanned the island comparing the mental pictures he'd conjured up when talking with Finch to what he saw in reality. It was remarkably close. The buildings were all located in the center of the island, at its widest point. To his right was the strip of land connecting everything to the mainland by bridge. He spotted the gap in the land he was expecting, and recognized the low bridge Finch had described. Easy pickings for Tim Chadwick and Christopher Dickinson, who would set the charges.

"You about ready, Sergeant?" The voice came from behind and above Saunders.

Saunders turned and looked up at the captain, who was on the conning tower. "Aye. We are, sir." Saunders raised a salute and the captain returned it.

"Best of luck."

"Thank you. See you soon."

When the two boats made it about fifty yards, the sub began its descent under the protective, comforting cover of the waters. It would rest there with a periscope up until Saunders and his boats were back in the water and returning.

The sun was leaning to the right on its midafternoon trek toward sundown. It was hot in the black boats and the men were sweating heavily as they rowed. Saunders was in one boat and Steve Barltrop in the other. After a few more yards of travel across the mercifully calm waters of the inlet from the Baltic Sea, Barltrop's boat veered to the southwest so as to land closer to the bridge.

Saunders' boat landed just west of the buildings, about two hundred yards from the complex. James Pickering and George Mills jumped out, grabbed the bow line and dragged the boat onto the sandy beach.

Saunders jumped out, followed by William Endicott and Edward Redington. Everyone pitched in to drag the boat ten yards across the beach. They dropped it under the lip of a grass dune, and then spent a few minutes covering it with a desert camouflage net and scooped-up sand.

When they were done, Saunders signaled 'forward.' He took point and wound his way carefully toward the sparse tree line that separated the complex from the beach. Saunders was in the middle of the five men who were fanned out a few yards apart. He knelt at the far edge of the trees and examined the buildings closest to him. They were all constructed of brick. One building farther back stood out because it was an enormous two-story structure. Saunders estimated it was one hundred by fifty feet. It loomed over three smaller-by-comparison buildings that formed a right triangle with the hypotenuse facing Saunders. The front doors all faced the inside of the triangle, as did a lot of windows. A grassy common filled that space along with a few trees, the nearest of which was about forty yards away. Intelligence had determined from the recon photos that one of these was likely the laboratory. The suspected housing was about thirty yards south of the center building and had an open lawn in front of it.

He could see no one moving around and was surprised by the lack of security. Nevertheless, he stayed in place for several minutes. When he was satisfied it was clear, he decided it was time to move.

"Building on the right," he said, just loud enough for all of his men to hear. He rose and sprinted toward the nearest tree, his men following in line behind him.

The narrow bridge connecting the island to the mainland was only fifty yards long running toward the southwest. It was supported by one set of wooden center pillars, which was where Chadwick and Dickinson were attaching the explosives. They were standing on a dry rock bed that ran the entire length and width of the bridge. Above them, tucked behind the short walls along the roadway were Barltrop, Geoffrey Kopp, and Arthur Garner, keeping watch primarily on the west, but every few seconds, checking behind them to the east; they were exposed from that direction.

Chadwick and Dickinson worked fast. They didn't want their teammates in the open long.

"God, I love my job!" Dickinson said as he inserted a detonator into a package of plastic explosive. "Have I ever told you that?"

Chadwick grinned without looking at his friend. "Only every bloody damn time we do this, mate."

"Huh. Really? I had no idea," Dickinson shot back. He pulled his hands back and then held them palm outward to Chadwick. "Ha. Done. Suds are on you."

"Sod off."

"Need me to finish that for you?"

"I repeat, sod off." Chadwick stepped back, done. "Let's get upstairs."

"Lead the way."

As they scrambled up the embankment, they heard the buzzing sound of a light plane's engine.

Barltrop motioned to Chadwick and Dickinson to stay down as he looked westward toward the sound. A half mile away, a two-seater German Storch was coming in for a landing. Barltrop immediately surmised that whoever was on the plane was going to be coming across the bridge pretty soon. Perhaps it would be the man called Teichmann.

Barltrop took a quick look to the east and picked out a couple of spots in the ditches running along each side of the road.

"Disconnect the charges," he told Chadwick and Dickinson. Then he gave instructions for the possible ambush to Garner and Kopp.

While Chadwick and Dickinson ran back under the bridge to disconnect the timers from the explosives, Barltrop and the others ran about thirty yards east. Barltrop and Garner flopped down in the north ditch and Kopp in the side opposite. When Chadwick and Dickinson finished with the explosives, leaving all in place, but unhooked, they made their way back to the road and took cover in the north ditch.

The wait was short. A German staff car came into Barltrop's view as he watched from the ditch. When the car reached the far side of the bridge, he gave a short whistle.

The car was moving at about twenty-five miles an hour. Barltrop calculated how much stopping time the car's driver would need. When the car was almost at the east end of the bridge, he whistled twice and jumped up. Garner and Kopp rose and ran to the middle of the road, weapons raised.

The driver saw them and while he was reacting the car traveled another forty feet. Then he stomped on the brakes. The car came to a rocking stop about fifteen feet from the British commandos, who held their ground. He stared open-mouthed for a few seconds as his brain tried to catch up with what he saw. The lone passenger, an SS officer sitting in the front seat, reacted first by shouting something at the driver.

The driver put the car in reverse and gave it the gas. He put his right arm over the seat to look backward. He slammed on the brakes again when he saw two more commandos standing on the north side of the road with weapons aimed, seemingly right at his head. The SS officer was still shouting, but now he was pointing toward the three commandos in front of the car, only thirty feet away. The driver evidently was more afraid of the SS officer than he was of the commandos because the car leapt forward. Barltrop and the other two commandos unleashed a barrage of nine millimeter rounds into the front of the car, low and into the engine compartment and the front tires, which exploded. The engine stopped running and the car coasted a few more feet on flopping tires before coming to a stop a yard from the unyielding British soldiers.

Barltrop stepped to the passenger's side as Kopp and Garner moved to the driver's side. Standing back a few feet from the car, Barltrop gave the SS officer a grim smile and said, "Hello, Major. *Sprechen Sie Englisch?*"

Chapter 45

German airfield, Paris
24 August, 1440 Hours

The *Ghost Devil* ground to a halt near Marston and Fontenot. Dunn jumped down and ran over to the British spy. They shook hands quickly, unwilling to spend more time than necessary.

Marston couldn't help himself, though and blurted out, "What are you doing with Sherman tanks?"

Dunn smiled. "Later, Neil. Tell me what you have."

"The Germans are unloading the airplane and we confirmed the plane's identification number. There's one truck, about twenty SS troops, and Teichmann is there, too."

"Show me."

"This way."

Marston led the way through the shrubs on his hands and knees. When they got to the other side, Dunn raised his binoculars. Some of the SS troops were staring in his general direction, perhaps having heard the clanking sounds of the tanks' treads, but they were uncertain. After a few more moments, they turned back to what they were doing, unloading the airplane, whose engines continued to run. Dunn thought perhaps their sound helped masked the tanks' clanking.

"I thought there was just one crate," Dunn said.

"Yeah, me, too."

Dunn shrugged. It didn't really change his overall plan. "Okay, that's all I need."

He wiggled backwards, then escaped the shrubs. Marston was right behind him.

"It'll be best for you and your buddy to get over there," Dunn pointed toward a couple of birch trees. "And stay down behind the trees."

"Whatever you say," Marston replied. He knew full well from experience that Dunn always knew what he was talking about.

"See you later." Dunn waved and ran back to the tank. Once aboard he said to the commander, Mike Lynch, "Okay, Sarge, are you ready?"

"We are."

"Just liked we planned."

Lynch gave his tank commanders the order to go.

Dr. Gebhard Teichmann happened to be returning to the plane when a tank crashed through a long line of bushes about two hundred meters away. Over the idling airplane engines, he could suddenly hear the roar of the gasoline engines, and the squeaking of the wheels against the tracks. He was frozen in place. This was a sight he never expected to see. A few seconds later, two more tanks burst through, one on each side of the first, but behind it, forming a triangle.

Teichmann got his wits about him, and turned and ran back to the truck. He climbed up in the back with the help of an SS soldier. Pulling a keyring from his pocket, Teichmann knelt next to a large wooden crate; it had taken two men to lift it into the truck earlier. On the front was a stenciled eagle and swastika. Below that was the crate identification number: NVH2351798. He unlocked and opened it quickly, even though his hands were shaking.

Inside, gleaming in the dim light inside the truck were the brushed aluminum canisters. There were six on the top shelf of the crate, embedded in soft material formed into the cylinders' shape. He plucked two and climbed down from the truck.

He was shocked to see, not only how close the American tanks were, but that there were five of them. They had already covered half the distance. He ran to the airplane, brushing past the SS soldiers who were attempting to do something, anything against the onrushing tanks. He ran up the small ladder and into the airplane. He came to a stop just behind the cockpit.

"Take off. Now!"

The startled pilot looked over his shoulder. "The loading door is still open," he protested.

"I don't care. Take off." Teichmann pointed to the copilot's window, facing west. "Tanks. Enemy tanks. Take off."

The pilot glanced out the window and immediately said, "Take your seat."

The pilot revved the idling engines and the plane began to move.

Teichmann planned to get the plane over central Paris, trigger both devices, and then with a few seconds left on the timers, toss them overboard through the open door. They would begin spewing their deadly virus on the way down to the ground. At least some Parisians would die. Horribly.

Dunn watched the man in the SS uniform climb into the truck, and then moments later reappear with two shiny objects in his hands, and then he got into the airplane. Dunn realized immediately what the Nazi wanted to do.

The plane began to pick up speed, moving right to left in front of the tanks.

"Can you catch that thing before it takes off?" Dunn shouted at Lynch.

Lynch was shaking his head. "No way." He pointed at the plane. "See it's already picking up speed." By now it was already one hundred yards down the airstrip, heading north. The tail was still on the ground; it hadn't reached take off speed yet.

Lynch grabbed the gigantic .50 caliber Browning machinegun, spun its barrel toward the plane, yanked back on the charging bolt, and aimed in front of the Junkers' left engine. He pulled the trigger and tracers flew downrange. They were a little high so he lowered the barrel. Nothing seemed to happen, even though it looked like the tracers were hitting the wing.

Dunn stared at the escaping airplane. "Can you hit that thing with the big gun?"

Lynch stopped firing and glanced at Dunn. He raised his eyebrows and shrugged a little as if trying to say, well, I don't know, but we can try.

"Gordy! AP round on the airplane." Lynch wanted the tracer that all the armor piercing rounds had on them. "Ted, slow down for Gordy."

"Roger," replied both the gunner and the driver.

If Rick Gordon, the gunner, was surprised by the order to fire at an airplane in flight, it didn't come over the headset to Lynch. The turret began to rotate at top speed. Dunn had the peculiar perspective of feeling as though he were aiming the largest rifle he'd ever seen as the barrel swept toward the diminishing airplane, which was now three hundred yards away.

The plane's tail wheel lifted off the ground.

The plane's main gear left the ground.

Gordon stomped on the firing pedal.

Chapter 46

Barltrop got the SS major and driver out of their car and into the grips of Kopp and Garner. Barltrop had relieved the major of his Luger, which Barltrop decided to keep. He had frisked the man, who had said absolutely nothing the whole time. Kopp had done the same with the driver, finding a Walther PPK, which he pocketed.

Barltrop turned toward Chadwick and Dickinson, and whistled three times. The men disappeared under the bridge for the third time and reconnected the timers and reset them for five minutes.

They rejoined their squad mates quickly and with the Germans in the middle, still in death grips by Kopp and Garner, the group marched up the road toward the central complex.

Saunders entered the front door of the right hand building first, followed by the rest of his men. They were met by a long hallway, with doors set all the way down on both sides. Only a few hanging lights were on, giving the hallway a distinctly cavernous feel.

It took three minutes to declare the building clear. Saunders had no idea what was done in this building. All of the rooms were empty, and when they checked the lower levels, they were found to be barren.

"Next building," Saunders said.

After examining the smaller open space between buildings one and two, Saunders led the charge and they entered the second building through a side door facing building one. As soon as Saunders entered the door, he knew they'd found something. He could hear faint voices coming from somewhere ahead. The building had an identical layout to the first, but all of the hallway lights were on making visibility much better. His nose wrinkled at a smell he immediately associated with the hospital where Sadie had spent so much time recovering from her wounds from the buzz bomb. *Disinfectant, that's what that is,* he thought.

Advancing, Saunders pointed to the opposite wall with his left hand. Pickering and Endicott slid across the hallway. Redington and Mills closed up behind Saunders.

Saunders continued to creep toward the voices. About half way down the hallway, he located the people. They were in an alcove off the hallway. He sidled up to the corner and peeked around the edge. Three men, who were wearing white lab coats, stood around a coffee pot in a semicircle.

The shortest of the group was the only one facing the hallway. He saw Saunders as the big redheaded commando burst into the alcove with his weapon raised. The German's mouth opened to say something, but by that time two more commandos had entered the room. The other two men twisted around to see what was happening. Their mouths gaped at the sight of British soldiers.

Saunders pointed at the floor with his weapon in a motion indicating for the men to get down on their knees. The men set their coffee mugs down on a table next to them and complied, fear etched on their faces.

Saunders examined each man carefully, deciding none of them was Teichmann. In his deep rumbling Cockney accent, Saunders said quietly, *"Sprechen Sie Englisch?"*

None of the scientists, for that's what Saunders was certain they were, said anything.

Behind him, Saunders knew Pickering and Endicott were just inside the room facing out, guarding against surprises from the hallway.

Saunders nodded to Mills, who stepped close to the shortest man. Mills pressed the barrel of his Sten submachinegun to the back of the man's head.

Saunders repeated himself quietly, *"Sprechen Sie Englisch?"*

The short man immediately said, "Yes."

"Where is Teichmann?"

The men involuntarily exchanged glances.

"Where is he?"

"He's not here. He left this morning," a man with horn-rimmed glasses spoke this time.

"Where did he go?"

"I do not know," said glasses man. "He doesn't tell us anything." The man's eyes slid to the left.

Saunders had grown up in a neighborhood full of liars and he knew a lie when he heard it. He lowered his weapon, letting it hang from his shoulder strap across his chest. He grabbed the lying glasses man and yanked him to his feet. The man was a few inches shorter than Saunders, and thinly put together. His knees seemed to have turned to rubber and Saunders had to help support his weight.

"For the last time, where is he?"

"I can't say."

Saunders nodded again to Mills. Mills clicked the safety button on and off making an ominous sound, similar to cocking a handgun's hammer, especially to the ears of the man with the weapon jammed against his skull.

"Paris. He went to Paris."

"He went to Paris with the biological weapon?"

All three of the men stared openmouthed.

Saunders had time to think, *that seems to be their only expression,* then said, "How many work here?"

"About a dozen, counting us."

"Who are you exactly?"

Before glasses man could answer, Pickering said, "Sarge, got a soldier coming this way from the back door."

To the Germans, Saunders immediately said, "Don't try to be heroes. You'll be dead heroes if you make any noise."

Saunders spotted a door leading into a room just off the alcove. "In there." He pushed his man ahead and the other two followed. Once in the room, Saunders closed the door and ordered them to lie down and be quiet.

Pickering moved over by the wall to stay hidden from the soldier coming down the hall. He slipped his Sten off his shoulder and laid it on the floor behind him. With his right hand, he pulled his commando knife and held it in the slicing, cutting grip, with the pommel between his forefinger and thumb, and the blade extending past his pinkie finger.

Endicott stood a few steps behind Pickering, his weapon up in case things went bad for Pickering.

Pickering leaned against the wall, listening. He could barely hear the soldier's footsteps, but it was enough.

Closer and closer they came.

Pickering crouched low.

The soldier came into view. He was looking straight ahead.

Pickering jumped toward him, his right hand pulled up in front of his own left shoulder, cocking the plunge to come. He took two quick steps.

The German detected the movement and started to turn toward Pickering.

The commando swung his arm in a full arc, left to right and the knife entered the soldier's chest just under the solar plexus. The German looked surprised, grunted, and fell to the floor, dying on the way down.

Pickering left the knife in place, wiping his hand on the man's shirt. Endicott and Pickering grabbed the soldier by the boots and pulled him into the coffee room.

Pickering opened the door and said, "All clear, Sarge."

Saunders told the scientists to stand. He looked at them, a smile on his face. "Which of you is in charge when Doctor Teichmann is gone on his trips?"

This time there was no hesitation from the thin man. "I am. Doctor Rikard Baer."

"Thank you, Doctor Baer." Saunders said. He glanced at his watch, calculating time. "I'm going to offer you a one-time only deal. If you take it, all three of you and all of your coworkers will live to see tomorrow. If not, well . . ." he shrugged.

Baer looked both scared and wary, but nodded. "What do we have to do?"

"Can you call your coworkers and get them to come here? Would they do that?"

Baer nodded enthusiastically. He wanted to see the next sunrise.

"Tell them you have a surprise from Doctor Teichmann and they have to come up right away."

"Yes, of course."

"No tricks or you all die."

"Certainly not."

Saunders looked at the other Germans and they seemed to be in agreement with Baer.

Baer stepped over to a metal desk and picked up a black phone. He dialed a two-digit number.

Saunders thought he heard the faint sound of a phone ringing from somewhere across the hall.

Someone answered. Baer spoke in a calm voice, in German, a risk Saunders knew, but what choice did he have? If he'd spoken English the person on the other end would still have known something was wrong.

Baer finished with, *"Danke Shoen."*

He turned to Saunders and smiled. "Five minutes. Where are you taking us?"

"It'll have to be a surprise."

"I see. But I have your word we will be safe?"

"Aye, as long as you followed my instructions."

Five minutes later, Saunders and his four men, and the three German scientists were waiting in the coffee room. A door directly across the hall opened suddenly and a man appeared, wearing a white lab coat.

Saunders made eye contact with the man, who gave his enemy an evil smile. Then he raised a bright, shiny brushed aluminum cylinder about the size of an eighty-eight shell and drew his arm back.

Chapter 47

German airfield, Paris
24 August, 1446 Hours

The armor piercing round's tracer flew under the Junker's left engine. Whether the pilot ever saw it was unknown, but he made no course correction.

"Too low!" Lynch shouted.

"I know," Gordon replied calmly. He adjusted his aim, the barrel rising imperceptibly. He received the kick in the shoulder from his loader. He stomped on the firing pedal and the 76 mm round screamed toward the airplane.

Dunn watched in silence as the tracer seemed about to miss high. Then suddenly the plane rose into it. The round pierced the aircraft's paper thin skin just to the right of the port engine. The Junkers 52 exploded in a huge bright orange fireball, the fuselage containing Teichmann and his precious two cylinders of death vaporized. Shredded, flaming pieces of the wing remnants that were no bigger than a shoe box flew in all directions and began to settle toward the earth.

Dunn whistled his approval of Gordon's shot. "Tell your gunner thanks! That was incredible."

Lynch was staring at the black smoke still hanging in the air where the Junkers had been until the moment it met its death. "I've never even heard of anything like this."

Dunn grinned. "Yeah, just goes to show what a guy can really do, huh?"

Lynch turned to look at Dunn, some awe in his eyes. Yes, his gunner had pulled off the impossible, but this guy, Dunn, had come up with the idea, and was now treating it as commonplace. "Who are you, really?"

Dunn shrugged. "Just a guy doing his job."

Lynch looked dubious. "Yeah. Right. Okay."

Dunn looked toward the hangar where the German truck was still parked. The SS troops had retreated in the face of the onslaught of five thirty-plus ton Sherman tanks bearing down on them. They were now inside the hangar, their weapons up and aimed, but no one fired. What was the point?

"We need two tanks to secure that truck. The rest are going to have to flush out those troops. Remind everyone that no one is to fire into that truck."

"Roger." Lynch spoke into his mike.

The two tanks farthest to the south wheeled directly toward the truck.

Lynch gave another order and the two left-most tanks turned toward the hangar. The *Ghost Devil* rotated in place and headed toward the truck.

When the tank farthest to the right reached the truck, it angled itself right in front of it like a police car blocking any escape, although it turned out there was no driver. The gunner depressed his barrel and swung it toward the SS troops caught in the hangar. The tank just to the left pulled in behind the truck and aimed its gun at the hangar, too.

The *Ghost Devil* stopped near the truck. Dunn motioned to Schneider, who was sitting on the cover over the right tread.

"Tell them to surrender. Throw down their weapons. Come out with their hands up."

Schneider shouted the instructions to the Germans.

One of the SS troops started to raise his MP40, but the man next to him put a hand out, forcing the barrel down. He lifted his own MP40's sling off his shoulder and dropped the weapon on the hangar's floor. He gave a gruff order. His men immediately did what they were told. A minute later, nearly twenty SS troops were standing in front of the hangar with their hands raised.

Lynch suddenly stiffened, listening to his headset. His head swiveled to the north.

A pair of troop trucks were barreling down the road leading to the airfield.

Chapter 48

All five of the British commandos fired at the same time, filling the man with so many holes his white lab coat turned completely red. The cylinder dropped from his hand and bounced once, then began to roll into the hallway.

At the far end of the hallway, where the first German solider had come from, the door burst open and a dozen more stormed through. They spotted the commandos, who were standing just barely in the hallway and started firing.

Pickering was hit in the neck and dropped.

Endicott took one in the side of his head.

Mills and Garner each threw a grenade down the hallway and shoved Saunders back into the coffee alcove. The booms stopped the Germans. All of them lay mangled, burned, and either dead or groaning on the shiny white tile floor, now turning red.

Saunders grabbed the glasses man, Baer, and shoved him into the hallway. The man stared at the cylinder, which caused

Saunders to do the same thing. It was doing nothing. Saunders wondered if it was a dud or if it was releasing the virus invisibly.

"I ought to kill you!" Saunders growled at Baer.

Baer recoiled and tried to run, but Saunders grabbed him by the collar.

"Let's go!" He pushed the scientists ahead of him toward the door they'd come in. Mills picked up a clearly dead Pickering, and Garner lifted Endicott over his shoulder.

The men ran as fast as possible toward the door.

Saunders suddenly heard a hissing sound. He turned and saw a mist spewing from the cylinder. His heart raced. "Faster!"

In seconds, the men surged at full speed though the exit and into the clean air. The door was stuck open from the force of their hit.

When they were across the grassy lawn and almost into the trees, Saunders turned to look over his shoulder once more. Was it his fearful imagination or did he really see the mist curling through the jammed-open door?

The three scientists had lost all interest in resisting the British soldiers and ran full steam in the direction Saunders was pointing, to the beach.

Saunders was surprised and pleased to see Barltrop and his gang on the beach already getting the boats into the water. To his surprise, they had two Germans with them.

Saunders checked his watch.

The charges Chadwick and Dickinson had placed exploded and the bridge collapsed in a pile of smoking rubble.

Saunders glanced toward the explosions and said, "Only ten minutes to spare, gents. Get a move on."

The commandos got everyone aboard the two boats in short order. The bodies of Pickering and Endicott in one boat together, handled with loving care.

As the boats left the shore of the island Insel Riems, Saunders muttered, "Shite, I hope the fooking American bombers are accurate."

No one had a reply to that.

Out in the waters of the Baltic Sea inlet, a black shape slowly breeched the surface, and soon the *HMS Spark* was sitting low in the water a hundred yards off. Sailors were on the deck facing the arriving commando boats.

When the boats were just about to the sub, a deep rumble filled the air. Saunders and his men turned to look westward. Black dots filled the sky. Saunders did a quick count and gave up at forty. He some quick math, based on his limited knowledge of bombers, multiplying forty by five thousand. Two hundred and fifty thousand pounds of explosives. A quarter-million pounds.

Once on board the sub, Saunders turned over custody of the Germans to the captain and his armed men. Saunders told his men they could either go below or stay and watch. No one left.

The first bomb struck the first building Saunders and his men had entered.

The men cheered.

Saunders watched as sticks from several different bombers hit the laboratory where the hissing cylinder had released it terrible death. More bombs hit the enormous building behind them all. Within five minutes, the entire complex was destroyed and aflame. Saunders hoped Finch was right and that the fire would destroy the virus.

The surviving British Commandos took a last look at the conflagration on the island, then set about getting their dead friends in the sub.

Ten minutes later, the *HMS Spark* slipped beneath the still waters and made way for England.

Chapter 49

German airfield, Paris
24 August, 1452 Hours

Lynch pointed at the troop trucks. "We have company, Dunn."

"Someone made a phone call," Dunn guessed.

Neither man could know the trucks were arriving as the support ordered by Choltitz in response to Hitler's last cable.

Lynch spoke into his mike.

The two left-most Shermans turned their turrets toward the incoming vehicles and fired. The lead truck burst into a ball of fire and the second one crashed into it, catching fire as it bounced off and rolled off the road, where it overturned. Flaming bodies were ejected into the air looking like grotesque fireworks.

"Fuck," Dunn said. It would be a long time before that sight faded from his memory, if ever.

"Yeah," replied Lynch.

Dunn patted Lynch on the shoulder. "Now to see what we can find."

"We'll be right here."

Dunn told his men to dismount the tank, and jumped down himself. He next told the men to secure the prisoners, and to take no chances with them.

He headed for the truck and heard his name from the west. He turned toward the voice. Marston and his partner were running across the field the tanks had just recently charged across. Marston was waving. Dunn waved back, then continued on to the truck.

Cross came up beside him. "I've never seen a tank shot like that."

"Yeah, Lynch and I thought the exact same thing."

Dunn climbed up into the truck and Cross followed. It was a no brainer to figure out which crate was the one they needed; it was still open. Dunn approached it cautiously, the way some people creep up on the edge of a cliff to peek over the lip.

"Damn. There they are."

Cross stepped up and peeked in at the silver canisters. There were four on what appeared to be a removable shelf. Dunn leaned over and noticed little leather handles on each side of the shelf. He slid his hands into the handles and lifted, and then rotated his upper body to clear the crate. Packed in the bottom of the crate were six more of the deadly cylinders. Dunn's hands suddenly started to shake and Cross stepped over to help guide the top shelf back into its resting place.

"Thanks."

"Don't mention it."

Dunn closed the lid, and reattached and closed the clasp lock with a loud snick.

Dunn jumped down from the truck, Cross right behind him.

"I feel like I should wash my hands," Cross muttered.

"I have a feeling it wouldn't do a bit of good with this stuff."

"That's a lovely thought. Thank you for that."

"Any time."

The SS troops had all been secured. They had been frisked and were now sitting on the ground, held in place by a half-dozen Rangers with Thompsons pointed in their general direction.

"Secure the truck, Dave."

"Will do."

Cross called out the names of a couple squad members. Waters and Wickham ran over to join him and to stand guard around the truck.

Dunn climbed up on Lynch's tank. "Can you raise Colonel Edwards?"

"Yeah, give me a minute."

After a bit, Lynch took off his headset and handed it to Dunn, who put it on.

"Colonel? Dunn here."

"What news have you?"

"We are secure. Ten items in hand, two destroyed. Location also secure. Have twenty SS prisoners."

"You're certain of the count?"

"Positive, sir."

"Okay. Wait for air transport to arrive within thirty minutes. One hour for trucks for the prisoners."

"Understood, sir. Uh, sir, how about an extra truck for my guys? I don't think we could stand any more travel by Sherman."

Edwards laughed. "As you wish. Hey, Dunn?"

"Yes, sir?"

"Incredible job. Thank you."

"You're welcome, sir."

"See you when you get back here. I'll buy you guys dinner."

"We look forward to it."

The C-47 Goonie Bird arrived twenty-nine minutes after Dunn hung up with the colonel. Dunn and Cross personally loaded it onto the aircraft, where a guard of a dozen MPs sat along the fuselage benches. The jumpmaster and copilot secured the crate to the floor of the plane with chains and locks, after first setting it on a couple of folded woolen army blankets to act as a cushion. The MPs' eyes widened at this lengthy procedure, but they were clearly unaware of the death they were flying with.

The plane took off ten minutes after landing. Where it was going, Dunn had no idea, but he assumed England. Then he thought about it for a moment and decided he didn't want to know.

Marston and Fontenot had been waiting patiently for Dunn to talk to them. Dunn had asked them to wait until the crate was airborne.

Marston was finally able to introduce Fontenot. The Frenchman shook Dunn's hand enthusiastically.

"So it's gone?" he asked.

"Yep."

"I don't even know how to thank you. You've done Paris and the nation such a service. I wish I could tell every Parisian what you've done."

"Well, look. First, I didn't do it alone. And second, saving Paris just had to be done."

"What now?" Marston asked.

"We have ground transportation coming for the prisoners, and for my squad. We're heading back to Patton's headquarters back that way." Dunn pointed west.

"Will you get to participate in the liberation? It's bound to happen any day," Fontenot said.

"Don't know. I just go where they tell me."

The French Resistance leader pulled a small piece of paper and a pencil from his pocket. He scribbled something on it and handed it to Dunn. He was grinning.

The writing was in French, so Dunn asked, "What's this?"

"My uncle's restaurant, still going after all the Germans have thrown at us. Dinner on me. It's near the Eiffel Tower, very nice view for you and anyone you want to bring with you."

"Thanks. Don't know if I'll get to use it." Dunn pocketed the note.

Fontenot gave a Frenchman's shrug. "It will always be there for you."

"Sergeant Dunn, it was great to see you again."

"You, too, Colonel Marston."

Marston laughed. It was a reference to Marston's role as an SS colonel during Operation Devil's Fire.

"We'll be heading off now. It's a bit of a walk back to the car." Marston pointed west.

"Hope to see you again, Neil."

"You, too, Tom."

The three men shook hands all around and then the British spy and the Frenchman walked away. Not until Fontenot drove their car away, did Marston realize he'd forgotten to tell Dunn about Madeline.

The trucks arrived more or less on time. The prisoners were loaded without problem, the soldiers sent along to guard them were somewhat awed by the sight of so many captured SS troops.

Lynch's crew had climbed out of the tank for a breath of fresh air. Each of the Rangers congratulated Gordon on his extraordinary shot. He'd given an aw-shucks grin, but was thrilled to receive accolades from these men, who were clearly extraordinary themselves.

"Don't want to ride back with us, I take it?" Lynch asked, nodding toward the third truck that was sitting empty.

"Don't take it personally, Sarge, but fuck no."

Lynch chuckled and held out his hand. "Good to know you."

Dunn grasped the hand and said, "Same to you. Maybe we'll see each other in Berlin."

"Could be."

Dunn shook hands with the rest of the *Ghost Devil's* crew, then called to his men.

Shortly thereafter, they were in the truck and it roared away to the west, toward Patton's headquarters, and hopefully a hot meal courtesy of Colonel Edwards.

Chapter 50

Liberation of Paris celebration
25 August, 1715 Hours

Madeline Laurent could faintly hear, but not see Charles De Gaulle, the President of the Provisional Government of the French Republic, as he gave an impromptu liberation speech in front of the Paris City Hall. Madeline was on a rooftop a block away. Snipers of unknown affiliation had become a problem during the early morning by indiscriminately firing on the throngs of gathering Parisians. Some French Resistance members believed they were communists who, everyone knew, hated De Gaulle. The feeling was definitely mutual. Madeline and several other Resistance members had taken it upon themselves to solve some of those problems.

De Gaulle had arrived in the city at four p.m. His first stop was the Montparnasse train station, where the German occupiers finally surrendered four years and a few months after their triumphant arrival. Following that stop he set up a new government headquarters at the Ministry of War building. Next was a quick visit to the Prefecture of Police, which was where the first Resistance uprising happened.

Speaking without notes, he delivered a speech to the liberated people, most of whom had never seen him in person, having only heard his voice on the radio for four long years. Cheers and clapping met every statement, prolonging the speech.

In Madeline's hands was a Mauser Karabiner 98k with a Zeiss Zielvier 4 power scope. The scope would come in handy in counter-sniper work across the rooftops where the range might be in excess of one hundred meters. She had a spotter with her this time who had a big pair of German field glasses. He went by the name of Jesper, which may or may not have been his real name. Madeline didn't know for sure and didn't care.

The streets were filled with people, old and young, male and female. The next day, there would be a parade that, unlike the one when the Nazis had marched into the City of Light in June of 1940, would be met with cheers, and tears not of a broken heart, but of joy and jubilation.

As she watched the rooftops, Madeline occasionally stole a glance down at the street. Part of her wanted to be there, but she knew this job was too important. She'd heard sporadic gunfire for the last fifteen minutes, and then being unable to find the shooter, grew frustrated. She was relieved though, when she didn't see anyone fall to the ground in a pool of blood. She did, however, see some people ducking underneath vehicles parked along the street.

"Ten o'clock," said Jesper, careful not to point, wanting to restrict his own movement to avoid detection.

Madeline searched to her left without the scope, and spotted a black form backlit by the brighter sky behind him. He was at the front of a four-story building. She brought the scope into play. The sniper was kneeling, using the top of the edifice as a weapon support. He had a non-scoped rifle aimed at the rear of the crowd facing the French president. Madeline glanced down at the spot. There was a big line of children standing there, trying to see over the much taller adults.

She sighted through the scope again and laid the crosshair on his right eyebrow.

"Distance?"

Jesper replied immediately, "Two-ten."

That was what Madeline had calculated. She turned a knob on the scope to adjust for bullet drop and sighted again.

Madeline's sight picture remained steady. She noted a small French flag flying nearby and gauged the wind out of the southwest, the right, at fifteen kilometers per hour.

The sniper activated his bolt, loading a high-powered round into the rifle's chamber.

Madeline squeezed the trigger and the Mauser barked and kicked back into her shoulder. She threw the bolt, loading the next round, while keeping her sight picture. The bullet struck the man a little left of where she expected, in the right ear. He dropped straight down out of view.

"Good shot, Madeline," Jesper said.

"Thanks."

Neither of them saw the man to their nine o'clock on a roof about two hundred yards away.

Because Madeline was right handed, she had her back to the second sniper. His bullet struck Madeline at a ninety degree angle, piercing her just under the right shoulder blade. She fell over with a grunt. Jesper ducked down behind the building's ramparts. He crawled over to Madeline and checked for a pulse. He found one. Her eyes fluttered and then closed and her breathing became labored.

"Madeline! Madeline!"

When she didn't respond, he rolled her onto her back and quickly checked her chest. No exit wound. The bullet was still inside her. He rolled her onto her stomach and checked the wound in the back. It was bleeding profusely. He tore off his shirt and folded it in half. He pressed it on the wound. Hard. Madeline groaned in her semiconscious state. Next he pulled off his belt and slipped it around Madeline's body, tightening it and buckling it in the last hole, right over the makeshift bandage.

He raised his head carefully and a stone near his head exploded in a puff of smoke. A split second later, the shot rang out.

Jesper picked up Madeline's rifle and crawled ten feet to the left of their original position. He slid the bolt back to make sure a round was seated. He took a deep breath and then rose to a shooting position. He acquired the sniper right away. The shooter was aiming at the crowd. Jesper squeezed the trigger and eliminated the coward.

Returning to Madeline, he set down the rifle; no way to carry her and it. He grabbed Madeline by her hands and pulled her to the roof's exit door. Once inside the stairwell, Jesper picked up Madeline and carried her piggyback down four flights of stairs.

At the street level, he wound his way through a back alley and turned west. He went two blocks and found his small four-door Renault. He gently laid Madeline in the backseat. He awkwardly rolled her due to the cramped space, and checked the bandage. It was bright red, but not completely soaked through. He double-checked the belt, and then laid a jacket that was in the front seat over her back. He made sure her face was pointed to the left, away from the seat back, so she would have fresh air.

He only knew of one thing that might save her. Finding a French doctor on this day of all days, would be impossible. That left the recently arrived British Field Hospital. He drew up his mental map and determined he was about five miles northeast of the hospital. As he started the little car, he prayed that they would get there in time, and then peeled away from the curb.

Chapter 51

Hitler's Office, The Chancellery
Berlin, Germany
25 August, 1728 Hours

Adolf Hitler slammed his phone back into the cradle. Lieutenant General Dietrich von Choltitz was a dead man as far as he was concerned.

Heinrich Himmler sat opposite the *Führer* in a wing chair.

"The governor of Paris is busy! Whoever answered the phone spoke English-accented German telling me that General Choltitz was being interviewed by the Americans. This confirms what you told me: that Choltitz had surrendered."

Hitler felt rage at the betrayal by Choltitz. He was even more furious than he'd been when Field Marshal Friedrich Paulus had surrendered to the Russians at Stalingrad, ruining Hitler's grand plan.

"Choltitz disobeyed my explicit order to leave Paris in a field of rubble."

"I don't understand how he could have done that, *Mein Führer*. He was so loyal to you."

"He's a coward. That's what he is. A disgrace to Germany. I should send someone to kill him."

Hitler glared at Himmler, as if daring the head of the SS to contradict him.

Himmler knew better. "I would be happy to set that in motion, should you decide on that course of action."

"I will think about it. How many men did we lose because of him?"

Himmler hesitated slightly, before saying, "In excess of twenty thousand men," he cleared his throat, then continued, "Plus all the equipment."

"I need some good news."

"I understand, but I don't have any. The Americans happened upon Teichmann and he was killed. All of the SS men there were captured. I sent several of my men to the airfield when I didn't hear from Teichmann. They found a few survivors of a crashed truck who said Teichmann's plane was blown up. They also report that the truck carrying the weapon was captured."

"Do you mean to tell me that the Americans now have my biological weapon?" He seemed unconcerned over Teichmann's death.

"Yes, they have the weapon."

Hitler stared at the windows on his left. His expression was somehow a mix of rage and disappointment. He sat like that for several minutes.

Finally he turned his attention back to Himmler. "Do you believe they will use the weapon?"

"Yes, I do."

"Incompetents. I'm surrounded by them. My generals, my scientists. Is there anything else you need to tell me? Bad news comes in threes, yes?"

Himmler nodded. "The weapon facility at Insel Riems has been completely destroyed. It was bombed by B-17s. There are no survivors, and no biological samples remain."

"It would take years to catch up, wouldn't it?"

"Yes."

"I long for the early days."

"Me, too, *Mein Führer*. Me, too."

Chapter 52

British Field Hospital
4 miles southwest of the Eiffel Tower
25 August, 1910 Hours, Paris time

Neil Marston pulled up a rickety wooden chair next to Madeline's hospital bed and sat down. Her red hair was splayed across the white pillow, and her skin was even paler than usual. Her eyes were open and focused, which made him feel hopeful.

Fontenot had come running into the safe house apartment in a panic. Marston was almost sick to his stomach when the Frenchman told him what had happened.

Marston drove Fontenot to the hospital right away, but Madeline was in surgery by the time they got there. The two men had taken a seat on the ground outside the tent and waited and waited. Finally, a beautiful British nurse with bright blue eyes came out and told them that Madeline had survived the surgery and was recovering.

"When can I see her?" Fontenot asked.

Marston glanced at the Frenchman, whose face was a mask of fear. Marston was certain he had been right about the two of them.

"Not until later. You can come back in couple of hours. The mess is not too far."

Fontenot thanked her and asked her name.

"I'm Pamela Dunn."

"Thank you, Miss Dunn."

"Mrs."

Fontenot tilted his head. "Mrs. Dunn."

Marston stared at her. "Ma'am, are you by chance Mrs. Tom Dunn?"

Pamela smiled. "Yes, he's my husband."

"Oh, I say! Congratulations!" He paused, trying to think of how to explain working with Dunn without breaking the law. "I've worked with Sergeant Dunn. I'm Neil Marston."

Pamela didn't recognize the name. Dunn never talked about the missions.

"I'm happy to meet you, Mr. Marston."

"You too."

Marston was in a quandary. Should he tell Mrs. Dunn he had just seen her husband the day before? It was a top secret mission after all. Just as he decided he could not tell her, Mrs. Dunn departed, returning to the interior of the tent. Marston and Fontenot wandered off in search of the mess tent.

Two hours later they came back and gained admittance to the recovery tent.

Marston had already decided he was going to make this quick, and leave the two alone.

"Madeline, I just wanted to tell you Paris is safe. The problem has been solved. Thank you for your help on this." Marston kissed her on both cheeks, and glanced at Fontenot. "And thank you, too."

Fontenot only had eyes for Madeline, but he replied, "Thank you, Neil."

"I can find my way back to Paris."

"You are sure?"

"Yes." Marston put a hand on Fontenot's shoulder and squeezed gently, then left. He glanced over his shoulder.

Fontenot was holding Madeline's right hand, his head bowed. Madeline caressed the back of his head with her left hand.

Marston made it back to Paris and once he was back in the safe house, he packed up everything. He'd received his new orders, which simply said, "Assist the French, the British and Americans in any possible way. Return to home is not, repeat, not imminent."

Now that he'd been back in the field, this suited Marston. Very much.

Marston stopped walking when he was a block to the south of the *Arc de Triomphe de l'Étoile*. The setting sun painted the white stone orange. He admired the structure for a few minutes.

The *Champs-Élysées* was full of people enjoying freedom for the first time in four years. Marston watched the joyful people for a few minutes, then marched the rest of the way to the monument.

He stood next to it and placed his hand against the cool surface. At last, he thought, I am here.

Chapter 53

10 Downing Street
London
25 August, 1945 Hours, London time

Finch stood up and stretched. It had been another long day and being up late to communicate with Marston and Saunders a few nights running was catching up with him. After a few trunk twists to finish up, he sat back down.

He was working on writing a summary of events that led to the capture of the Nazis' biological weapon. They had all ten of the devices secured on St. Georges Island, a tiny speck in the waters twelve miles west of Plymouth. A small facility was hidden in the forest covering the northern center of the island. British and American scientists were busy unlocking the weapon's secrets. The island, only twenty-two acres in size, was only accessible by boat. This suited Finch and the scientists very well.

Early on in the quest to destroy or capture the weapon, Finch had been briefly uncertain about his own government having the weapon, and the possible use of it. Then he recalled the terrors the Nazis had sent to the British people by bomber. If the time came, he would be fine with it. What was the difference between that and the atomic bomb, anyway? Anything that would end the war was fine by him. The sooner the better.

As he continued to write, he included the details as he knew them of Dunn's ingenuity. The man never ceased to amaze Finch. He added a note suggesting a medal for Dunn and Saunders for their parts in this mission. He knew neither the Ranger nor the Commando would be interested in receiving any accolades, but they had to be singled out. As did Reggie Shepston and the young woman, Eileen Lansford.

The phone rang and Finch jumped, so intense was his concentration on his work. He lifted the receiver.

"Finch here."

"Hi Finch, Shepston."

"Hi there. Funny you should call."

"Why is that?"

"I'm writing about you and Eileen in my report to the Prime Minister."

"Oh. Good things, I hope."

"No. I've decided you should go back to college."

"Always the bloody smart arse."

Finch shrugged, even though his childhood friend couldn't see it. "What can I do for you?"

"Dinner. Tonight. In fact right now. We're waiting downstairs."

"We?"

"Eileen and I. She brought a friend."

Finch was quiet long enough for Shepston to ask, "Still there, old boy?"

"I told you I wasn't ready to see anyone."

"I know you did. It's been four years, Alan. Maggie wouldn't want you to be alone so long. Come on, it's just dinner. You don't have to propose tonight."

Finch's jaw clenched and he involuntarily glanced at his late wife's photo.

Some time passed and Shepston asked, "Still there?"

Finch's throat suddenly closed up and his eyes leaked tears. He knew Shepston was right. Maggie would want him to live.

"Alan?"

Finch croaked a reply, "Yes, I'll go to dinner. I just . . . need a few minutes."

"Sure."

Finch hung up and closed his leather notebook with the handwritten report in it. He dropped it into a drawer and locked his desk.

He rose and picked up Maggie's photo. He touched her face with a finger, and stared into her lovely face for a long time.

He put the picture back on the desk.

And then he removed his wedding band and laid it on the desk in front of the picture.

Chapter 54

British Field Hospital
4 miles southwest of the Eiffel Tower
25 August, 2058 Hours

True to his word, Colonel Edwards had bought dinner for Dunn and his men the previous night. They had a hot meal of chicken something or other and warm biscuits and hot coffee. Some cinnamon apples were thrown in for dessert.

Patton's headquarters were located just west of Boulogne-Billancourt, which put it about four miles from the Eiffel Tower, according to the colonel. After a decent night's sleep, the next day found the squad getting some unexpected downtime. Sleep was the dominant activity.

During tonight's dinner, Dunn was surprised when one of the other staff officers sitting nearby mentioned hoping to get a date with a nurse at the new British Hospital. This caught Dunn's attention and he found out where the hospital was; only a few miles south. He'd finished his meal in quick order, excused himself to the colonel, explaining he needed to see if his wife was at the hospital; she was a British nurse. Edwards granted Dunn his departure with a smile.

Dunn parked the borrowed jeep outside a large tent amongst many of all sizes. He had to ask three different people, but he eventually made his way through the tent maze.

He stepped into a shadowy tent, a large one with rows of occupied patient beds on both sides. A few lights were on. He spotted Pamela right away, even though her back was to him. She was walking away, but he recognized everything about her. Dunn took a couple of steps inside to follow her, but she stopped suddenly, and whipped around to face him, as if she'd known he was there.

Her eyes widened and her hand flew to her mouth. She burst into a run. Dunn took off toward her, careful not to run over anyone or hit the beds. Just as they were about to crash into each other, Pamela pulled up short and held out a hand. Dunn nearly fell over at the sudden stop.

"Wait. I'm sterile." She leaned close, her mouth ready. "Kiss my lips only. Don't touch me."

Dunn admired the view of his wife all puckered up and leaning toward him. He refrained from chuckling. Gently, he leaned in and kissed her carefully and only on the lips. After a lengthy, awkward, yet satisfying kiss, Dunn pulled back and grinned at his wife.

"You look great."

"You do, too." She tilted her head a bit to the left. "I'm happy to see you, but I don't understand what you're doing here."

"It's a bit of a long story. I've been in France about a week or so. Heard the hospital was here and got some time off."

"Right. Well, I'm glad you did." She stepped past him and went to a table. She picked up some things and returned to her husband. "Let me put these on you."

Dunn stood patiently while Pamela dressed him in white scrubs. She was careful not to touch him or his uniform. She turned him around and examined him. "Okay. Not exactly nursing material, but you'll do. Follow me. I still have patients to check."

"Okay."

Dunn was curious to see her working even though he'd met her when he was a patient himself.

They walked slowly through the tent, and she stopped at several patients, checking them for fever and reading their charts, all the while speaking to them in a soothing tone that Dunn definitely recognized from his stay in the hospital.

At the point when Dunn thought they might be nearly finished, Pamela approached a bed with a smaller figure lying in it. Dunn realized it was a woman, but Pamela blocked his view of the patient's face. A young man who was also wearing white scrubs was sitting in a wooden folding chair next to the bed. He was leaning over so his head was lying on the pillow and he was holding one of the patient's hands. His face was obscured by Dunn's angle.

Husband, thought Dunn.

Then Pamela bent over to listen to the woman's chest and a flash of red caught his eye. He looked quickly at the red and thought, *can't be!*

He stepped around Pamela and stared at Madeline, whose red hair was spread over the white pillow. "Oh, my God. Madeline."

Madeline opened her eyes.

Pamela stood up and stared at Dunn.

"Tom?" said both women.

To Madeline, Dunn said, "Yep, it's me."

Fontenot sat up straight and spotted Dunn. He jumped to his feet and hugged Dunn.

"Good to see you again, Fontenot."

"You, too."

Pamela overcame her surprise, and said, "I take it you all know each other."

Dunn spoke first. "Yes. I met Madeline back in June when we went over to France on a mission. She and her Resistance members gave us a . . . uh, hand." Dunn turned to look at Pamela, whose expression was difficult to read, although there did seem to be something in her eyes, including a raised eyebrow.

"You never mentioned you worked with such a beautiful woman."

"Er, no, I suppose not." Dunn glanced at Madeline, who was grinning at his sudden problem. He raised both eyebrows at her, hoping to get some help.

Fontenot sat back down and was taking in everything with an amused expression on his face.

"Pamela." Madeline said her name as if trying it on. "Let me see if I can help."

Pamela and Dunn looked at her, Dunn with trepidation all over his face.

"When you told me your name, Pamela, I didn't make the connection: you are Mrs. Dunn. Yes, Tom and I worked together, but in spite of my wily attempts to attract him, his heart was already given. To you. He had just discovered that in France."

"Hm," Pamela said, noncommittedly.

Fontenot chuckled lightly at Dunn's predicament.

"Tell me, did he ask you to marry him soon after he returned?"

Pamela's eyes widened. "Why, yes. Well, it was following his next mission, but then it was right after he returned."

"There you have it. That's all. He was honest with me, he was honest with you. A good man in love, with but only one woman, you."

Pamela turned to Dunn and gave him a look that told him two things: okay, I understand, but you should have mentioned this.

Dunn nodded his understanding and said, "I'm sorry, Pamela."

"You're forgiven." Pamela turned back to Madeline. "Thank you for your honesty."

"You're welcome."

"You seem to be recovering nicely."

"Am I?"

"Yes, the bullet punctured your right lung, but doctor fixed it. You'll make a full recovery."

Pamela patted Dunn on the shoulder. "I have one more patient. Why don't you stay and talk with Madeline for bit, catch up, while I finish?"

"You sure?"

Pamela gave him a "really?" look.

"Okay, I will."

Pamela moved on to the next patient, a soldier with a deep scalp wound from a supersonic bullet. He was awake, but in pain. Pamela touched him on the shoulder and then helped him take something for the pain.

Dunn took a knee and touched Madeline's shoulder. "Are you okay?"

"Sounds like I will be." She smiled. "So when did you two tie the knot?"

"July twenty-ninth."

Her brows furrowed. "What is today?"

"August twenty-fifth."

"Oh! Coming up on your first month anniversary." She gave him a stern look. "You do have plans don't you?"

Dunn grinned. "As a matter of fact, I do. She doesn't know yet, but I'm taking her to some fancy restaurant in Paris."

"Oh, you. What a good boy you are. What's the restaurant's name?"

Dunn told her.

"But . . . that's Fontenot's uncle's place." She glanced at Fontenot. "How did you hear about it?"

Dunn dug into his shirt pocket and pulled out the scrap of paper. He handed it her. "I met him," he tilted his head toward the Frenchman, "with Neil Marston yesterday."

"What? Oh, you were the one London was sending to help with the, em," she paused and lowered her voice, "the thing?"

"The one and the same."

"Can you tell me what happened?"

"Sure, I don't see why not. I mean Fontenot here could tell you himself." So Dunn told her.

When he finished, she said, "I don't know whether you're brilliant or crazy."

"That's okay. You're not the first."

They visited a little longer. Dunn avoided asking what she had done to Luc the traitor during Operation Devil's Fire, and she didn't offer.

Dunn rose and said, "It was great to see you."

"And you. I wish you and Pamela all the happiness in the world."

"And the same to you." Dunn smiled, leaned over and kissed her on the forehead. He stepped back, but didn't leave. He tilted his head slightly. "Are you two together?"

Fontenot answered with a wide grin.

Madeline's expression didn't change. "You are such a detective."

Dunn grinned. "You can't fool me."

"No, I suppose not. But, you know, that's the problem with really smart people: they think they know everything."

Dunn chuckled at her bluster. He recognized it for what it was. Reluctant pride.

Dunn was happy to see the fire back in her lovely emerald green eyes. Deciding to get a little even with Madeline for her telling Pamela everything, he said, "Have you set a date?"

Madeline's mouth dropped open, and then she snapped, "You are so irritating!"

Pamela walked up in time to hear the last exchange. "You have no idea."

The women looked at Dunn, who just grinned and shrugged. Then everyone laughed.

Pamela told Dunn, "Go outside. She needs to rest."

Dunn waved at Madeline and Fontenot, who both smiled.

Then he asked Pamela, "When do you get off work?"

Over her shoulder, Pamela threw a smile and said, "I'm off now, sailor."

Chapter 55

Saunders glanced at Sadie's three younger brothers sitting across the dinner table from him. They were six, nine, and eleven. He couldn't help but think of Pickering and Endicott, whose deaths had hit him and the squad hard.

Robbie, the middle boy in age and seating, frowned and asked in a worried voice, "Are you okay? You look sad."

Saunders realized he hadn't hidden his thoughts very well. "I'm okay." He thought he might deflect the boy.

Robbie was not to be deterred. He loved Saunders too much. He made Sadie happy and that made Robbie happy. "No, you're not. I can tell."

Saunders looked at Sadie, who was sitting on his right, and she nodded. She knew about his loss of men.

The *HMS Spark* had docked at London earlier in the day, just after noon. Saunders and squad gladly handed off the prisoner scientists from Insel Reims, and as soon as they arrived back in

Camp Barton Stacey, Saunders tried to give everyone a couple of days' worth of passes for London, saying he would take care of Pickering and Endicott. Barltrop had told his friend to go on and see Sadie, and that he would take care of the men. Saunders didn't argue.

After making himself presentable, Saunders grabbed a car and took off.

"I lost two men on my last mission. It upsets me."

"Were they your friends?"

"Yes. They were my friends."

"Were they killed by the horrible Nazis?"

"Yes."

"I wish I was old enough. I want to fight."

"Me, too," chimed in the other two boys, Freddie and Johnny.

"It would be smashing!" Robbie said.

Saunders heart sank. *No, Lord please, no, don't take these boys, too*. He held up a hand as if a stop sign. He spoke softly, so the boys wouldn't think he was mad at them. "No. It's not 'smashing.' " I do this because I have to. I'm doing it for all of you." Saunders swept his arms wide to include everyone at the table. "I pray every day that you never have to go where I've been. See what I've seen. I want you to live normal happy lives. I want you to grow up to be old men. Do you understand what I'm saying?"

The boys seemed surprised by Saunders words, and were perhaps a little disappointed. It was far different from all the posters they'd seen everywhere and the radio broadcasts.

Robbie wasn't to be shut down so easily, though, and he persisted, "But I thought there was glory and honor in going to war to defend our country. Right?"

Saunders didn't say anything for a long moment, wanting to make sure he answered this question properly.

"It is an honor to go to war defending your country. It can make you proud. Of yourself and your friends. But glory is a different matter. Glory is bestowed on those who are successful. Most men are not looking for glory, and in fact I have an American friend who tries to stay away from it, but he's so good at his job, it comes to him often.

"I know for a fact, that if you asked him why he does what he does, for our country and America, he'll just shrug and say, 'because it has to be done.' Will you all three promise me that you'll remember that?"

The boys each held up a hand and spit into it, which made Mrs. Hughes say 'tsk tsk,' but with a smile. Each boy placed his hand over his heart. "I promise," they said.

"Any more questions?"

Freddie, the eldest brother, gave a mischievous grin. "When are you and Sadie getting married?"

Mr. and Mrs. Hughes laughed out loud, and Saunders and Sadie joined in.

When the laughter died down, Sadie said, "I get out of this blasted cast late next week."

"The doctors think it'll take several weeks of hard work to get so I can walk around again, with crutches at first. Johnny, go get the big calendar by the stove."

While her youngest brother ran off, Sadie leaned into Saunders and he put his big paw on her right shoulder giving her a gentle squeeze.

Johnny ran back in the dining room and gave the calendar to his sister. She flipped the page to September. She turned to Saunders. "Shall we say September twenty-third? It's the second from last Saturday in the month."

Saunders didn't even look at the calendar. "Yes. Let's"

The boys let out whoops and hollers and ran around the table to give Sadie and Saunders hugs.

The rest of the dinner was spent talking and laughing well past the time when the meal had been devoured.

As he looked around at Sadie's family, Saunders suddenly realized he had never felt so relaxed. Or so happy.

Chapter 56

Les Fontenot Restaurant on the Seine
Paris
27 August, 2000 Hours, Paris time

Dunn had driven back to Patton's headquarters earlier in the day, and spent some time with the men. He arranged with Colonel Edwards for them to have twelve-hour passes in Paris, and the colonel made sure that Dunn did, too. Dunn was more than happy to oblige. He left it up to Cross to handle anything that might come up, and made sure to thank and congratulate the men on another job well done. He scrounged up a clean uniform with the correct stripes, washed up, and returned to pick up Pamela. She wore a simple blue dress, which accented her eyes.

Mortimer Fontenot's uncle, Pierre, owned the Les Fontenot Restaurant, which was situated on the north shore of the Seine River. It was directly north of the Eiffel Tower, which rose just a mile away.

Fontenot seated Dunn and Pamela personally, leading them straight to a table next to the huge windows facing the Eiffel Tower. After they were comfortable, he introduced an older man wearing a black tuxedo, who had followed them from the door, as their waiter, Francois, and wished them to have a good meal.

Later, as the sun settled lower in the sky and the shadows grew longer across their spectacular view, Pamela stopped eating and laid her fork and knife down on her plate, even though her meal was but half-eaten.

"Tom?"

Dunn was in mid-chew, and had to shove the food into his cheek so he could speak. Was there something in her tone? "Everything all right?"

She smiled and reached her hand across the table. Dunn took it automatically, his underneath hers. "Yes. I have some news."

Dunn continued to look at her. Were her cheeks pinker than usual? "What is it?"

"How do you feel about having a little Thomas running around?"

Dunn wasn't following. "What? A little Thomas? What?"

"I'm expecting."

Dunn's eyes widened. "You're expecting? You mean a baby?"

"Yes. We're going to have a baby."

Dunn's eyes traveled down trying to see her belly, but the table blocked his view. It had seemed as flat as ever earlier. When do women start to show, he wondered. "A baby. You and me? Are having a baby?"

"Well, I'm having the baby, but close enough."

"Oh my God, Pamela! Are you all right? Do you need to lie down? Or something?" Dunn's heart was suddenly racing.

Pamela rotated her hand to put Dunn's on top. She laid her other hand atop Dunn's, sandwiching it between hers.

"Everything is all right. Don't worry."

Her words had an immediate effect on Dunn. He calmed down and felt as if it was okay to breathe.

"This is wonderful."

"Yes, it is."

"Do you know how far along you are?"

Pamela leaned forward so as not to upset any people at the nearest table with personal information. "I missed my time of the month about ten days ago."

"Is that enough to go on?"

"I've always been like a clock." Her eyes brightened. "Plus, I feel different. I'm positive."

Dunn lifted her hands to his lips and he kissed the top one gently.

"I love you."

"I love you more."

Dunn laughed. "I love you morest."

"Right. Good enough."

"What now? With work and all?" Dunn was hoping she'd say one thing in particular.

"I can work for a few months, but I'm required to tell my supervisor. They will send me home by the end of October."

Dunn was relieved. She would be back in England, away from the dangers here on the continent.

"Have you told your mom?"

Pamela shook her, her blond hair swaying. "I wanted you to be the first to know."

Dunn beamed. "Thanks. Okay for me to write my mom and dad, and my sisters?"

"Of course. Send my love."

"I will." Dunn calculated in his head, and then said, "So is the baby due in May?"

"I see you can still do arithmetic. Yes, it's May." Her eyes suddenly welled with tears.

"What is it?"

"Percy was born in May."

Pamela's brother had been killed at Dunkirk in May 1940. A member of the Royal Norfolk Regiment, 2nd Battalion, his unit had provided rear guard protection for the more than three hundred thousand men who'd escaped in the Miracle of Dunkirk, as Churchill called it.

"Oh, I forgot. If it's a boy, do you want to name him after Percy?"

"Maybe his middle name. He will be a Thomas, Junior."

Dunn grinned. He liked that. "Really?"

"Yes, really. You are the finest man I've ever known."

This caused Dunn to hiccup slightly with a little squeak as he stifled a sob of joy. When he got his voice back, he said, "That means so much to me."

"Well, it's true. Always remember that."

Dunn nodded.

Pamela let go of his hand. "Let's finish this excellent meal. I don't know when we might get another one like it."

"Okay with me."

They dug back in and just as Dunn finished chewing the last of his meal, the waiter returned.

In fair English, he asked, "Might I bring you a dessert? We have pies and cake today for the first time in years."

Dunn looked at Pamela and she nodded.

"Do you happen to have any chocolate cake?"

"Coming right up, sir."

The cake was half eaten on Dunn's plate when the waiter returned with a leather bill holder in his hand. Dunn raised an eyebrow; he thought dinner was on the French Resistance leader, Fontenot. The waiter opened the holder with a bit of a flourish, and turned it so Dunn could read the paper inside. It was not the bill. The message was hand printed in careful block letters on heavy stationary, written in excellent English.

Sergeant Dunn,

My nephew, Mortimer, wouldn't give me the details of what you did, but he did tell me you saved the people of Paris somehow, and not just because you are an American among hundreds of thousands of others, but for some specific Nazi danger.

Thank you!

I am honored to provide you and your lovely wife a meal tonight. As you Americans say, 'Your money is no good here' and that is for the rest of your life, should you ever pass this way again.

For the People of Paris, of France
Vive la France!
Pierre Fontenot

Dunn's eyes teared up and the waiter stuck out his hand. Dunn rose to shake it, but the Frenchman pulled Dunn into a hug and kissed him on both cheeks. The waiter stepped back from the table and cleared his throat loudly. The two dozen other customers all looked his way. He began clapping his hands, slowly at first. When the customers joined in and stood up, the clapping increased until it reached a crescendo.

Dunn held up his hands to stop the clapping, but it only increased. Two full minutes later, it finally died down. Dunn reached into his pocket and pulled out some cash for a tip and started to lay it on the table.

The waiter looked mortified and pointed to the letter, saying, "No, sir! Your money is no good here!"

Dunn put the money away and sat down. "Thank you."

"No, it is we who thank you."

Dunn handed the letter over to Pamela and she read it in silence. She began to cry and handed it back to Dunn.

"What did you do?"

Dunn shrugged his shoulders. "Something that had to be done."

Pamela nodded. She knew he couldn't tell her. Maybe someday, sitting in their rocking chairs on the porch in Iowa, or perhaps Chicago.

She took a deep breath and wiped her eyes with a fine linen napkin. And then she looked at Dunn with her bright blue eyes and smiled. "Take me home, Tom."

And so, Sergeant First Class Tom Dunn, not being entirely stupid, got up and took his beautiful wife's hand.

RONN MUNSTERMAN

Author's Notes

The German Wehrmacht was running for its life in August 1944. The horrific losses they suffered in the Falaise Pocket set the stage for all that followed until they reached their fatherland's border. This book takes place largely during this pell-mell rush to safety when the Wehrmacht's structure almost completely failed in places.

The Germans really did have a biological weapons laboratory at Insel Riems. The Japanese facility in China, and Unit 731, are real, and horrifying. The first commander, Shiro Ishii, in exchange for his knowledge about biological weapons, was never tried for war crimes.

I always mention the research I do for each of the Dunn books, but for this one I had to do something unusual: not watch a couple of shows for fear of tainting my version. The first is the British TV show *Bletchley Park*, which I so wanted to watch. Maybe now I can sit back and enjoy it. You'll have noticed I didn't go into detail about Enigma. That's because I didn't want Shepston's story flow to get derailed with tons of information you can find elsewhere and here: Bletchley Park. Eileen's character is representative of the brilliant, dedicated women who worked at Bletchley Park.

The other was Brad Pitt's movie, *Fury*, which is about a Sherman tank crew. I did finally watch it after I wrote the main chapters with Mike Lynch's *Ghost Devil*. All of the details I included came from other sources, but as I watched the movie, I was satisfied that I got stuff right.

Dunn smothering his breakfast in catsup is based on me. It's a major food group, right? I should get the T-shirt that says "I put catsup on my catsup."

The scene where a soldier directs Lynch's fire onto a Tiger over the hill is based on a true story. While watching *Patton 360*, I learned that Sgt. John Hawk, of the 90th Infantry Division, did that very thing, *while wounded*, and two tank destroyers killed three King Tigers near Chambois, France. He received the Medal of Honor for his clarity of thought and action, and courage.

Writers make many, many decisions while writing a book including not only what to include, but what to leave out. For this book, I really wanted to include and weave into the book an incredible story about an American soldier who single-handedly saved the almost 700-year-old (then) Cathedral of Our Lady of Chartres from destruction.

Forty-two-year-old Colonel Welborn Griffith, of Quanah, Texas, was a logistics and liaison officer in Patton's Third Army. On 16 August 1944, he learned of an order directing artillery to begin shelling the cathedral. It was feared that German observers and snipers might be located in one of the almost four-hundred-foot-tall spires. This was not an unjustified concern because the cathedral sits upon a hill about one hundred feet higher than the surrounding terrain, and anyone up there would have a view that stretched for miles.

Col. Griffith understood the historic importance of the cathedral, which was constructed between 1194 and 1250. On his own initiative, he, along with a non-com driver, made his way through the German held city, climbed the spire, determined there were no Germans there, and returned to friendly lines where he rescinded the artillery fire order.

Later that day, he was killed in action in Lèves, a village just north of Chartres. He was on board the exterior of a tank, which he successfully directed to destroy a machinegun nest. For his courage and action, he was posthumously awarded the Silver Star, the Distinguished Service Cross, and the French Croix de Guerre.

I couldn't directly include this brave man's story because the date of 16 August didn't work with Dunn's and Saunders' action at the bridge, which had to be on date of the liberation of the city,

18 August 1944. So I had the French grandfather tell Dunn about him for you.

The character Leonard Bailey is named for the late, great Spock, Leonard Nimoy. The character Rob Goerdt is named for my friend Robert A. Goerdt, SFC (U.S. Army Retired), who helps me with tactical questions. The character Rick Gordon is named for the Kansas City Royals gold glove player, Alex Gordon.

During a plot conversation with Steve Barltrop, he mentioned using captured French river boats to get the men to Chartres. Since we couldn't have any engine noise, the idea morphed into using the standard army assault boats (human powered). So Steve gets the credit for that idea.

Hitler did indeed give the "rubble fields" order to General Dietrich von Choltitz, the governor of Paris. All religious and historical buildings were to be destroyed, as well as the bridges over the Seine. Raoul Nordling was the real Swedish ambassador, and he did help broker a truce with Choltitz. Some historians believe Choltitz was the savior of Paris, but others vehemently oppose this view. In his memoir, Choltitz says he deliberately disobeyed Hitler's orders because he loved the city. I chose not to emphasize his role due to the controversial points of view, and I leave it to you to read more about it and draw your own conclusions. Choltitz's headquarters was located in the beautiful Le Hotel Meurice.

The Germans did put young boys on the front line as seen in the chapter where Dunn rescues the French husband from four young Nazis. I first thought of including a scene like this one when writing *Behind German Lines*.

The Palace of Versailles is truly an incredible sight as seen by Dunn.

I like to introduce interesting machines and equipment and that's why the photo recon plane is the marvelous de Havilland Mosquito.

I hope you enjoyed seeing Madeline, Finch, and Marston again. Credit my son Nathan for suggesting bringing Madeline back. Credit Steve Barltrop for getting Dunn in the same room with Madeline and his wife, Pamela. Oh, the discomfort . . .

Speaking of Pamela. You'll have noticed I didn't go into a lot of detail about the nursing work Pamela did during surgery. That's on purpose. I only know what I see on TV, and that's too modern for the book. The hand-cranked blood pump machine is real, however, and that's the extent of my research. I'm far more interested in how Pamela reacts to the surgeries and the men who are living and dying under her care than I am in the medical details.

Likewise with the story taking place at Insel Riems where Teichmann was killing innocent people for testing. I didn't want to make the book about the virus itself, there are plenty of other good books about that kind of story. You may have noticed when Teichmann and his helpers were taking the temperatures of the victims, it says "one hundred six." When writing units of measurements, I use the system the point of view character would use, metric for most of Europe and Imperial (American and British). I felt the imperial measurement would make more sense to more readers. Most everyone would know an untreated fever of one-oh-six could lead to death.

The Bontard watch given to Dunn by the grateful French grandfather is like this one:
http://www.bogoff.com/pocket/8048.html.

The Eiffel Tower and the *Arc de Triomphe de l'Étoile* are mentioned several times because they are the most well-known structures in Paris. That's why it was important for Dunn and Pamela to have dinner with a view of the Eiffel Tower. Marston's need to touch the monument is based on my own experience with architecture: I have to touch a building or monument because then it feels personal to me. Someday, I hope to touch the Pyramids of Egypt.

A personal note. You may have read in my Amazon bio that I'm an IT professional of over twenty years. As of 18 December 2015, I'm a retired IT professional! I've worked day jobs since 1973 and now I get to have my dream job: fulltime writer! What I hope this means for you is that I'll be able to publish Sgt. Dunn books more often, as well as another World War II series I have in mind that takes place in the Pacific. Just so you know, I already have the next Sgt. Dunn book (number 5 – no title yet, so it is sd5) plotted and ready to start writing after Christmas.

I really would love to hear from you. Please email me at sgtdunnnovel@yahoo.com. You can also sign up for my infrequent newsletters so you'll be among the first to know when something new is coming. The signup form for the newsletter is on my blog.

RM
Iowa
December 2015

Please consider following me on my blog and or Twitter to get up-to-date info on what's happening with upcoming books.

www.ronnmunsterman.com

http://ronnonwriting.blogspot.com/

https://twitter.com/RonnMunsterman
@ronnmunsterman

The Sgt. Dunn Photo Gallery:
http://www.pinterest.com/ronn_munsterman/

About The Author

Ronn Munsterman is the author of four Sgt. Dunn novels. He also writes short stories, two of which have been published by magazines. His lifelong fascination with World War II history led to the writing of the Sgt. Dunn novels.

He loves baseball, and as a native of Kansas City, Missouri, has rooted for the Royals since their beginning in 1969. He and his family jumped for joy when the 2015 Royals won the World Series. Other interests include reading, some more or less selective television watching, movies, listening to music, and playing and coaching chess.

Munsterman is a volunteer chess coach each school year for elementary- through high school-aged students, and also provides private lessons. He authored a book on teaching chess: *Chess Handbook for Parents and Coaches*, available on Amazon.com.

Munsterman retired from his "day job" in December 2015. In the latter half of his career he worked as an Information Technology professional with everything from Microsoft Access to PowerBuilder to web development and finally, with SAP. His new "day job" fulfills his dream: to be a full-time writer.

He lives in Iowa with his wife, and enjoys spending time with the family.

Munsterman is currently busy at work on the fifth Sgt. Dunn novel.

RONN MUNSTERMAN

RONN MUNSTERMAN